MW00333798

DARK SPIRITS

DARK SPIRITS

A DAISY GUMM MAJESTY MYSTERY, BOOK 8

ALICE DUNCAN

ePublishingWorks!
love what you read.

Without limiting the rights under copyright(s) reserved below, no part of this publication may be reproduced, stored in or introduced into a retrieval system, or transmitted, in any form, or by any means (electronic, mechanical, photocopying, recording, or otherwise) without the prior permission of the publisher and the copyright owner.

This is a work of fiction. Names, characters, places, and incidents either are the product of the author's imagination or are used fictitiously, and any resemblance to actual persons, living or dead, business establishments, events or locales is entirely coincidental.

The scanning, uploading, and distributing of this book via the internet or via any other means without the permission of the publisher and copyright owner is illegal and punishable by law. Please purchase only authorized copies, and do not participate in or encourage piracy of copyrighted materials. Your support of the author's rights is appreciated.

Copyright © 2014 by Alice Duncan. All rights reserved.

Book and cover design by eBook Prep

www.ebookprep.com

April, 2019
Paperback ISBN: 978-1-64457-061-6
Hardcover ISBN: 978-1-64457-062-3

ePublishing Works!
644 Shrewsbury Commons Ave
Ste 249
Shrewsbury PA 17361
United States of America

www.epublishingworks.com
Phone: 866-846-5123

DEDICATION

For Mimi Riser (who is forever helping me), Lynne Welch, Sue Krekeler, Andie Paysinger, and my very old friend, Jim Hull, in thanks for their input. Without their help, I couldn't have written the blasted book. Also, I truly appreciate the help given me by Rosalie Jaquez, reference librarian at the Pasadena Public Library. Librarians are my heroes, and Rosalie went way above and beyond. By the way, I had a very good friend named Marshall Armistead, with whom I graduated from John Muir High School donkeys' years ago. I used his name in this book because he was a wonderful person, a great photographer, and he died far too young.

ONE

I f I'd read the *Pasadena Star News* that morning at the breakfast table, as was my habit, Sam Rotondo wouldn't have known how disturbed I was by the news it carried that day. As it was, he was right there in the living room when I finally got a chance to pick up the newspaper.

"What's wrong?" he said, frowning at me. Sam frowned at me a lot. He'd been my late husband's best friend. Until recently, I'd considered him my worst enemy, but now I wasn't sure what I thought of him.

I shook the newspaper at him. "What's this about some of your cohorts in the police department being suspended for insubordination because they belong to the Ku Klux Klan? Why would anyone with half a brain join that brutal group?"

Sam's frown deepened, which didn't surprise me any. Sam was a detective with the Pasadena Police Department, and I guess he didn't like my description of some of his officers. "They aren't my cohorts. And at least the City of Pasadena has an ordinance against any of its employees belonging to the KKK."

My father, with whom Sam had been playing a peaceful game of

1

gin rummy, as the two men did several evenings every week, stared at his cards. Guess he didn't want to get involved in the discussion.

I huffed, still upset and indignant. "But really, Sam. How can officers sworn to uphold the law belong to an organization that's dedicated to eliminating people who aren't precisely like they are? And violently, too! Why, I read the other day that the governor of Oklahoma actually had to declare martial law because of violent attacks by members of the Klan. And I don't blame him. The Klan burned down an entire Negro section of Tulsa a couple of years ago!"

"The Klan isn't Governor Walton's only problem," grumbled Sam, trying to squirm out of a conversation he didn't want to have.

"I don't care what his problems are. What I want to know is why people here in Pasadena, California, and police officers at that, join such associations as the Ku Klux Klan. Why, did you know that Jackson's brother and his family actually had to move to Pasadena from Oklahoma to escape the Klan?"

Sam's nose wrinkled. "Who's Jackson?"

I slapped the newspaper onto my lap and glared at Sam who, naturally, was still frowning. "Who's *Jackson*? How long have you known Mrs. Pinkerton anyhow, Sam Rotondo?"

My mother said, "Daisy," in the voice she uses at me when she thinks I'm being rude. However, being rude to Sam Rotondo was sort of like being rude to a granite statue, so I didn't back away from this conversation. I did modify my voice slightly.

"What does Mrs. Pinkerton have to do with anything?" asked Sam, looking genuinely puzzled for a second before he resumed scowling.

Although it was generally Sam who rolled his eyes at me, I turned the tables on him and rolled mine at him. Which brings up another issue I'll go in to later, actually.

"Jackson, Sam, is Mrs. Pinkerton's gatekeeper and has been for as long as I've been working for the stupid woman."

My mother said, "Daisy" again, drat her.

I heaved a sigh. "I'm sorry, Ma, but she really is kind of dim."

2

"That's true, Mrs. Gumm," said Sam in defense of my opinion of Mrs. Pinkerton if not his brothers at the police department. "But that doesn't have anything to do with anything. I've never been formally introduced to Jackson, and I'm sorry about his family's troubles, but they don't have anything to do with me, and neither do the policemen who joined the Klan. *And* who have been suspended, don't forget. I don't like the KKK either, if that's any comfort to you."

Now he was being sarcastic. Fine. "Have there been any lynchings in Pasadena?" I wanted to know.

"Daisy!" My mother again. Even my father looked up from his hand of cards.

"No! No, there haven't been any lynchings in Pasadena. And there aren't going to be. The officers who joined the Klan were suspended, and if they don't quit the Klan, their jobs are history."

I sniffed. "Well, I'm glad to know that. But Jackson's brother has had a good deal of trouble since he moved here from Tulsa. Jackson thinks the Klan's after him. He thinks Klan members followed him all the way from Oklahoma. I thought he must be exaggerating, but after reading this article"—I waved the newspaper at him again—"I'm not so sure. Especially after what happened the other day."

Sam's frown, which had been aimed specifically at me, now took on a more universal aspect. "What do you mean, he's been having trouble? What kind of trouble? What happened the other day?"

"People following him and his children. Someone tried to run his children down last week—Jackson's brother's children, not Jackson's. They burned a cross on Jackson's lawn the other night. That sounds like the Klan to me, and it worries me that some of the people who are supposed to protect Pasadena's citizens might be doing the dirty work themselves."

"They burned a *cross*?" My father had evidently lost interest in the gin rummy game. He laid his cards, face-down, on the table and stared at me with dismay. Made sense to me.

"Goodness gracious!" said my mother. It was about the most forceful thing she ever said.

"Yes. They burned a cross. And if that's not the most evil, blasphemous thing to do, I don't know what is, unless they actually lynched someone. Which they've done in other parts of the country."

Sam's eyebrows dipped so steeply they reminded me of fuzzy caterpillars. "I never heard about any cross-burnings. When did this happen? Where? Didn't Jackson or his family report it?"

"It happened the night before last. Monday night. I don't know if Jackson or anyone in his family called the police. You should be able to check your records. And Jackson lives on Mentone. Anyway, what with half the Pasadena Police Department in league with the Klan, why *should* they report it? To whom?"

"It's not half the force," Sam said, growling slightly.

I sniffed. "Perhaps, but I can understand Jackson's reluctance to report harassment if all he can expect from the police department is more of the same, if not worse."

"Hmm. Maybe I ought to check into this."

"Would you?" Instantly my irritation with Sam evaporated. "That would be nice of you, Sam. I know you're a detective and this probably doesn't fall into your line of work, but it's not fair of the Pasadena Police Department to ignore a segment of Pasadena's population. We all live here, after all."

"You don't know we *are* ignoring them," he said giving me my own personal frown once more. "For all you know, the crime was investigated and the perpetrators arrested."

I tilted my head, not believing a word he said. "Well, it would still be nice of you to check into the matter."

"I will."

"Fine. Thank you."

"You're welcome."

Sam and my father resumed their game. My mother went back to reading the book I'd obtained for her from the Pasadena Public Library—*The Girl from Montana,* by Grace Livingston Hill, in case you wondered—and I lifted the newspaper again. I read the article

4

once more and then stared at the print until the words began to waver and slide around before my eyes.

Darn it! Jackson's problems were real, whether Sam thought so or not, and the mere thought of policemen, the very people who were supposed to uphold the law and arrest the breakers thereof, belonging to such an organization as the vile and merciless Ku Klux Klan worried me a whole lot. And here in Pasadena, of all places! My own fair city! I'd always thought we Pasadenans were slightly more civilized than people in other parts of the country. Heck, we'd had telephone service and electrical lighting and paved streets since before the turn of the century, and the city was full of rich people. Why, we had more automobiles than horses and buggies in Pasadena, for Pete's sake.

Mind you, my family and I weren't rich. But we worked for rich people. At least my aunt and I did. My dad used to until he had a heart attack a few years before. Until then, he'd been a chauffeur to rich people. Ma worked as chief bookkeeper for the Hotel Marengo, which, in its way, catered to folks who were at least rich enough to travel. Aunt Vi worked for Mrs. Pinkerton, who, as you've probably guessed by now, is wildly wealthy. Nobody but rich people can afford to have huge iron fences around their property and gate-guarders like Jackson to keep the riffraff out.

Now I expect I'd better tell you why the notion of turning tables brought something else to my mind. You see, since my tenth year, when Aunt Vi was given an old Ouija board by Mrs. Pinkerton, who was then Mrs. Kincaid but that doesn't matter, I've been a practicing spiritualist medium. It started out as kind of a joke I played on my relations at Christmas time, but it gradually turned into a full-time profession. Via spiritualism, and particularly my own special spirit control, a thousand-year-dead Scottish guy named Rolly whom I made up when I was ten, I've been making a darned good living for my family and me for years now.

My skills as a spiritualist came in extremely handy when my husband, Billy Majesty, whom I'd loved since my earliest years, went off to war, got shot and gassed in France, and came home disabled and in a wheelchair so he couldn't earn a living for us. His army pension was a veritable pittance. Therefore, I earned a living for the both of us, even though Billy didn't like it. Five years after the Great War's end, he finally died. He did so on purpose, but everyone who knew him, including our family doctor, Dr. Benjamin, understood that Billy was a casualty of that wretched war.

Which comes to the reason I hadn't been able to read the *Pasadena Star News* at the breakfast table that morning. I'd just eaten the delicious meal Vi had cooked for us, washed the dishes, put the last one up, and was about to sit at the table and read the paper before I took Billy's darling doggy, the black-and-tan dachshund Spike, for a walk, when the telephone rang.

Whenever the telephone rings in the morning, the whole family knows it's for me. And it's always Mrs. Pinkerton, who's always in a dither, and she always wants me to drop whatever I'm doing and go summon Rolly, use the Ouija board, or read tarot cards for her. Therefore, when I was supposed to be reading the paper and/or walking Spike, I was at Mrs. Pinkerton's house, trying to calm her down because she'd had a disturbed night. More about that later.

By the way, Billy had been dead for about a year and a half when my conversation with Sam took place. My worries about Jackson and his family had plagued me for not quite that long.

You see, Jackson and I were old friends. Ever since I made my first appearance as a spiritualist for Mrs. Pinkerton, he'd been teaching me about spiritualism where he came from, which was New Orleans, Louisiana, with roots somewhere in the Caribbean. Well, I suppose technically his ancestors came from somewhere in Africa, but they were captured and brought to the Caribbean and then moved to Louisiana. Boy, we white folks have a lot to answer for, don't we? Well, never mind about that.

Talk about fascinating! Jackson was a spectacular source for a spiritualist medium. Not that I could use too many of his teachings in my own work, because folks in Pasadena didn't want any truck with voodoo and haints and tiny dolls and so forth. What they wanted me to do for them was chat with their dead relatives. So I did.

Billy used to revile my line of work. He even told me once or twice that what I did was wicked, but I chalked up his lousy attitude to his state of health, which was pitiful.

After Billy died, I went into a steep decline. In fact, I still didn't feel as well, emotionally, as I had before Billy's death, but at least I no longer looked like a skeleton—although, come to think of it, that might have been appropriate, given my line of work. However, it took me a long time to resume my spiritualist job. I couldn't summon up the energy to deal with the idiots who believed the malarkey I fed them. I know, I know. I shouldn't disparage those who pay me for my services and, thereby, keep food on the table, but that's how I felt for a long time after Billy's suicide.

Eventually I got back to working again, and I was still making money hand over fist by fooling people. The people who paid me wanted to be fooled, though, so I didn't consider my line of work sinful. In fact, I honestly and truly attempted to help people by assuring them their late loved ones were happy on the Other Side (which, I presume, is heaven) and they wanted their still-living associates to be happy in this world until called to the next by God Himself. I absolutely did *not* want anyone to commit suicide on my watch.

Wish I could believe that rubbish myself, but oh, well.

By the way, the food I put on our table was cooked for us by my own darling Aunt Vi, my father's brother's widow, who is possibly the best cook in the world. In fact, if Vi were a man, she'd be called a chef and make lots more money than she does. But we were happy to have her cook for us. In fact, if either Ma or I had been called upon to perform the duty, the entire family would no doubt have starved to death or been poisoned long since. Neither Ma nor I could cook anything more complicated than toast. And I even burned that most of the time. Vi says it's because I don't pay attention to what I'm doing when I cook, and that's why I'm so bad at it. *I* say that we're

7

each born with certain gifts. I was born with a gift for spiritualism and a gift for sewing, and I do both of those things to perfection. God gave Vi the gift of cooking, and she does it to perfection.

Anyhow, none of that matters. I just wanted to give you some background and to tell you why I was concerned about Jackson and his family, and why I was outraged that so beastly an organization as the Ku Klux Klan had managed to gain a foothold in my hometown, Pasadena, California.

When I first saw D. W. Griffith's *Birth of a Nation*, I'd thought it was a swell picture. After talking to Jackson during the past couple of months, I now think Griffith did the world a disservice when he presented Klan members as fine, upstanding citizens.

Very well, perhaps the Klan had served, or had intended to serve, a noble purpose when it was first started. I'm sure those southerners whose way of life was ruined after the Civil War felt pretty bad about the carpetbaggers and scalawags who moved in and took over their land. I don't agree with them, perhaps because my ancestors are from New England, and my side won.

Besides that, the only way those rich southern white folks could sustain the way of life they so loved was if they continued the practice of slavery. Yes, I know there's no mention in the Bible that slavery is an evil institution. However, I also know that in ancient Rome, at least slaves could earn their freedom. And yes, I also know the old lady in *Adventures of Huckleberry Finn* freed her slave, Jim, but he sure didn't have an easy time convincing anyone else he was a freed man. It probably boiled down to color. In Rome, I suspect slaves looked like Romans. In Missouri in the 1840s, freed slaves didn't look like their white former owners.

Anyhow, if there ever had been a logical reason for the Klan to exist, it seemed to me their goals had been perverted beyond all reason. Anyone who'd terrorize someone's children, try to run down a little old man or burn a cross on somebody's front lawn, while hiding behind a white sheet and a stupid dunce-cap thing, was bad. Not misguided. Not a little silly. Not merely misbehaving.

Bad.

And now they'd begun sending Mrs. Pinkerton threatening letters, telling her that if she didn't fire Jackson—who, by the way, had worked for her family for years longer than I'd worked for her—she'd face serious consequences. Which was why I'd had to go to her house when I should have been reading the newspaper that morning.

And to think that members of the Pasadena Police Department actually belonged to that evil organization made me sick. I tell you, I was worried to death.

TWO

On Thursday morning, my mind was still unsettled about Jackson's problems, but I tried not to worry my father who, as usual, went with Spike and me for a walk after breakfast.

In fact, it was he who brought up the subject as we walked along our pepper-tree-lined street, Marengo Avenue, in the gorgeous city of Pasadena. Spike didn't have a care in the world. After all, nobody hated him just because he was black. Well, he was black and tan, but you know what I mean.

"Did someone really burn a cross on Jackson's lawn, Daisy? You didn't just say that to make a point, did you?"

I stared at my father. "What? I'm not in the habit of creating nasty scenarios to make a point, Pa. Well, except when I'm working." The full meaning of his words sank in, and I could hardly believe he'd said them. "In fact...in fact...darn it, why would you think I'd ever do such a thing?" My feelings were hurt. And by my *father*, of all people. My father, who is probably the most wonderful human male on the face of the earth!

"Don't get upset, sweetheart. It's just...well, it's troubling that you know someone who's in bad with the Klan. I know some of those folks, and they take themselves pretty seriously."

"You know *Klan* members?" Shocked doesn't half describe my condition at this piece of information.

Pa heaved a big sigh. "Yeah. I'll never understand it, either. These guys aren't bad people."

"They must be stupid, if they're not bad," I said. "Heck, the Klan hates everybody who doesn't believe precisely as they do, and they believe they're God's chosen people. Why else would they terrorize Negroes, Jews, Gypsies, Indians and Roman Catholics? That's insane thinking, Pa."

"Don't get mad at me about it," said Pa, not sounding angry but, rather, frustrated. "I agree with you." He peered down at me, a puzzled expression on his face. "What's this about Jews and Gypsies and Indians and Catholics? I thought they only hated Negroes."

"No. I actually asked Miss Petrie at the Pasadena Public Library to guide me to some reference materials about the Klan when Jackson first talked to me about his brother's troubles. The library's periodical room has newspapers from all over the country. I read a bunch of them that had articles about the Klan. The KKK hates everybody who isn't them. If you see what I mean. And they've done some perfectly horrible things in a lot of states."

"So you said. Wonder why they're so rampant in Oklahoma?"

I shrugged, feeling helpless. "I don't know. The governor of the state seemed particularly concerned about Tulsa and some city that begins with an O. It's an Indian name, I believe." I huffed. "Which is probably the only remnant of the Indian culture left in the state." The unfairness of the world often got my goat. Which is an odd expression, but I don't suppose it matters. "Um...oh, yes, it's Okmulgee. I guess both Tulsa and Okmulgee are kind of near Arkansas and Texas, and there's been a lot of Klan violence in Texas, but I'm not sure why they're so...raucous, I guess is an all right word, in Oklahoma. They claim they're fighting for Americanism, whatever that is. They don't like immigrants of any stamp."

"Heck, if you go back far enough, we're all immigrants." Pa shook his head. "And if they hate immigrants, then I really don't understand why Charlie's a member. He's the most peaceable fellow I know. Anyhow, his parents came here from Germany in the late 'eighties, so wouldn't he be sort of an immigrant?"

"I should think so. Do his Klan buddies know he's a first-generation American?"

"Don't know, sweetheart. The Klan sounds crazy to me. My family came here with the Pilgrims, but I don't have anything against other folks coming here to make better lives for themselves."

"Have you talked to...what's his name? Charlie who?"

"Charlie Smith."

"Smith? That doesn't sound German to me." Ever since the war, I'd held a particular grudge against Germans because they killed my husband. Not quickly and kindly, but slowly and painfully, with mustard gas, which has got to be one of the most hideous weapons ever perpetrated against anyone, ever. I tried not to hate Charlie because he came of German stock, but I was perfectly willing to detest him for his Klan affiliation.

"I expect the name started out Schmidt or something like that."

"Probably. Those guys at Ellis Island weren't great spellers."

Pa chuckled. "No. I guess they weren't." His expression turned serious once more. "Still, I can't figure out why Charlie joined the Klan."

"Have you asked him?"

"Yeah. He said the Klan's patriotic."

"Patriotic?" I think I snorted, not a very feminine or spiritualistic sound, but really! Patriotic? Lunatic, maybe. "Perhaps he should pay a trip to the library and do some research," I said wryly.

"Maybe he should, at that."

We spoke no more about unpleasant things as we walked among the dripping pepper trees. I love those trees even if they are kind of messy. Spike was in his glory, snuffling through all the fallen pinkish seeds and dead leaves. I once asked Vi about those seeds, which look sort of like red peppercorns, but she said they aren't edible so I've never eaten one, proving that even I can follow advice once in a while.

When we got back home, the telephone was ringing. Since every now and then I can not only take advice, but can even occasionally display common sense, I didn't rush to answer it. Rather, I hung Spike's leash in the kitchen, took off my sweater, hung it in my closet, and told myself that if the 'phone stopped ringing by the time I did all that stuff, the call wasn't important.

It didn't. Stop ringing, I mean. I exchanged a glance with my father, who shrugged. We knew it was Mrs. Pinkerton on the other end of the wire, and the persistence of that dad-gummed ringing also told us she was in another taking. Or perhaps this taking was left over from that of the day before. I hate to admit it, but I almost didn't blame her for being upset about what had happened the day before.

With slumping shoulders, I walked to the telephone, which was on the wall in the kitchen, and picked up the receiver. "Gumm-Majesty residence, Mrs. Majesty speaking."

Perhaps I'd best explain about the Gumms and Majestys at this point. I was the only Majesty extant at the time this story took place. My Billy was the last of the Majestys on his limb of the Majesterial family tree. My family name is Gumm, and the rest of the residents in our snug little bungalow on South Marengo Avenue were Gumms.

"Daisy!" shrieked Mrs. Pinkerton.

I pulled the receiver an inch or so away from my ear in an attempt to forestall deafness.

"Good morning, Mrs. Pinkerton," said I, in my soothing spiritual-ist's voice. We spiritualists have to use all the tools available to us, and a low, purring voice is *de rigueur*. In this instance, my tone of voice didn't help. Not that I'd expected it to. When Mrs. Pinkerton was this upset, it would take a brick upside the head to get the woman to calm down. Or a tarot-card reading by yours truly. I suppressed my sigh. I did, however, take a moment to shoo our party-line neighbors off the wire, including the annoying Mrs. Barrow, who absolutely loved listening in on my conversations. I'm sure my conversations were a good deal more interesting than hers, but still....

I heard the last click, and said, "Please, Mrs. Pinkerton, try to calm down." This advice was akin to telling the Pacific Ocean to stop making waves, but I tried it every now and then for form's sake. Didn't work this time any more than it usually did.

"Daisy! They planted a bomb!"

I jerked up from my slump and stared at the receiver in my hand. "I beg your pardon?" My spiritualist voice had risen an octave and no longer purred.

"They planted a bomb!" she repeated. "In the mailbox! It blew up the box and the pillar and shattered Jackson's gatehouse windows!"

Very well, the time for shilly-shallying was over. "Did you call the police? If you didn't, do so instantly. Right this minute." I remembered with whom I was speaking and said, "Never mind. *I'll* call the police."

"Oh, Daisy, *thank* you! I knew you'd know what to do!"

An idiot would have known what to do if someone planted a bomb in her mailbox, but I didn't say so to Mrs. P. "I'll telephone Detective Rotondo right this minute and then come to your house. Is that all right with you?"

"Oh, yes. Yes. Yes! Thank you, Daisy! You're so good to me!"

She was right about that. For once, the woman didn't keep thanking me but hung up the telephone on her end of the wire. As soon as I depressed the receiver on our 'phone a couple of times, tested the wire to make sure Mrs. Barrow hadn't sneaked back on, and sucked in a deep breath for courage, I dialed the Pasadena Police Department. As the 'phone rang on the other end, I glanced at my father, who stood at the kitchen table, watching me, a troubled expression on his face.

"Somebody planted a bomb in Mrs. Pinkerton's mailbox. It blew up."

Pa's eyes widened, and I wanted to ask him what he thought of his pal Charlie's Klan affiliation now. But someone answered the other end of the wire, so I couldn't.

"Detective Rotondo, please," I said to the policeman who'd answered at the station. "This is Mrs. Majesty calling."

I strained to hear a snicker on the other end of the wire, but couldn't. Sam came in for a good deal of ribbing by his fellow policemen because of me, which wasn't fair to either of us, but I'd recently begun to believe that human beings were almost always irrational and often bestial creatures who gave ourselves too much credit just because we didn't belong to some lower form of life. Last time I looked, it wasn't amoebas or dogs or raccoons or elephants or hippopotami that were causing the world's troubles. It was people.

Sam picked up the telephone on his end, so my reveries ended abruptly. "What is it?" he barked into his receiver. He would.

"Darn you, Sam Rotondo. Why aren't you ever polite to me when I telephone?"

"Because a call from you always means trouble," he said as if he meant it. Huh.

"Maybe, but this time it's not I who am in trouble. Someone planted a bomb in Mrs. Pinkerton's mailbox, and it went off, shattering that concrete pillar it stood on and breaking the windows in Jackson's gatehouse. Mrs. Pinkerton is in a tizzy."

"*What?*"

It was a bellow, and yet once more I had to yank the receiver away from my ear. "Darn it, Sam, don't yell at me! I didn't do the evil deed. I suspect the Klan members who have been harassing Jackson and his family are the culprits here."

"God damn it."

"And it's no use swearing at me, either. I'm headed to Mrs. Pinkerton's house right now, and I suggest you get a wiggle on and get some men on the job as quickly as you can. Mrs. Pinkerton, unlike Jackson and his kin, is white and has money, don't forget." Very well, that was snide of me. But it was also the truth. I knew from personal experience that the PPD paid more attention to the city's wealthy citizens than they did to the rest of us. Or the Jacksons who lived here. A dirty shame, that.

"God damn it," said Sam once more, and then he slammed the receiver down. Politeness was not one of Sam's major personality characteristics.

Since I was used to it, I merely hung the receiver up on my end of the wire and turned to speak to my father. Spike was there, wagging at me, so I knelt and gave him a vigorous petting. "I have to go to Mrs. Pinkerton's place. Lordy, I hope this doesn't mean more trouble for Jackson. You know, Pa, his only sin is to be a Negro. He's a very nice man. That Klan is a wicked thing."

"You don't know the bomb was planted by the Klan," Pa said, as if he held on to some faint hope.

I said, "Huh. Until Jackson's brother moved here from Oklahoma, nobody ever bothered Jackson or his family. In fact, I saw his son Jimmy playing the cornet in—" Nuts. I'd seen Jackson's son playing the cornet in a band in a speakeasy, but I didn't want to tell Pa that. Not that I'd been doing anything wrong in that stupid speakeasy; I was there on Mrs. Pinkerton's behalf. I swear, sometimes that woman loomed large as perhaps my biggest problem as well as my best client.

"In what?"

"In August," I replied lamely. Then I got to my feet and lammed it out of the kitchen and into my bedroom, which was right off the kitchen. Billy and I used to share that room because it was the easiest room for Billy to get in and out of. I remained there after his death because...well, why not? Spike joined me in staring at my well-stocked closet.

"What should I wear, Spike?"

A chill hung to the September morning, which was somewhat unusual, since September in Pasadena is generally a scorcher. In fact, the first day of school has traditionally been the hottest day of the year, and we kids felt compelled to carry all our textbooks home to show the folks. We'd be walking with a hundred pounds of books under our arms in a hundred-degree heat, some of us for miles. Occasionally I wonder why we didn't all die of heat prostration. Not that the weather has any bearing on the present story, but I thought I'd mention it.

Spike voiced no opinion regarding my wardrobe question, so I opted for a rusty-brown, ankle-length day dress with a low waist and long sleeves that gathered into cuffs at the wrist. My hair is sort of rusty-red, and the color of the dress went well with it. I opted for black accessories: hat, handbag, and low-heeled pumps with a strap over the arch. I always had a sensation of something akin to glee when I managed to put myself together in so fashionable a manner, because I'd made the dress, hat and handbag with my very own skillful fingers. I'm no shoemaker, so I had to buy the shoes, but I got them on sale at Nash's. I expect the entire outfit, which was perfect for the day and my occupation, probably cost me no more than a buck and a half. Well, with the shoes, maybe you could add another half-dollar to the total cost.

After I got my outfit assembled, I retired to the bathroom, where I washed my face, combed my hair into submission—it wasn't hard to do, since I'd had it bobbed a year or two earlier, and kept it short—and dabbed a bit of light-colored rice powder on my cheeks to cover my freckles. No lipstick. I always aimed for the pale and spectral image appropriate to my profession, but I did use a little mascara and a little eyebrow pencil. And then I was ready to drive our family's almost-new Chevrolet to Mrs. Pinkerton's house and face even so unpleasant a scene as I expected to find there.

I was right about that last part.

THREE

Boy, what a mess. The bomb had taken out not merely the cement pillar into which the mailbox had been stuck by some clever craftsman years earlier, but some of the black iron fencing leading up to the gatehouse, as well. Shards from every single one of the windows in Jackson's gate-guarding sanctuary lay on the ground or inside the gatehouse building.

The police had arrived before me. That's because they didn't have to worry about dressing appropriately. They wore uniforms or cheap suits every time they went out to investigate a crime. I wasn't pleased to see Sam Rotondo standing there, fists on hips, glaring at the shattered remains of the pillar. He was surrounded by uniforms, and poor Jackson looked as if he wished he were elsewhere. I didn't blame him.

Therefore, I decided to begin my work here, at the scene of the crime, and leave Mrs. Pinkerton to stew in hysterics for another few minutes. I parked the Chevrolet in the drive and got out.

Sam looked up at me and scowled. Jackson looked up at me and smiled. "Miss Daisy! Thank the good Lord, you come. Mrs. Pinkerton's in a real state. Thank you, child."

"There's no need to thank me, Jackson. I'm your friend. And these men"—I swept my arm in a broad gesture meant to include the entire police contingent—"are going to help solve this terrible crime." I speared a couple of uniforms with a sharp look. "Aren't you, gentlemen?"

One of the uniforms shuffled his feet and muttered, "Yes, ma'am."

I nodded sharply. "Good." Turning to Sam, I said, "I presume this was a Klan crime?"

"We don't know anything yet except that it happened," he all but snarled at me. "We're at the preliminary stages of our investigation."

"Nuts. You know as well as I do that someone in the Klan planted that bomb, Sam Rotondo. Mr. Jackson and his family have been harassed for weeks by those horrible people."

Jackson nodded. Sam grunted. I kept an eagle eye on the rest of the policemen and noticed a couple of them exchange what looked to me like guilty glances. I turned to one of the policemen who'd glanced guiltily at the other policeman.

"What? Do you know something about this terrible crime?" I asked him. He was a young man, probably younger than I, who was twenty-three at the time. "I know some of you in the police force are members of the KKK. Are you? If you are, you're breaking a city ordinance, you know."

Very well, while it's true I can sometimes hold my tongue, most of the time I can't. I didn't really mean to accuse the young man, but I was madder than a wet hen at the moment. To see Jackson there, amid a sea of white men in uniforms, all of whom probably thought they were somehow superior to him, just made me mad.

"No, ma'am," said the young policeman, whose name, I saw, was Officer Petrie—I instantly wondered if he was related to *my* Miss Petrie, a librarian at the Pasadena Public Library—stammering slightly.

"Hmph," said I.

"Daisy, get out of here. Go and hold Mrs. Pinkerton's hand, will you? We have work to do."

I ignored Sam and turned to Jackson once more. "Are they treating you all right, Jackson? Do you want me to stay here and make sure they do their jobs?"

Sam said, "God damn it."

I continued to ignore him. I was worried about Jackson, darn it.

"No, ma'am. I'm doin' all right here. These gentlemen are treatin' me okay."

"They'd better be," I said, raking the assembled policemen with one last good glare. "You be sure to tell me if they don't."

Sam cursed again. Again I ignored him. However, I did get into the Chevrolet, pressed the starter button and continued up the long, deodar-lined drive to the front of the house. It had been a couple of years since I'd felt obliged to enter through the back door like a tradesman. I, Daisy Gumm Majesty, spiritualist medium, entered through the front door or I didn't enter at all.

Very well, perhaps my indignation was a wee bit high that morning. I tried to tone down my anger and resentment as I stomped past the marble lions, walked up to the gigantic double doors, and whacked the knocker with a good deal more force than was strictly necessary.

Featherstone, Mrs. Pinkerton's incredibly correct butler, answered my knock almost as soon as I dropped the knocker.

"Good morning, Featherstone. I expect Mrs. P is in a frenzy."

Featherstone would no more answer me in kind than he would fly to the moon. Rather, in his superb butlerish way, he said, "Please come this way, Mrs. Majesty."

He always said that. No matter that I could have found my way blindfold to what Mrs. Pinkerton called her drawing room and the rest of us mere mortals on this earth would have called a living room. Featherstone always, always led me there. So I followed.

I have to admit to a wave of aghastness, if that's a word, when I entered the room to encounter not merely a weeping Mrs. Pinkerton, but her son (and one of my best friends) Harold, as well as Mrs. P's horrid daughter, in attendance. Anastasia "Stacy" Kincaid had been a thorn in my side for more than a decade at that point in time. She wasn't as much of a weasel as she had been a year or so ago when she'd been aspiring to become one of F. Scott Fitzgerald's "flaming youths", but she was still plenty awful.

Evidently there had been a family discussion in progress because Mrs. Pinkerton, her overstuffed self huddled in an overstuffed chair, wailed, "But I simply *can't*! He's been with me for *years*!" Mrs. Pinkerton is probably the world's best wailer.

"Besides," Harold said, frowning at his sister. "This isn't his fault."

Stacy threw her arms in the air in a gesture of frustration. "If he weren't here, all the problems would stop!" She wore her uniform as a Salvation Army maiden. I don't know what her rank was, but she was definitely rank. One of my dear friends, Johnny Buckingham, had drawn her into his fold when she got picked up in a raid on a speakeasy and proceeded to batter a couple of coppers. I remained friends with Johnny and his wife, Flossie, in spite of their kindness to Stacy.

From the comments flying around the room, I presumed Stacy had suggested her mother fire Jackson. To test my theory, I first cleared my throat in order to gain everyone's attention. It worked like a charm.

Mrs. Pinkerton squealed, surged to her feet and aimed herself toward me at a dead run. I braced myself against a sturdy piece of carved wooden furniture so I wouldn't topple over when she hit. I admit to staggering slightly, but shoot. The woman was twice my size.

"Daisy! Oh, Daisy! I'm *so* glad you're here!"

"Me, too," said Harold. His gaze paid a trip to the ceiling, and I could tell he was about at the end of his patience.

"I don't know what *you* can do," said Stacy. Nastily, of course.

I managed to free myself from Mrs. Pinkerton's embrace and as I led her to the chair from which she'd just risen, I said to Stacy, "I suppose you suggested your mother get rid of Jackson?"

"Well, *yes*! Of *course* I did! Nothing like this would have happened if *he* didn't work here!"

See? Told you she was a pill.

"Jackson has worked here for years and years, Stacy. It's not his fault some misguided people have decided he's not human because his skin is dark."

"True," said Harold. What a pal that man was. "He's been in Mother's employ longer than you've been alive, Stacy. And he's contributed considerably more to Mother's tranquility than you have, too."

I wanted to stick my tongue out at Stacy like a schoolkid, but I didn't.

"Harold!" wailed Harold's mother.

"He only spoke the truth, Mrs. Pinkerton," I said, giving Stacy a quelling look. She remained unquelled. She would. "Jackson has never caused you a moment's trouble, has he?"

"What do you call an exploded mailbox?" screeched Stacy.

"A crime. And one for which Jackson isn't responsible." Sometimes I had the truly evil wish that someone would drive a stake through Stacy's heart and give the rest of the world a break.

"And Mother's received two threatening letters!" Stacy told me.

"I'm sure neither of them was penned by Jackson," said Harold, who was rational under almost all conditions.

"Your mother and I talked about the letters yesterday. From what I've gathered through news reports and in talking with Detective Rotondo," I said, "the Ku Klux Klan has invaded Pasadena. I'm sure the Klan is responsible for the letters and the damage to your mother's property."

"Well, then? If you got rid of Jackson, those horrid Klan people would leave you alone. Don't you *see* that, Mother?"

I was fed up to the back teeth with Stacy Kincaid. Mind you, this wasn't anything new or unusual, but I didn't generally call her on her meanness. I lost my temper that day. "For someone who purports to be a good Christian girl, Stacy Kincaid, you certainly don't sound like

22

one at the moment. You're honestly advocating Jackson's dismissal because some heathens don't want him around? He's lived in Pasadena, California, for years and years. Ever since he moved here from New Orleans in the late eighteen hundreds, for heaven's sake!"

"How do you know that?" Stacy demanded.

"Because he told me so. Jackson is a friend of mine. His family was originally from the Caribbean, then they moved to New Orleans. Well, I expect they were slaves at some point, but...oh, never mind." I don't know why I tended to babble when I was upset, but I did.

"He's from New Orleans?" Harold said, sounding fascinated. "That's where Del's from. I'd love to go there one day."

Very well, I suppose this is as good a time as any to tell you about Harold Kincaid and Delray Farrington. Del was Harold's...oh, bother. I don't know what to call him. The two men were lovers. There. I said it. They lived together in San Marino, and they were two of the nicest folks I knew. Many people believe men like Harold and Del to be somehow evil—I'm sure the Klan did so, and would dearly love to lynch them—but I called them good friends. Also, near as I can figure, neither of them had ever had a choice in the matter of which sex attracted him.

Besides all that, it was Mr. Del Farrington who saved Harold's father's bank when Harold's father, the wretched Mr. Eustace Kincaid, stole a bunch of bearer bonds and headed to Mexico with them. If he hadn't been caught, and if Del hadn't worked so hard to repair the damage Mr. Kincaid had done, the bank would have folded and hundreds of people would have lost their life's savings. So say what you will about people of Harold and Del's stamp; if you dislike them because of their inclination, you're just wrong.

Boy, I'm not usually so forceful. But by that morning, I'd had my fill of bigots.

"And this only started because Mr. Jackson's brother moved here from Oklahoma. I believe, from what Mr. Jackson has told me, that members of the KKK followed his brother to Pasadena and are determined to ruin him, if not outright kill him."

Everyone in the room goggled at me for a moment. Then Harold said, "Really? I didn't know you knew the guy so well."

"Yes, well, I do. And Jackson's been awfully worried lately. I don't know why the Klan is after his brother, but it is. Did you know that some of those idiots actually burned a cross on Jackson's front lawn on Monday night?"

"Good heavens!" cried Mrs. Pinkerton. "Perhaps I *should* let him go." She turned frightened eyes upon me and instantly said, "I mean, perhaps I should give him a leave of absence. In order to sort out his problems at home, I mean."

I knew what she meant. And I didn't intend to let her get away with it. "Mrs. Pinkerton, do you value my services and advice?"

Stacy made a rude noise.

"You know I do," Mrs. P said, grabbing my hand as if to keep me from running away.

"Then please don't let Jackson go. Don't even give him a leave of absence. If you give in to those awful people, they'll have won. You need to be an example to the rest of the *good* people in Pasadena. Don't you see that?"

"She's right, Mother," said Harold, bless his heart.

"Gawd," said Stacy.

I turned on her. "Speaking of God, it wouldn't hurt you to ask for His advice before you advocate people turning other people out of their employment for the sins of other people." I hope she understood that. I was rather upset when I said it. "And it also wouldn't hurt you to talk to Captain Buckingham about this. I'm sure he'll be of guidance to you, since your own humanity doesn't seem to be working very well these days."

Harold grinned at me. Mrs. Pinkerton gulped audibly. Stacy stamped her Salvation-Army-sanctioned shoe. The carpet was so thick, her stamp didn't make much noise.

And then Featherstone appeared at the door to the drawing room and announced in a voice that would have done the Grim Reaper proud, "Detective Rotondo to see you, madam."

24

Mrs. Pinkerton groaned.

Harold heaved a sigh of relief. He and Sam knew each other of old. Neither much cared for the other, but they respected each other. Heck, Harold once shot a man who'd helped kidnap Sam. He'd fainted immediately thereafter, but Sam owed Harold a good deal.

Stacy, naturally, made an ugly face and said, "Well, *I'm* not going to stick around here if I'm not wanted."

"Good riddance," said Harold.

"Wait a minute, please, Miss Kincaid," said Sam. "I want to take statements from everyone before you go."

"Why me?" Stacy said with a whine. "I didn't see or do anything."

"Routine," growled Sam, his voice as full of menace as I'd ever heard it.

For once, Stacy obeyed another person and sat as if Sam had pushed her. Inwardly, I applauded Sam. Outwardly, I said, "Good morning, Detective Rotondo."

If we were in any place other than Mrs. Pinkerton's grand drawing room, I'm sure Sam would have asked what was good about it, but he only nodded at me and turned to a subordinate. I'd met the other copper before. His name was Officer Doan, and I don't believe I'd ever seen the man smile. Then again, I suppose police work isn't awash in gay abandon and frivolity, so he'd probably earned his dour expression. He had his notebook out and his pencil poised.

"Please be seated, gentlemen," said Harold. "And you, too, Daisy. Come here and sit by me." He patted the place next to him on a sofa. The room was enormous and full of chairs, so Sam and Officer Doan each pulled up a medallion-backed chair and got to work.

After about an hour or so, he was finished with all of us. Turned out nobody knew anything worthwhile, which I could have told him in less than a minute, but the man had to do his job after all.

I was the one who told Sam Stacy had begged her mother to fire Jackson. Stacy flounced in her chair—bet you didn't know people could do that, but you don't know Stacy. Sam's scowl deepened.

"That's not a good idea, Mrs. Pinkerton. We need to keep an eye on Jackson, and the best way to do that is to have him go about his daily routine in as normal a fashion as possible. From what he told us, and from what we've learned from other sources, this bomb was probably planted by a member or members of the Ku Klux Klan, which has recently made inroads into Pasadena."

"Rotten organization, the Klan," I said because I couldn't help myself.

"Yes, well, we intend to capture and jail the perpetrators of this crime. We don't approve of people planting bombs in Pasadena," said Sam, frowning at *me*, for heaven's sake!

"Don't forget the threatening letters," said Stacy.

I'm probably the only one in the room who noticed Sam's slight sag. He straightened instantly. Then he drew in a deep breath and used it to say, "You've received threatening letters? You should have telephoned the police department, Mrs. Pinkerton."

"Oooooh," said Mrs. Pinkerton, sobbing into her already-damp handkerchief.

Sam, who knew a lost cause when he saw one, turned to Harold. "Do you know what these letters said, Mr. Kincaid?"

"I didn't see them. Mother burned them, but I believe they threatened her with bodily harm if she continued to employ Jackson." He looked as if he wanted to add something else, but he shut his mouth with a click of teeth and didn't.

"Huh," said Stacy, crossing her arms over her chest.

"Is that the gist of them, Mrs. Pinkerton?" asked Sam.

Mrs. P nodded, still sobbing.

"Why didn't you keep them, Mrs. Pinkerton? The police could have possibly garnered clues from them." I don't know why I asked her that question; truly, I knew better. Mrs. Pinkerton was the silliest woman on the face of the earth.

"I-I didn't know," she wailed softly.

Sam and Harold and I exchanged a few looks. Harold shrugged. Sam shook his head. Which looked to me as if it was overdue for a haircut. Sam is of Italian extraction, has olive skin, dark brown hair, dark brown eyes, has to shave and cut his hair a lot. We went to the same barber, although we didn't know that until we met there one day.

"If you get any more letters, please keep them, Mrs. Pinkerton. And please also telephone the police department." Because he knew Mrs. Pinkerton well, he said, "Or ask Featherstone to call the department. Or Daisy."

It galled Sam that so many people were more apt to call me with their problems than they were to call the police department. I'd told him, in truth, that it was because I'm nicer than he is, but he still doesn't like it.

"I will," promised Mrs. Pinkerton in a shaky voice. "I will. I'm sorry I threw the other letters away."

"Is it all right for Mother to call workmen in to repair the fence and replace the mailbox?" asked Harold, who kept to the point, bless him.

"Yes. We've taken enough photographs and talked to Jackson and Featherstone and most of the family. I suppose I ought to speak with the rest of the staff. Is that all right with you, Mrs. Pinkerton?"

"Of course. Of course," she said.

"What about Mr. Pinkerton?" asked Sam. "Do you think he knows anything more about these happenings than you do?"

"I don't think so," said Mrs. Pinkerton.

"Hmm." Sam frowned again. "I'd still like to speak with him. Do you know when he'll return to the house?"

"Algie?" said Mrs. Pinkerton, as if she had more than one husband. "He should be back home this evening. He's at the stables now."

Mr. Algernon Pinkerton, Algie to Mrs. Pinkerton and their friends, had two grown sons from his first marriage, and they both played polo. Guess Mr. P still liked horses, although he was round as a rubber ball by then and probably couldn't have mounted one if he'd wanted to.

"Is it all right with you if I come round this evening to speak with him?" asked Sam politely (for him).

"Of course. I don't think he'll be able to help you, but you never know."

"Thank you. I'll speak with Featherstone and ask him to round up the rest of the staff." Sam rose, Officer Doan closed his notebook, the two men bobbed their heads in a sort of farewell gesture and aimed themselves at the drawing room door.

I was about to toddle after them when Mrs. Pinkerton turned pleading eyes upon me. "Oh, Daisy, please stay with me when the police are questioning everyone. Please! I need you to call upon Rolly for me."

Rats. I wanted to be with Sam when he questioned the staff. But I knew my duty. Besides, Aunt Vi would reveal all that evening at our own dinner table at home.

Sam, as I'd expected him to do, turned to give me gave an irritated eye-roll before he exited the room.

Harold winked at me.

Stacy said, "Well!" and left, which was about the only good thing to happen that entire day.

FOUR

"Goodness," said Aunt Vi as we dug into the pork chops, fried cabbage, potatoes and carrots she'd cooked for our delectation, "I do feel sorry for Mrs. Pinkerton. She's such a...a..."

"Nitwit?" I asked. Not kind of me, I know.

My mother said, "Daisy!"

Sam, who had, at Vi's invitation, come to dinner that night, said, "Nitwit about covers it. Ineffectual describes her pretty well, too."

"Well," said Ma, who didn't like to hear people insult other people, "I suppose she may be a rather ineffective parent, but she's still your best client, Daisy, so I don't think you should be talking about her like that."

"Sorry, Ma. You're right."

"Say, Daisy, you're pals with Jackson, right?" said Sam.

I looked up from my plate and eyed him across the table. "You know I am. Why?"

"I want to talk to the rest of his family, but I don't want to take another policeman with me." His lips tightened as if he didn't want to say what he said next. "I'm afraid they'll all clam up if a bunch of uniformed officers come to call."

I sniffed meaningfully and took another bite of my carrots.

"Anyhow, I thought you might be willing to come with me. Jackson knows you, and the two of you seem to be friendly."

I straightened in my chair as if someone had shot a bolt of electricity through me. "Oh, Sam! Do you mean it? Of *course*, I'll come with you! I'd love to. In fact...oh, bother. Tonight's choir practice." I sang alto in the choir of the Methodist-Episcopal Church, North, on the corner of Marengo and Colorado Boulevard, and we met every Thursday evening for rehearsal.

"What time does choir practice begin?" asked Sam.

"Seven. We meet from seven to nine."

"Hmm." Sam looked at his newfangled wristwatch. "It's six now. I don't suppose that would give us enough time to visit with Jackson and his family before practice."

"I could go with you tomorrow evening," I said brightly, hoping he'd go for it. He more often than not didn't want me anywhere near his cases, so this was a definite departure for him.

Scowling, Sam carved a piece of pork chop, stuck it in his mouth and chewed. As soon as he swallowed, he said, "I guess that'll be all right. The sooner, the better. Anyhow, I have to go back to the Pinkertons' place this evening to talk to Mr. Pinkerton."

"That's fine with me," said I, happy to be included. Besides, I'd like to see where Jackson and his family lived. He'd told me his mother had moved to Pasadena from New Orleans a couple of years prior, so I'd get to meet her and his brother and his brother's family, too. I was always happy to broaden my horizons. Which reminds me of the time I told Billy I wanted to broaden my horizons, and he told me my horizons were already broad enough. That was in the good old days, when he was still whole and happy and I weighed a tiny bit too much. Ah, memories. Bittersweet, they were.

"By the way, Sam, Pa knows someone who belongs to the Klan," I said.

Everyone at the table stopped chewing and stared at me. I felt as if I'd just burped or something.

"Well, you do, don't you, Pa? You told me your friend, Charlie Smith, is a member of the Klan."

"Charlie didn't have anything to do with planting a bomb," said Pa with great force.

"How do you know? Anyone filled with enough hate to join the KKK might be persuaded to do almost anything."

"Not Charlie. He's a good, decent man."

"Huh. Your good, decent chum joined an organization that only exists because its members hate everyone who isn't one of them."

"Daisy," said Ma, darn it.

Sam turned to Pa. "If you know someone in the Klan, Joe, it might be really helpful if I could talk to him." He held up a hand when Pa opened his mouth to say something. "And no, I'm not accusing your friend. But he might know something or someone who has information about who's been harassing Mrs. Pinkerton and Jackson."

"Well..." Pa looked mighty unhappy. I was sorry to have put him in the middle of a muddle, but not sorry enough to regret having flung Charlie the Klansman into the conversation.

"He just wants to talk to him, Pa. For all you know, Charlie will be as horrified as we are that people in an organization to which he belongs are bombing people's mailboxes, burning crosses and sending threatening letters."

"That's a good point, Joe," said Ma, much to my surprise.

Pa heaved a sigh. "All right. I'll get Charlie over here. He works for the city—"

"Then he's violating a city ordinance by belonging to the KKK," I said triumphantly, interrupting my father, which wasn't very nice of me, but oh, well.

With a tilt of his head, Pa glanced at me somberly. "Wonder if he knows that. You know, it might be a good idea if you *did* talk to him, Sam. I suspect he doesn't realize he's breaking the law."

"That's true, Pa. Why, he might lose his job." I know I shouldn't have felt such glee when I said that, but I did anyway.

"Right. I'll ask him to come over to the house at five tomorrow evening. That time all right with you, Sam?"

"Fine. And then Daisy and I can visit the Jacksons."

"Oh, but it might be getting dark then," said Ma. "I don't know that I want Daisy in that neighborhood after dark."

"Peggy," said Aunt Vi, pinning my mother with a frown, which was a most unusual thing for her to do. "Jackson is a fine man. I'm sure his family are good, upstanding citizens. Just because the man's a Negro doesn't mean his neighborhood is dangerous."

"Well, but..." Ma hung her head. "You're right. Of course. I, of all people, should know that."

"Why you of all people?" asked Sam as if he were genuinely curious.

"Why, because of our history, of course," said Ma, as if everyone should know what she was talking about.

Sam still appeared confused, so I enlightened him. "Crispus Attucks," I said. "The first man killed by the British during the Boston Massacre at the beginning of the Revolution. He was a black man."

"You're kidding me," said Sam, incredulous.

"Am not. Both of my parents are descended from Revolutionary stock. They taught my brother and sister and me all about it before we even started going to school."

"I'll be dam-uh-darned," said Sam.

I had no doubt about that, although I didn't say so.

Choir practice that evening went quite well, and I was pleased to be asked by my friend and fellow singer, Lucille Spinks, if I'd be willing to be a bridesmaid when she married her fiancé, Mr. Albert Zollinger. Mr. Zollinger seemed to be a fine man, but he was a good deal older than Lucy and kind of stringy. Then again, the Great War had wiped out so many young men that a girl had to take what was available if she ever wanted to be a wife and mother. That doesn't sound awfully romantic, but Lucy was making the best of it. And she sure loved flashing her diamond engagement ring around. She'd darned near blinded me with it a time or two.

October was almost upon us, the weather was cooling down some, and Mr. Floy Hostetter, our choir director, had us practicing "For All the Saints" already, even though we wouldn't be singing that one until the end of the October. That was all right with me, because I love that hymn. I also loved the anthem for the upcoming Sunday, which was "Amazing Grace." In fact, Lucy and I were scheduled to sing a duet during the second verse of that one. Mr. George Finster (bass) and Mr. Lou Ballantine (tenor) were singing a duet during the fifth verse (it's a long hymn). As Lucy's and my voices blended during practice (she's a soprano), my mind wandered to the vexed question of the Klan.

Here we were in church, supposedly good Christians all. How could anyone who called him or herself a Christian belong to an organization devoted to hate? Why, the Klan even *murdered* people. I'm sure Jesus Himself would loathe the tenets of the KKK. I decided I'd ask Mr. Charlie Smith if he was a Christian, and if he thought being a Christian was compatible with being a Klansman.

Sam would be furious. Probably Pa wouldn't much like it, either. And I sure as anything hoped Mr. Smith wouldn't.

"When we've been there ten thousand years," we sang with gusto during the last verse, "Bright shining as the sun, We've no less days to sing God's praise Than when we've first begun."

Hmm. It was difficult for me to imagine ten thousand years of anything at all, and singing for ten thousand years sounded as if it might hurt one's throat. However, that's clearly not the point of the hymn. I have a really good imagination, but sometimes I'm a trifle too literal. Then I remembered that "Amazing Grace" had been penned by a repentant slave-ship captain, John Newton. I'd bet he'd detest the Klan, too, if he knew about it.

Mr. Hostetter interrupted my musings, which was a good thing, since I was supposed to be thinking about God and His mercies and stuff like that.

"Very well done, everyone. Miss Spinks and Mrs. Majesty, your voices blend beautifully. Mr. Ballantine and Mr. Finster, you also sounded quite good. Mr. Finster, you need to be just a trifle louder, and you went a little sharp on the second line. Let's go over your verse again."

Lucy and I exchanged a look of triumph. We were better than the men! I know what you must be thinking. We were in church, which is no place for vanity. Still, we were proud of ourselves.

People. There's no doing anything with them. Anyhow, my vanity received another boost when Mr. Hostetter changed the order of the duets. On Sunday, Lucy and I would be singing the fifth verse, and the two men would sing the second. I guess our choir director didn't want to leave the congregation on a sour note. So to speak.

When I drove the Chevrolet down the hill to our little bungalow —yes, it's an easy walk, but I don't like walking alone at night—I wasn't sorry to see Sam's big black Hudson sitting in front of our house. In fact, I rushed into the house via the side porch, pausing only to scoop up Spike, who greeted me with his customary exuberance, and proceeded to the living room. I'd expected to see Pa and Sam playing gin rummy, but they weren't. In fact, they seemed to be having a serious discussion, which broke off instantly when they saw me.

"What?" I said. "Keep talking. Don't let me interrupt you." Even as I spoke the words, I knew they wouldn't work. The men in my life seemed determined to keep me uninformed about the good stuff.

Standing, Sam said, "I was just leaving."

"Thanks for stopping by, Sam," said Pa.

"Oh, no you don't!" I told them both. "What were you talking about? It was about Mr. Pinkerton and Jackson and the Klan, wasn't it?"

Pa and Sam exchanged a glance, then looked at me, and looked at each other again. After several uncomfortable seconds, Pa said, "You might as well tell her, Sam. She'll find out anyway."

Hugging Spike to my chest—he was quite a largish bundle—I said, "That's right, Sam. So spill it." Then something truly horrible occurred to me. "Please don't tell me Mr. Pinkerton has joined the Klan! He's such a nice man!"

Naturally, Sam frowned at me. "No, he hasn't joined the Klan."

"Thank goodness." I sank onto the sofa and set Spike in my lap. Before Billy's death, my arms had been strong and muscular, because I'd had to wrestle with his wheelchair and Spike and him on a more or less daily basis. I wasn't as strong anymore, and my arms ached. I shook them out. "What's wrong, then?"

"Nothing's wrong," said Sam. Grouchily, I'm sure I need not add. "But Mr. Pinkerton knows the Pasadena Klan's exalted cyclops. He's a member of one of Pinkerton's clubs."

I squinted at Sam. "He knows the *what*?"

With a sigh Sam said, "He knows the exalted cyclops of the Klan in Pasadena."

"What in the name of Glory is the exalted cyclops? I've never heard a more ridiculous title in my entire life!" I felt like giggling.

"The exalted cyclops is the big shot in a particular group of Klan members. This guy leads the Pasadena chapter," said Pa.

"Good Lord. And these guys take themselves seriously?" I thought about all the articles I'd read in various newspapers, and any notion of laughter fled. They may call themselves silly names, but they killed people. And burned crosses. And hated *everyone*.

"Yeah," said Sam. "They do take themselves seriously. Very seriously. And now I know one of them is a prominent Pasadena businessman."

"Good Lord," I said again. "This sounds grim."

"It is grim," agreed Sam.

Pa nodded.

Spike and I saw Sam to the door, and I stepped outside with him. I hadn't removed my sweater, so I wasn't uncomfortable in the chilly night air. Spike, who loved being outdoors in the front yard, instantly raced after the Wilsons' cat. The Wilsons are our neighbors on the north. They have not only a cat, but also a young son, whose name is Pudge. That's not his real name, which, I think, is Richard, but everyone calls him Pudge, probably because he's as big around as a broom straw.

"So is this exalted cyclops person going to be a problem for you?" I asked Sam.

He heaved a huge sigh. "I don't know. If you're asking if he's going to affect the way I do my job, the answer's no."

"Could he cause you any trouble?"

"I expect so. He's a bigwig."

"That's so unfair," I said, feeling enormous sympathy for Sam in that moment.

He shrugged. "It's all part of the job."

I peered up at him. Sam was a large man, solid as an oak, and about as mobile. When we first met, we disliked each other. Sam thought I was a fraud, and I thought he was a bully. We were both kind of right, but...well, our relationship changed a lot after Billy's death. In fact, Sam had once, in the heat of a verbal battle, told me he loved me. Talk about shocked. My mouth had fallen open, and I'd almost keeled over. We hadn't discussed the love angle of our relationship since that time, but we'd grown closer in the ensuing year and a half or thereabouts.

"Why'd you decide to become a policeman, Sam?" I asked, honestly curious.

"I wanted to help people."

Oh, boy. You sure can't tell what a person's like inside from looking at the outside, can you? Sam Rotondo, who appeared about as approachable as a fire-breathing dragon, had gone into police work because he wanted to help people. "That's a noble reason," I said, meaning it.

I should have expected that Sam would think I was making fun of him. "It's the truth," he growled.

"I believe you, Sam. It's just...I only wondered, was all. Did Margaret approve of your line of work?"

Margaret was the name of Sam's late wife, who'd died of tuberculosis shortly after the two of them had moved to Pasadena from New York City. I knew for a fact that Sam felt guilty about her passing, even though he wasn't to blame for her poor health or her death. I felt guilty about Billy's poor health and his death, too, so I understood his sensitivity on the Margaret issue. Even though I knew the matter was a moot one, I still believed I was more culpable than Sam, because of how much Billy and I used to argue, even though I *knew* he was only grumpy because he was in pain and couldn't breathe or work at a job that could have supported us. Poor Billy. Poor me. Poor Margaret. Poor Sam.

Another shrug. "She didn't like the hours. It's probably a good thing we didn't have any kids."

This wasn't the first time he'd said that, and I understood his reasoning, even if I always experienced the urge to wince when he said it. If his marriage to Margaret had born fruit, his children would now be living with his parents in New York City. Sam might or might not have been able to move back to New York, but he still wouldn't have had the rearing of his children to himself.

"I guess so. Billy and I wanted children, but...well, if we'd had any, I probably wouldn't have been able to support them. Not and rear them, too."

"Right. That's exactly right. And your mother and aunt both work away from home, too, so you couldn't be off reading palms somewhere and leave the kids with either of them."

Crude, but true. "Yes," I said, and left it at that.

"Well, I'd best be off." He turned to me, and for a moment, I thought he might kiss me. He didn't. I wasn't sure whether to be disappointed or not. He said, "Your father talked to his friend Charlie this evening, and the time of our meeting has changed. We're going to go to his house tomorrow at one. Will that be all right with you?"

"Sure."

"Also, I talked to Jackson this evening when I went to the Pinkertons', and he said if we got to his place at seven, he'd be there, and so would his brother."

"That's fine with me."

A mad eruption of barking from Spike interrupted us at that point, so I'll never know if our discussion would have led to anything more revealing of a personal nature. I called, "Spike! Come!"

Spike, well-behaved dog that he was—because I'd taken him to the Pasanita Dog Obedience Club two years previously, and we'd both learned our lessons well—came. And Sam, after petting Spike and calling him a good dog, which he was, left. I watched his big, blocky Hudson roll away down Marengo and wondered for about the six-thousandth time where he lived.

FIVE

Friday morning dawned overcast and foggy. The weather suited my mood, since I woke up feeling down in the mouth. I wasn't sure why until, after slipping on a faded blue day dress and shoes and stockings, I made my yawning way into the kitchen and saw Pa.

Oh, yes. It all came back to me. The exalted cyclops of the Pasadena chapter of the Ku Klux Klan was a rich businessman, and Mr. Pinkerton, husband of my best client, knew him. Presumably well, although I didn't really know that for certain. Not only that, but the Pinkertons' gatekeeper, a friend of mine, was being harassed by that same Klan. And, perhaps most distressing of all, some of my father's friends belonged to the Klan. Dismal, all of those things.

"Morning, sweetheart," said Pa.

"Morning, Pa," said I. My heart brightened marginally when I saw that my wonderful aunt had fixed French toast and sausage patties for breakfast. Vi herself was upstairs getting ready to go to Mrs. Pinkerton's house and begin a day of cooking. Bless her heart; then she'd come home and finish the day with more cooking for us, her family.

"Your aunt outdid herself this morning," said Pa as he watched me take a couple of pieces of French toast and a couple of sausage patties from the plate in the oven where Vi had put them to keep them warm for late-rising me. Well, it wasn't all *that* late, being approximately seven-thirty at the time, but both Vi and Pa rose distressingly early.

"Where's Ma?" I asked.

"Getting primped up for work."

"Golly, I don't have anything to do this morning, do I?" I'd been haunting—so to speak—Mrs. Pinkerton's house ever since she'd received that first threatening letter from the Klan, but I hadn't heard from her today. Yet. A glance at the clock told me there was still plenty of time for her to annoy me. "Let's eat up quickly and walk Spike, Pa. I want to be gone if Mrs. P calls again today."

With a chuckle, Pa said, "I've finished breakfast. You eat up, and we'll go. You can wash the dishes when we get back from our walk."

Spike, who was already excited about breakfast, almost had a spasm when he heard the word "walk". Smart dog, Spike.

"Will do." I dug in, buttering my French toast and pouring real New England maple syrup over same. Our relatives back East always sent us genuine maple syrup for Christmas, which was very nice of them. In between bites, I said, "Sam said we're going to Mr. Smith's house this afternoon."

"Yeah. I talked to Charlie, and he asked if we could visit him instead of him coming here. He gets off at noon on Fridays, and he asked if we could come earlier than we'd planned."

"Sounds good to me."

Ma and Vi both walked into the kitchen just then. Both of them were clad appropriately for their jobs: Ma wore a sober gray suit; Vi wore a sober gray day dress. As soon as she arrived at Mrs. P's house, she'd don an apron. Both ladies wore sensible shoes. I was the only clothes-horse in the household.

"Good morning, Ma. Good morning, Vi."

"How are you today, Daisy?" Ma asked. She had a distinct

twinkle in her eye. I think she suspected I'd been spooning with Sam the night before.

"Fine, thanks. You?" Darned if I'd tell her Sam and I had been talking about the KKK as we'd dallied on our front porch. Let her keep her romantic notions.

"Fine, dear. Glad it's Friday and that I only have to work until noon tomorrow."

"I think everyone should go to the five-day workweek," I said.

"You sound like a Socialist," said Pa, grinning at me.

"Phooey. People shouldn't have to spend their entire lives at work."

"People have been spending their entire lives at work forever, sweetheart," said Ma.

"Maybe when we all lived on farms and stuff," I said. "Not these days. These days, with all our modern conveniences, we can get more done in less time. Well, except for me, but my hours are my own. More or less."

"I'd rather work at my job than yours," said Ma. "At least I don't have crazy rich people calling me all the time."

Vi said, "And isn't *that* the truth!"

"Exactly," said Pa.

It was nice to know my family didn't think I loafed for a living. I guess.

And then the telephone rang. My mother, father and aunt all turned their heads to stare at me. I stared at the dad-blasted telephone and didn't move until I'd finished chewing and swallowing the bite of sausage I'd just taken. Then, with a sigh on my lips and doom in my heart, I rose and went to the 'phone.

I didn't even get through the whole "Gumm-Majesty residence. Mrs. Majesty speaking" speech before Mrs. Pinkerton started wailing at me.

"Daisy! Someone splashed paint all over what's left of the gatehouse!"

I waited until I'd swallowed my wrath, much as I'd swallowed my sausage, before I asked mildly, "And you called the police, right?"

"The-the police?"

I allowed my shoulders to droop and my head to fall back. When I saw my relations still staring at me, I straightened and managed to speak gently into the receiver. "Yes, Mrs. Pinkerton. It's against the law for anyone to deface anyone else's property. That's called vandalism. You need to telephone the police." Sanity struck, and I amended my last statement. "That is to say, have Featherstone call the Pasadena Police station. Ask for Detective Rotondo. If he's not there, talk to whoever's on duty. I mean have Featherstone talk to whoever's on duty."

A big gulp sped from Mrs. P's end of the wire to my ear. "Oh. Of course. Of course, I can do that."

"Excellent." My heart lifted for a split-second, which was silly of it, since I knew Mrs. Pinkerton of old. It plummeted when she spoke again.

"Oh, but Daisy, can you come over today? Please? I *need* to speak to Rolly through the Ouija board. This morning?"

I considered my morning's plans for a moment before answering her. Realizing I didn't really have any (plans, I mean), I said, "I can be at your house at ten thirty, Mrs. Pinkerton. I'll have to leave before noon, because I have an appointment at one."

"Ten thirty?" She sounded sorry, as if she thought I should drop everything and rush to her side. Phooey.

"Yes." I said the word firmly.

"Very well. I'll see you at ten thirty. Harold said he wants to talk to you, too."

"He does?" Her message surprised me. Harold was always telephoning me; why hadn't he conveyed his interest in talking to me via the telephone wires? Well, mine was not to wonder why, as some poet or other said once upon a time.

"Yes. He told me it's important. I think he wants to talk to you about what's been going on with that wretched Klan."

Puzzled, I said merely, "Very well. I'll be happy to talk to Harold." That was true. I loved talking to Harold. He was a great guy.

"I'll see you at ten thirty then, dear."

"Yes. I'll be there on the dot." Whatever that means. There are a whole lot of idiomatic expressions in the English language that don't make a particle of sense to me.

After I hung the receiver in its cradle, I turned to find my family staring at me with great intensity. I shrugged. "Somebody splashed paint on the Pinkertons' gate house and gate. I suspect the Klan again."

"My goodness!" said my startled mother.

"Good heavens," said Aunt Vi.

"The police really need to catch whoever's doing that stuff," said Pa.

I agreed with all of them. Then I finished my breakfast, washed and put up the dishes—there was no reason to leave them for later since I'd already received Mrs. P's telephone call—and went with my father to take Spike for a walk.

As I'd suspected she would be, Mrs. Pinkerton was in a lather as, at the stroke of ten thirty, Featherstone let me in to the drawing room. She saw me, leaped to hear feet, and would have run me down had not Harold stopped her.

"Let Daisy come in and sit down, Mother. There's no need to bowl her over every time she comes at your call."

I blinked at Harold, who didn't generally speak to his mother in such sharp tones or with such pungent words. They worked, however, and Mrs. P plunked herself back down onto the sofa from which she'd only seconds earlier risen. I walked over to her and held out a hand. My hands are well manicured and soft. Mind you, I did a lot of the gardening around our Marengo home, but I always wore gardening gloves and slathered on cream every time I washed them. My hands, not the gloves.

"I'm so sorry you've had more trouble, Mrs. Pinkerton," I said in a voice as smooth as my hands. I meant what I'd said, too. I'd seen the ugly red splashes against what was left of the formerly white gatehouse and the black iron fence next to it, although both were mainly rubble at the moment. Workmen had already arrived, however, to fix the fence and resurrect the gatehouse.

Taking my hand in hers, Mrs. P proceeded to bury her face in them—my one hand and her two. I glanced at Harold, who rolled his eyes. I felt like doing the same thing. I didn't appreciate having my hand wept upon.

That being the case, I gently removed it from her grip and said, "Let me set out the Ouija board, Mrs. Pinkerton, and we can consult with Rolly."

"Oh, yes! Yes. Thank you, dear."

"You're most welcome. Did you have Featherstone call the police?"

"I called the police," said Harold in a voice a good deal gruffer than his normal, happy-go-lucky tones. "And I told them about the paint. This has gone far enough."

"It's gone too far, if you ask me," I told him.

"Oh, yes! It has," agreed Mrs. Pinkerton. "But I won't fire Jackson."

Her voice was so firm, it startled me. I've come to expect lots of things from Mrs. Pinkerton, but seldom firmness of purpose. I shot Harold a glance, and he nodded. Aha. That explained it. Harold was always a good influence on people. Well, except his sister. No one seemed able to affect her behavior, with the one exception of Captain Johnny Buckingham of the Salvation Army and, after listening to Stacy the day before, I even had my doubts about Johnny.

"Excellent," I said. "Jackson is not at fault here. I suspect the Klan has taken against him, and all this mischief is their doing."

"I'm sure you're right. Do you suppose Detective Rotondo will come himself today?" asked Harold.

Again, I turned to Harold. Something was clearly wrong in his life, and I doubted it was his mother's troubles. Then I thought about the Klan, and about how they hated everyone who was in any way different from a so-called "normal" white Protestant person, and I sucked in a quart or so of air. Good Lord! Could the Klan be after Harold because he and Del were...?

Harold must have seen the speculation and appalledness (if that's a word) in my eyes because he gave his head a short shake and said, "But I want to speak with you after you deal with Mother."

"Of course," said I, my heart pounding out funereal dirges in my breast. It kept beating out: *not Harold, not Harold, not Harold.* Or maybe I'm just being dramatic. That's what it felt like, though.

However, my curiosity would have to wait. I sat in a chair across from Mrs. Pinkerton, and together we plied the planchette. Rolly told her not to worry (stupid advice, given the recipient, but I couldn't help myself), and that the police would solve the crimes committed against her property and her gatekeeper soon. I prayed I was right about that and that neither the Pinkertons nor Jackson and his family nor, heaven forbid, Harold, would run afoul of the Klan again.

Unfortunately, after Rolly was through assuring Mrs. P she had nothing to worry about and that others were scurrying around behind the scenes to make sure she wouldn't be bothered again, she wanted me to read the tarot cards for her. Blast the woman. I wanted to talk to Harold, darn it.

I dealt out a Celtic cross pattern. The cards told Mrs. Pinkerton precisely what Rolly had told her. Mind you, the cards aren't as easy to manipulate as the Ouija board, because when you shuffle those things, you never know what you'll uncover when you lay out your pattern. Oddly enough, however, that day they worked out precisely the way I wanted them to. Would that the rest of life would follow suit.

As soon as I'd finished interpreting the cards for Mrs. Pinkerton, I stuffed them and my Ouija board into the pretty carrying cases I'd sewn for them and rose. Mrs. Pinkerton's face took on a tragic demeanor.

"Oh, Daisy, do you have to leave *now*?"

"I'm afraid I do, Mrs. Pinkerton. My day is full. I only had a short space of time in which to visit you. But I'll be happy to come again soon."

"Tomorrow!" she said instantly. She would.

I had to pause and try to think what day tomorrow would be. Saturday. Blast. I wanted to separate irises and pick oranges on Saturday. And then read the rest of the day away. Fiddlesticks. Maybe I could squeeze an hour out of my not-too-strenuous schedule to do another Rolly reading for Mrs. P. After all, she's been my best client for more than half my life, and she truly did have something to complain about at the moment. Generally speaking, while she was always in a dither about something, her somethings didn't seem all that awful to me. The Klan, however, was another kettle of fish. A stinky one, at that.

So I mentally fumbled through the hours of the day and finally said, "I'll be happy to visit you tomorrow at eleven o'clock, Mrs. Pinkerton. Unfortunately, I can only give you an hour." Actually, I'd sell her an hour, but there was no point in quibbling over wording.

"That will be so sweet of you, Daisy. I know what a busy life you lead."

She did, did she? I doubted it. But I smiled serenely at her and said, "It will be my pleasure." Very well, I'd just lied. Sue me.

Harold followed me out of the drawing room, and shut the door as soon as we hit the hall. I turned abruptly. "Don't tell me you and Del have been getting—"

"No," he interrupted me. "But I'm afraid someone might catch on to our relationship, and then we'll be in the soup. Rotondo's *got* to stop those bastards before they tear our family apart!"

"Oh, dear." Laying a hand on Harold's arm, I said, "I'm so sorry, Harold. Sam and I are going to visit a Klansman today, and maybe we can ferret out some information from him about this whole situation. We're also aiming to visit Jackson and his family, so I hope we can put an end to this rash of vandalism before you and Del become involved."

"If those sons of bitches hate Jackson just because he's a Negro, can you imagine what they might do to Del and me?" Harold took his handkerchief from his coat pocket and wiped his perspiring brow. Harold was usually the jolliest of fellows, so I know he was truly worried.

"They're evil," I said, although I don't know why. We already knew that.

"Would you like my help with anything? Rotondo probably wouldn't like it, but I'm offering myself as a sacrifice for the police if they need me."

He meant it. He'd proved himself in battle, so to speak, before now. "I hope you won't need to become involved, Harold. Pa and I are going to visit a friend of his who's in the Klan right now...well, after lunch, and then maybe I'll know more."

"Your *father* knows a Klan member?"

"Yes. Maybe more than one. Actually, so does your stepfather. In fact, your stepfather knows the exalted cyclops of Pasadena's chapter of the Klan."

Although I hadn't planned it, the title of the Klan's leader jolted Harold out of his worry. "The exalted *what?*"

I heaved a sigh. "The exalted cyclops. He's the head of Pasadena's chapter."

"Good God."

"Indeed."

"Do you know who he is?"

"No, curse it. Sam didn't tell me, and neither did Pa."

"Well, I guess I don't blame them. They don't want to get you involved."

"Not you, too!" I fear I lost my temper a bit. "I'm so sick of the

47

men in my life thinking I'm an idiot, Harold Kincaid! I didn't know *you* were among them!"

"I don't think you're an idiot," said Harold hotly. "But I don't want you getting hurt!"

"I won't get hurt!"

"You don't know those people."

"You don't, either," I pointed out.

"Yeah, but I'm a man."

I only stared at him. After several seconds of that, we both burst out laughing. I know, I know. There wasn't much to laugh about, but my comment hit us both on our funny bones. You can sue me for that, too, if you want to.

SIX

By the time both Harold and I had dried our eyes, we decided to visit Aunt Vi and see if we could scrape up something for lunch. As I might have expected, Vi lavished food upon us. Therefore, when Harold and Vi and I finally parted that Friday, it was a stuffed Daisy Gumm Majesty who drove the Chevrolet back to our home on South Marengo Avenue.

Sam Rotondo had already arrived at our house when I drove the machine into our driveway and came to a stop next to the side porch. I heard Spike barking with joy even before I exited the car. It was so nice to come home to a being that *always* appreciated me, even when I was in bad with the rest of the world. I think dogs are Mother Nature's perfect gift to us poor, flawed human beings.

When I opened the door and knelt to embrace my wriggling pooch, I felt a presence looming over the both of us. Sure enough, when I glanced up, there was Sam, fists planted firmly on his hips, frowning at Spike and me.

Irked, I said, "What? I'm right on time!"

"I didn't say you weren't," said the exasperating man.

With one last stroke for my best buddy, I rose to my feet with something of a grunt. Shoot, I never used to grunt when I got up from the floor. Maybe I'd better walk more briskly on my daily toddle around the neighborhood. It had been more than a year since I'd had to wrestle with Billy in his wheelchair, and I guess I'd lost muscle tone. Perhaps I should check out a book on Swedish exercises next time I went to the library.

"Well, then, stop frowning at me," I snapped at Sam.

I noticed my father, who stood behind Sam and who smiled at the both of us. Well, the three of us, if you count Spike. Nuts. I don't know why everyone thought it was "cute" when Sam and I sparred. I sure didn't.

But never mind that. "Are you two ready to go? I'm all set." And it was only a quarter to one; so there.

"All set," said Pa. "I think Sam will drive us."

"Yeah," said Sam. "My Hudson's out front."

"I saw it," said I with something of a sniff.

So we all trooped out to Sam's automobile, leaving a disconsolate Spike behind. We sometimes took him with us on auto trips, but this day was reserved for Charles Smith/Schmidt. Sam opened the back door and Pa instantly scrambled in, leaving me to sit next to Sam on the front seat. Fine. If this was a ploy on Pa's part to drive Sam and me into each other's arms, it wasn't going to work.

Perhaps I was a teensy bit defensive that day.

Anyhow, we arrived at Charlie Smith's place, which was on a street called Madison Avenue. Madison Avenue was nothing like New York City's Madison Avenue, if what Sam had told us was correct, and for once I saw no reason to doubt him. Rather, our Madison Avenue was a residential street much like Marengo Avenue, where middle-class folks like the Gumms and Majestys lived.

Charlie Smith's house was kind of like ours, in that it was a bungalow. There were scads of bungalows in Pasadena. I do believe the architects Charles and Henry Greene were responsible for a whole bunch of our bungalows. The Greene brothers' bungalows, however, were much fancier than our little bungalows. Other architects had built the houses that now belonged to us plebeians. Not that our houses weren't nice, but they weren't massive and wildly expensive, like most of the Greene brothers' homes. Still, I liked them.

But that's not the point. Sam parked his Hudson in front of Charlie Smith's neighbor's house, because someone had already parked in front of Mr. Smith's place on Madison Avenue, and Sam actually got out of the auto on his side and walked to my side to open my door before I could do it for myself, thereby proving that he could behave in a gentlemanly manner every once in a while, even if he did maintain his scowl as he did so.

"Cute house," I said, just because I thought I should say something. "Kind of like ours, only smaller."

"Right," said Pa.

"I like the flowers," said Sam, surprising me. For some reason, every time Sam propounded a sentiment of any kind, he surprised me.

"Yes. 'Tis the season for chrysanthemums, all right. I like those bronze-colored ones." Mind you, the chrysanthemums at our house were prettier and more plentiful, but still, at least someone in the Smith household cared about making his home look good.

"Is that what those are? Chrysanthemums?" asked Sam.

I refrained from rolling my eyes at him, but only said, "Yes. Aren't they pretty, all blooming together like that?"

"Yeah."

Well, what can you expect from a fellow who grew up in New York City, where, I'm sure, nobody's seen a chrysanthemum grow for a hundred years or more? On the other hand, what I know about New York City could be written with a wide fountain pen on the head of a sewing pin, so I may be wronging the city.

We all walked together, I in the middle, up to Charlie Smith's front door, and Pa gave the doorbell a twist. We waited for a very few minutes before the door was answered by a plump woman in a house dress and apron, who invited us in with a smile. Luscious smells emanating from the kitchen announced an apple pie was baking. Bet it wouldn't be as good as one of Aunt Vi's.

Oh, dear, now I was maligning a woman I don't even know, right after I'd maligned New York City. I really ought to be more kindly disposed toward the rest of the world.

"Good day to you, Joe. And is this Daisy? Why, I haven't seen you since you were knee high to a grasshopper, young lady." Yet another odd idiomatic expression. "And this must be Detective Rotondo. Please come into the living room and have a seat. I'll get Charlie."

"Thanks, Marge," said Pa.

"And I'll bring a little snack and some tea, too," said Marge. For a Klansman's wife, she was certainly hospitable. My judgmental nature suffered a slight dent.

"Joe!" a man who was at least as plump as Marge, bellowed, walking into the living room and making Pa and Sam rise from the chairs they'd just taken. I rose, too, not because it was expected of a woman, but because I didn't want to meet the enemy sitting down.

Whoops. That dent just got fixed in a hurry, didn't it?

"Hey there, Charlie. I want you to meet my daughter, Daisy, and Detective Sam Rotondo, from the Pasadena Police Department."

Charlie shook my hand and Sam's, although he appeared a trifle belligerent when he took Sam's. "Glad to meet you both," said he. I don't think he meant it about Sam.

"Thank you for allowing us to come over and talk to you about the Klan, Mr. Smith," said Sam formally.

"There's nothing wrong with the Klan," said Charlie Smith. "It's a patriotic organization dedicated to purifying America."

"And cleansing it of immigrants, Negroes, Catholics, Chinamen, Gypsies, and everyone else who isn't a white Protestant man or woman?"

Very well, I know I should have kept my fat mouth shut. I have a deplorable tendency to speak when I shouldn't. Naturally, Charlie Smith stiffened up like a setter on point and frowned at me. I was used to receiving frowns from the males in my life, so I only smiled sweetly at him.

"And just what do you know about the Klan, young woman?" demanded Charlie.

"A lot. I've studied all about it at the Pasadena Public Library," said I smartly.

Sam elbowed me in the ribs like the fiend he was. Nuts.

"Listen, Charlie, we didn't come here to argue." Pa shot me a shut-up-and-be-still look, so I decided I'd better do it. I really hadn't meant to start an argument. Well...maybe I had, but I shouldn't have.

"I'm sure you didn't, Joe," said Charlie, sending me a look much like the looks my mother gave me when I misbehaved.

"But I think it's important that you and Detective Rotondo have a chat," Pa went on. "Because he has some information you might find important. And we'd like to learn if you know anything about some recent incidents in Pasadena that might relate to the Klan."

"The Ku Klux Klan is a benevolent organization created to promote patriotism," said Charlie in a sententious voice.

I could hardly believe my ears. Because Pa and Sam both shot me looks this time, I didn't protest this blatant and ridiculous misrepresentation of the Klan's purpose in life.

We sat again. Then Mrs. Smith came in with a tray, and we all stood once more. I tell you, social rules are really silly sometimes.

"Here are some nice ginger snaps and some lovely tea. There's milk and sugar if you want it," said Marge.

"Thank you very much," said I, trying to redeem myself. It didn't work. Sam and Pa both gave me another look. Sometimes—quite often, in fact—I can't win.

She left the room, and we all sat again. I took a ginger snap and a cup of tea in order to keep my mouth busy. The ginger snaps were nowhere near as good as Vi's, and I felt somehow vindicated, although I have no idea why.

"All right," said Sam after Marge had left the room once more and the four of us were huddled in a circle, "will you please tell us about your Klan affiliation? What are you required to do?"

"Well, I go to meetings."

"Did you have to buy a white sheet?" I asked. Darn me, anyway!

"Of course. That's one of the requirements. And the initiation fee is ten dollars."

Whew! That was a lot of money. "Out of curiosity, how much did the sheet cost you?" I know. I should have just shut up, but I was fascinated by this whole Klan culture. One of the articles I'd read at the Pasadena Public Library said that a sheet-maker in Atlanta, Georgia, had reignited the Klan for business purposes and was raking in the lettuce by selling sheets to the idiots who wanted to join the "patriotic" Ku Klux Klan.

Charlie Smith added his frown to those of Pa and Sam, but I was still curious. "The official Klan sheet cost six dollars and fifty cents."

Holy jumping cats, as my Uncle Ernie used to say! If I wouldn't have hated myself for it, I could have made a mint on my own by selling cheaper sheets to those Klan idiots. Nevertheless, I decided to be still and let Sam continue his interrogation of Mr. Smith.

"How long have you been a member of the Klan, Mr. Smith?" asked Sam politely.

"Only a couple of months. I've been to six meetings so far." Shooting me a glower, he said, "And we've discussed nothing except keeping America up to the standards our founding fathers expected of us."

"The founding fathers, all of whom were born in other countries, if I'm not mistaken." Very well, so I wasn't still for long.

"The English are a far cry from the Irish and Greek and Italians that are cluttering up the streets these days!" cried Mr. Smith indignantly.

I smiled sweetly at Sam, who, I think, would have liked to slap some tape over my mouth. "Detective Rotondo's of Italian descent," said I.

"Well, I didn't say they're all dirty immigrants," muttered Smith.

"That's not the point," said Sam stolidly. "We need to know who's causing mischief at the Pinkerton home."

Charles Smith appeared positively shocked. "Pinkerton? Isn't he that rich fellow who lives on Orange Grove?"

"Yes, that's the one. His wife has been getting threatening letters, and someone planted a bomb in their mailbox. Their gate keeper is a Negro fellow, and some people burned a cross on his lawn last Monday."

Mr. Smith's mouth opened and closed a couple of times. Then he said, "Th-that's terrible. That's not what the Klan is all about."

I pressed my lips together so as not to blurt out anything else of an incendiary nature.

"The letters addressed to Mrs. Pinkerton told her to get rid of Jackson unless she wanted to face dire consequences. There was a Klan symbol at the bottom of the letter. Naturally, there was no name appended thereto." Sam's voice was as bland as custard, but his face was set like concrete.

"Also, Mr. Smith, you work for the City of Pasadena, don't you?"

Charlie, who appeared a trifle beleaguered, said, "Yes. The water department. That's why I only work half days on Fridays, because I have to work Saturday afternoons. What does that have to do with anything?"

I was about to enlighten him, but Sam, after (naturally) shooting me a fierce look, said, "Any city employee who belongs to the Ku Klux Klan is in direct violation of a city ordinance, and can lose his job."

"What?" Charlie's startlement seemed unfeigned.

Sam handed him a sheet of paper upon which was a lot of type-writing. "Here's a copy of the ordinance. The Klan's caused major problems in several states, and California is attempting to nip the problem in the bud."

Glancing from the paper to Sam and back again, Charlie said, "But...but I don't understand. What problems are you talking about?

I swear to you, we've never discussed anything except how to be a good American at the Klan meetings I've attended."

I scrutinized his face carefully and could detect no hint of prevarication. On the other hand, I'm not good at reading faces, so what did I know?

"Aside from the burning cross, the mailbox bombing, and the threatening letters, red paint was splashed on the Pinkertons' ruined mailbox last night."

"Oh, my goodness," Charlie said, clearly appalled.

No longer able to help myself, I said, "Goodness has nothing to do with it. Aren't you a second-generation German? I'm surprised the Klan allowed *you* through their hallowed doors, given the feeling folks have about Germans these days, myself included. Germans killed my husband, you know."

In novels, people are always reported as going deathly pale when they hear something they don't want to hear. I've never seen that phenomenon myself, but Charlie Smith definitely narrowed his eyes and flattened his mouth after my speech.

"I-I-I," he stammered. "I-I don't think I ever mentioned my heritage at the meetings. Which is Swiss, by the way, not German."

"Swiss or German, you'd better not mention it, if you don't want a cross burned on your front lawn or your mailbox bombed." Me again. Told you I couldn't hold my tongue.

"Daisy," said Pa.

But I was fed up. "Darn it, Pa, it's the truth! If those Klansmen knew Charlie's parents were from Switzerland, they'd probably burn *him* and forget the cross entirely. Or lynch him."

"L-lynch?" stammered Charlie in something of a whisper.

"So far there have been no lynchings in Pasadena, Mr. Smith," said Sam, giving me the fish-eye. "But some Klan members are creating mischief, and the chief of police is not happy about it. Six members of the Pasadena Police Department who joined the Klan have been suspended. If anyone learns about your Klan affiliation, I have no doubt you'll be suspended, too, if not dismissed permanently."

"Good God."

"As nearly as I can tell," said I, irking all three men, "God has nothing to do with anything the Klan does."

"But we believe in God!" cried Charlie in a last-ditch effort to redeem an unredeemable cause. "We love God and our country. We're all good Christian men!"

"Tell that to Jackson," I said. "He was born in the United States, and his family has lived here for generations. As slaves, of course." Very well, I sneered. Sometimes there's no doing anything with me.

"But those blacks, they cause trouble." Still trying to turn a sow's ear into a silk purse, our Charlie.

"Nonsense. The only trouble Jackson and his family have had has been caused by your beloved Ku Klux Klan. Why, did you know that the Klan burned down an entire Negro district in Tulsa, Oklahoma, two years ago? And that the governor has had to declare martial law because the Klan is perpetrating so much violence? That's why Mr. Jackson's brother had to move to Pasadena."

"But-but that's only because those jigaboos want our white women."

"Oh, for heaven's sake!" I said, totally disgusted. "Jigaboo is a disparaging, belittling term for people who are just like us except for being of a darker complexion. Anyhow, if you believe that, I expect you'll believe the moon is made of green cheese and that the cow actually *did* jump over it."

"Daisy," said Pa again.

He had a point. Charlie Smith was old enough to be my father, and I was being disrespectful. Therefore, I apologized. Sort of. Jigaboo, my left hind leg. "I beg your pardon, Mr. Smith. However, I recommend you visit the Pasadena Public Library and do some research on the organization you claim is benevolent, patriotic and good-natured. There are hundreds of relatives of lynched persons who would disagree with you."

"Daisy," Sam said through clenched teeth.

I huffed.

"However," Sam said before I could do anything else, "Mrs. Majesty has a point. Not only are you violating the city ordinance against city employees belonging to the KKK, but at its roots, the clan promotes violence and even murder. So far, we haven't had that kind of trouble in Pasadena, and I aim to see that we never do."

Charlie buried his head in his hands. I didn't feel sorry for him. Perhaps if he'd only been a Klansman *or* had a German name, I might have. The combination was too much for me, however, and I wanted the man to suffer. Mean of me, I suppose, but there you go.

"I don't know what to say," said Charlie. "I honestly didn't know all that stuff about the Klan. I believed the kleagle—"

"The *what*?" Me again.

Frowning at me, Charlie said, "The kleagle. He's a representative from Klan headquarters who goes around the country recruiting people."

"Ah," said I. First an exalted cyclops and now a kleagle. Could this organization come up with any more ridiculous names for its various positions? I didn't ask the question aloud.

"Anyhow," Charlie continued, "I believed what the kleagle said about the Klan being a patriotic organization." He looked up with a pleading expression on his face. "We're against bootlegging," he said, as if that made a particle of difference to anything.

"So am I," said Sam, "but I'm willing to live and let live. However, that's neither here nor there. The point is that you're violating the city ordinance and can be fired from your job."

"I don't want that," muttered Charlie.

"None of us wants that," said Pa. Untruthfully. I didn't give a rap if this nitwit lost his job or not.

"Very well. You don't want to lose your job. That makes sense to me. So that means you can quit the Klan—"

"I can't do that!" cried Charlie, suddenly looking frightened. Past time, if you asked me.

"Why not?" asked Pa.

"They-they don't like people to quit the Klan. They...well, I understand that can be quite...um, nasty to people who quit the organization."

"How patriotic of them." I swear, sometimes I can't keep my trap shut for anything.

Giving me a frown, albeit not as mean a one as his priors, Charlie licked his lips and said, "Well, maybe they're not as benevolent as the kleagle said they were."

I'd have rolled my eyes if I hadn't already caused so much trouble.

"That being the case," said Sam, "I have a proposition to set before you."

I swiveled my head to stare at him. Good heavens, he wasn't going to allow this man to continue in his evil ways, was he?

As it turned out, he was. But Charlie Smith wasn't out of the woods yet.

SEVEN

"Actually," I said after thinking about Sam's proposal to Charlie Smith for several silent moments as Sam, Pa and I went back out to Sam's black Hudson, "that's not a bad idea."

"So glad you approve," said Sam as he opened the back door for my father and the front door for me.

"Don't be snide," I advised him. As if he'd ever take advice from me.

"You were quite intrusive in there, Daisy," my father told me, making my heart squish painfully. "Although you did impart some useful information." That made me feel a trifle better, although not much.

"I'm sorry I butted in so much," I said, feeling like two cents.

"Actually," said Sam in a thoughtful tone of voice, "although I was peeved at the time, you do know more than the rest of us about the Klan, so maybe it's good that you did interrupt."

I goggled at Sam. Sam Rotondo, who disapproved of nearly everything I did, had just paid me a compliment. Kind of. "Oh," I said, because I couldn't think of anything else to say.

"I just hope I haven't put the guy in danger," said Sam, still musing aloud.

"Do you really think he might be in danger?" asked Pa.

"Maybe. Those Klan folks play for keeps, and they aren't nice people. If they ever find out your friend is a spy for the PPD, they're apt to do anything."

"Jeepers, Sam, do you honestly think they might hurt Mr. Smith?" I wasn't altogether sorry to hear it, which means I'm definitely at least a semi-bad person if not a totally bad one.

Sam shrugged. Then he said, "On the level. This character, Smith, might think his fellow Klansmen are patriotic gentlemen, but someone in that organization is causing trouble, and I'm hoping Smith will help us find out who it is."

"Who's the exalted cyclops? I mean, what's his name?" I asked. Not that I expected either Sam or my father to answer me.

They both surprised me, and a duet of masculine voices said, "Stephen Hastings."

"For crying out loud!" I more or less bellowed. "The very man whose own son was murdered last year?" And who had been of Harold's ilk, something I'm sure the KKK would frown upon as much as they frowned on Negroes, Jews and American Indians.

"That's the one, all right," said Sam, sounding glum. "He's a high muckety-muck in lots of civic organizations. Guess he considers the Klan one of them."

"The man's a gorgon," said I, having had dealings with people who knew him. "I feel sorry for his wife. Again. Still, actually."

"Yeah, well, he's rich and we're not, so we're going to have to tread carefully."

"Why? Wouldn't the good citizens of Pasadena rise up and refuse to use his legal services if his Klan affiliation were known?"

Both Sam and Pa looked at me as if I'd grown a second head, and I heaved a sigh. "Right. You're right. Of course they wouldn't." I sat silent for a few minutes, which I'm sure was a relief to Sam and Pa, as

I muddled through this latest mess to intrude upon our lives. Finally, after thinking the matter over thoroughly, I said, "I don't believe it."

"You don't believe what?" asked Sam, irked.

"I don't believe Stephen Hastings is the exalted cyclops."

"Why not?" said Pa.

"I...I don't know. It just doesn't sound like him. He doesn't strike me as the type who'd hide under a sheet. I imagine he has dirty dealings all over the place, but he's probably fixed them so that they look legal. And he's certainly no shrinking violet. Besides, if he were the Klan leader, he'd have to mingle with the peasants. You know, like us. Well, not like us, because we wouldn't join the Klan, but...oh, heck, you know what I mean."

Sam said, "Well..."

Pa said, "I don't know. Maybe she has a point."

"Maybe," admitted Sam, although he didn't sound as if he meant it.

Nuts to him. In fact, nuts to everyone. I was downright sick of the human race, and I burst out, "Why can't people be like dogs?"

"Run in packs and kill each other?" said Sam. He would. "That's pretty much what the Klan's doing, isn't it?"

"Applesauce. Dogs only run in packs and kill each other if they have to. People join the Ku Klux Klan because they want to. There's a huge difference."

"If you say so."

That pretty much killed the conversational theme for the rest of that drive. After promising to come by for dinner at six—he and I would then go to Jackson's house to interview him and his family—Sam dropped Pa and me off at home, and he returned to his office at the police department, probably to write up his interview with Charlie Smith and detail the plans he intended for Smith to follow.

Pa and I walked into the house and were ecstatically greeted by Spike.

The rest of Friday passed pleasantly enough. I'd already visited Mrs. Pinkerton, so I didn't expect to hear from her again unless something else related to Klan activities intruded upon her serene existence.

Stephen Hastings. The name always made me cringe a bit, mainly because everything I'd learned about him when I was investigating his son's death had led me to believe he was an overbearing son of a she-dog. His wife was a lovely woman who cultivated orchids, and she deserved better than he. Then again, lots of women did. There weren't many specimens of manly wonderfulness wandering around loose, especially in those days after the Great War. I've always felt fortunate that my mother and father had found and married each other, because they were both swell. In fact, my father is one of the world's best people. So few people were as fortunate as I.

Well, except for having lost my husband when he was only twenty-four. He'd been a good man, too, until the Kaiser's men got hold of him. But never mind that.

It still boggled my mind that Stephen Hastings might don a white sheet and terrorize people. Especially if he had to do it amongst common folks like Pa's friend and Pasadena coppers. I wondered if Mr. Pinkerton might have been mistaken. After all, Mr. P *surely* wasn't the sharpest nail in the barrel. He'd married Mrs. Pinkerton, hadn't he? That alone told me, if it didn't tell Sam or Pa, that he wasn't precisely a genius.

Nuts. I couldn't figure it out all by myself. I'd just wait for further information, which was sure to come soon.

I spent the remainder of that day cleaning house and reading. Spike and I napped for an hour or so late in the afternoon, then I got up to set the dinner table when Vi got home and began preparing dinner.

Sam, who always arrived on time for one of Vi's meals, knocked on the door at precisely six o'clock. Spike and I greeted him and, before he knelt to say good evening to Spike, Sam handed me a bunch of store-bought chrysanthemums. He didn't wait for me to thank him before petting Spike, which was typical.

"Thank you, Sam. These are beautiful. I'll put them in a vase."

"You're welcome." He stood, much to Spike's disapproval. "They don't smell very good."

"They're chrysanthemums, Sam. Chrysanthemums smell like chrysanthemums, not roses or gardenias."

"Huh."

Also typical of Sam.

"Well, come along. I'll find a vase, and you can talk to Pa while Aunt Vi and I get dinner on the table."

"I couldn't remember what they were called," Sam said at my back.

I stopped my trek to the kitchen and turned to face him. "You couldn't?"

"Naw. But the flower shop was full of 'em, so I just asked for a bunch of them. Mixed colors, because you said you liked the different colors."

Sam had bought flowers he couldn't remember the name of because I'd mentioned I liked the various colors. That was...well, it was downright sweet of him. I told him so. "Thank you, Sam. That was very sweet of you."

I had the satisfaction of seeing his olive complexion take on a magenta hue. I swear, I could argue with the man all day and never raise a blush, but if I told him he was sweet, he turned to goo. Satisfied with the results of my words, I finished walking to the kitchen and listened to Ma and Aunt Vi ooh and aah about the pretty bouquet. I filled a vase with water, added the flowers, put the flowers on the dining room table and finished helping Vi serve dinner.

Dinner. I stared at a big pot of cornmeal mush, trying to hide my astonishment. I guess my efforts were for naught, because Vi laughed.

"Don't worry, Daisy. I'm not serving cornmeal mush for dinner."

I pointed at the pot. "It looks like cornmeal mush to me."

Mind you, I had nothing against cornmeal mush. We had it for breakfast with butter, brown sugar and cream often, and sometimes Vi poured it into a loaf pan and let it set, and we had it fried in the morning with butter and maple syrup. It was good stuff. But I'd always considered it a breakfast food.

"Well, it may look like cornmeal mush," said my aunt with a superior twinkle in her eyes, "but this, my dear, is called polenta, and it's Italian."

"Polenta? Is that Italian for cornmeal mush?"

"Yes. But you serve it while it's still hot and before it sets, and pour an Italian sauce over it."

"Who in the world did you get this recipe from?" I asked ungrammatically.

"Sam."

I goggled at my aunt. "*Sam?*"

"Yes. Sam. He even told me how to make the sauce."

I sniffed appreciatively. "So that's what smells so good?"

"That's it, all right."

"I had no idea Sam knew how to cook."

"I didn't, either, but we chatted the other day when he came to Mrs. P's to talk to the staff about poor Jackson's problems."

"Well, I'll be hornswoggled." Yet another inexplicable idiomatic expression.

"Smells like home in here," came Sam's voice from the door leading from the dining room to the kitchen.

"It smells great," I said. "And I understand it's all your fault, too." I smiled to let him know I was joking.

"I feel honored that Mrs. Gumm decided to use one of my mother's recipes," said Sam, sounding as though he meant it.

"Feel free to give me any other of your mother's recipes, Sam Rotondo. If they're as good as this one smells, we'll all be fat in a trice."

He only smiled.

Oh, boy. I'd had spaghetti with a red sauce kind of like the one Vi served us that night, but this was the best I'd ever tasted in my life. And it was served over cornmeal mush, of all unlikely beds!

"I didn't know Italians liked mush," I said after swallowing a bite of my dinner. Vi served some of her delicious bread and a green salad with the mush and sauce.

"We call it polenta," said Sam, clearly peeved.

"I guess polenta does sound better than mush," I admitted.

"In New York City, we Italians eat this red sauce with everything. In fact, the kids call it gravy."

"Really!" I said, my imagination instantly beginning to work. I glanced at my aunt. "Hey, Vi, I imagine you can serve all sorts of other things with mush. Like creamed chicken and stuff like that."

"Creamed chicken and polenta doesn't sound as if it would taste as good as this nice spicy Italian sauce," said my mother who, I might have mentioned already, wasn't an adventurous eater, although she was sure tearing into her dinner that night.

"I understand southerners call cornmeal mush grits," said Pa.

"They do? I had no idea," said I.

"That's what I read somewhere," said Pa.

"French folks eat snails," I plopped into the conversation for no perceptible reason.

"I prefer what the Italians eat," said Ma.

"But mush mixed with cooked shrimp and cheese sounds pretty good," said Pa. "I think I read somewhere that they eat that in the south somewhere."

"Where in the south?" I asked him.

He shrugged. "In a costal state, I imagine. There are lots of southern states with long stretches of coast."

"Shoot, California has a huge coast, too, and you don't hear about people eating mush with cheese and shrimp here. At least, I don't think they do." What did I know?

"And in Louisiana, they eat something called 'jerked chicken'," said Sam.

"What's that?"

"I don't know, but I bet your friend Jackson can tell us."

"I'll ask him when we get to his place. Boy, you can sure learn a lot of things around the dinner table, can't you?"

Everyone agreed, and we continued to enjoy our meal. For some reason, knowing we were dining on a meal suggested by Sam made me feel proud of him. Irrational, I know, but everyone is irrational sometimes.

After dinner and dessert (floating island, if anyone cares), Ma and Vi told me not to bother with the dishes, but to go with Sam to Jackson's house. So I did.

When we were rolling westward on Colorado to Mentone Street in Sam's Hudson, I patted my stomach. "That meal was great, Sam. I'm so glad you told Vi how to make it."

He shrugged. "It was nothing. We ate that all the time when I was a kid back home. My mother was a pretty good cook. You can use the same sauce with any kind of noodle, too."

"Any kind of noodle? What kinds of noodles are there? I've heard of macaroni and spaghetti, but...I guess I'm too much a Yankee. We eat stuff like baked beans and brown bread and cornmeal mush and syrup."

"Oh, there are many different shapes of pasta. There's ziti and penne and fettuccini, and there's even a kind of pasta made from potatoes called gnocchi."

"Good Lord, really? I'd probably really like the potato one."

Sam actually smiled. "New York City is home to pretty much every variety of people in the world. When I was a kid, we ate Italian, East Indian, Chinese, Arabian, German and all sorts of other kinds of foods."

"I remember you said something about you eating at an Indian friend's house and had curry a lot."

"Yeah." Sam smiled reminiscently. "I do miss all the different kinds of food available in New York. I don't suppose you've ever heard of falafel."

"What?"

"Falafel."

"No. I've never heard of falafel."

"I'm kind of surprised you didn't encounter falafel when you went to Egypt."

I shuddered, my automatic reaction when reminded of that dreadful trip. Harold had meant well when he'd dragged me off to Egypt and Turkey, but I'd been grieving for Billy and sick as a dog almost the entire time.

"I know that trip was rough on you," said Sam, sounding amazingly sympathetic for him. Sam Rotondo was a big, rugged policeman. He wasn't as a rule given to sentiment.

"Yeah," I said and hoped he'd drop the subject.

Naturally, he didn't. "Falafels are made of chickpeas or fava beans. They're ground up, mixed with garlic and other stuff—I don't know what—and fried. They're delicious. My buddy Armen used to bring them to school for lunch."

"Armen? What kind of name is that?"

"Armenian. Then there were the Swedish kids. Their food was kind of bland if you were used to East Indian, Arabian and Italian food. The Germans, too. Helmut used to bring something called sauerbraten to school. It was kind of sweet. I didn't like it much, although he also brought some great sausages. His dad was a butcher."

"My goodness. Maybe I should visit New York City someday. Sounds like a great place to eat." Well, except for the German cuisine, but I didn't want to spoil the evening by bringing up my grudge against Germans.

Sam actually turned in his seat and smiled at me. "It is."

For some reason, my heart fluttered. Stupid heart.

EIGHT

The part of Mentone Avenue where the Jacksons lived wasn't all that far from where the Pinkertons lived, geographically. Financially and socially, it was about three worlds away.

Not that the street in any way looked run down. In actual fact, although it was dark as night—because it *was* night—I could see small houses impeccably kept with small lawns bursting with fall flowers that I would have bet looked pretty during the daytime. Mentone sits in between Fair Oaks Avenue and Lincoln Avenue, and is north of Colorado Boulevard, where the north-south separation of Pasadena begins.

"I can't see any street numbers," grumbled Sam as his gigantic Hudson lumbered slowly up the street.

"I can't, either, but Jackson said he'd keep the front porch light on for us."

"How do you know that?"

"Because when I left Mrs. Pinkerton's house today, I asked him to."

"Oh."

Oh, my foot. "By the way, don't be surprised by Jackson's mother," I said to Sam as I squinted out the passenger-side window.

"Why should I be surprised by Jackson's mother?"

"I guess she was some sort of big voodoo queen or something back in New Orleans. Jackson called her a mambo, but he said she's not dangerous. She just dresses a little oddly for a Pasadena person, and Jackson says she likes to put on an air of mystery. And she makes those little dolls that people stick pins in."

The Hudson came to a sudden stop and I asked, "Are we there?"

"She's a *what*? And she does *what*?"

"There's no need to yell at me, Sam," I told him tartly. "Jackson said his mother is a voodoo mambo. I guess that means she's a bigwig in the voodoo set. Or she was when she lived in New Orleans. Evidently she has a growing number of followers here in Pasadena now."

Sam laid his forehead on the steering wheel for a moment.

I frowned at him. "What? It's not my fault Jackson's family is full of interesting people. Why, I've been talking to Jackson for years about the spiritualist trade. It's...well, it's definitely different in New Orleans. I don't think the Mrs. Pinkertons of the world would like it much. I read a really interesting article at the library about an old voodoo mambo named Marie Laveau, who was called the voodoo queen in New Orleans. She lived in the last century, and she—"

"Stop!" Sam said. "You're telling me we're going to the home of a practitioner of voodoo?"

"Well...yes. I guess so. Jackson's mother is the practitioner. I think Jackson goes to the Baptist Church on Lincoln where a lot of Negroes attend."

Lifting his head and pinning me with a look I didn't deserve, Sam said, "Daisy Gumm Majesty, you know the most...appalling kinds of people."

Defensive, I said, "*I* prefer to think of them as interesting. Jackson helped me a whole lot when I started out in the spiritualist business."

"How old were you when you decided to become a spiritualist?" The question seemed to be asked out of true curiosity. At least I didn't detect any sarcasm or condemnation in it. On the other hand, Sam had asked it, so I trod carefully.

"I didn't actually *decide* to become anything. It just sort of worked out that way. Turned out I had a knack with the Ouija board."

"A knack."

"Yes. A knack. But why are we talking about this now? Where's Jackson's house?"

Sam shook his head. "I don't know, but it's got to be in this block. I'll just park the machine, and we can walk."

"Sounds good to me."

So he parked his automobile, and I swear I heard him mumble something about "voodoo mambos" when he exited the vehicle and walked around to open my door for me. I thought he was taking Jackson's mother's vocation entirely too seriously. What the heck. If the woman was making a living practicing voodoo, more power to her, is what I thought. Still do, in fact.

It turned out that we were smack across the street from Jackson's house, so Sam and I walked across Mentone and were heading up the walkway to the porch when Jackson, who'd been sitting in a rocking chair on the porch smoking his pipe, stood and approached us.

"Evening, Miss Daisy, Detective," he said, smiling his big, white smile.

"Good evening, Mr. Jackson," I said, pleased to see him looking happy.

"Evening," said Sam in his usual gruff way.

"Can you show us where those evil creatures burned the cross?" I asked.

"Daisy," said Sam.

Nuts to him. I wanted to see for myself. Even if it was too dark out to see much.

"Yeah. Right over here. Woke up the whole neighborhood, it was so bright." Jackson led us to a black patch on his well-groomed lawn.

I shook my head in sorrow. "That's really horrid of them."

Jackson shrugged. "I 'spect it is, though they might've done me some good. My mama says it's good to burn the grass every year or so. Says burnin' it makes it grow better next season. Not that we have what you might call seasons here in Pasadena."

"Boy, that's the truth. I didn't know that about burning grass."

"We're not here to talk about grass," Sam snarled.

"Right, right," said Jackson. "Come on in the house, please. But first, let me tell you about my mama. She's a good woman, my mother, but she's from New Orleans, and she has some funny ideas." He pronounced the city's name "Nawlins."

"Daisy mentioned that," said Sam, sounding grouchy. Then again, he generally did.

Jackson and I exchanged a smile. "Well, she's like Miss Daisy here, in that she deals in the spirit realm. Only she do it the New Orleans way, where there's a lot of voodoo goin' on."

"She told me that, too."

Grinning widely, Jackson said, "Just don't be alarmed, is all. She don't dress like most ladies in Pasadena dress."

Boy, he could say that again! As soon as Jackson opened the front door to admit us, I saw a large woman, dark as soot, dressed in a fabulously colorful robe, and with an extravagant turban-like thing on her head. She frowned at us as soon as we stepped foot in Jackson's house.

"Here's the kind folks who're going to help us find out who's been plaguing Henry and us, Mama," said Jackson, using an almost pleading tone with the magisterial female seated beside the fireplace. She was ever so much more regal than any of the Majestys I'd met in my life to date. In fact, she'd have appeared right at home on a throne.

"I can do my own juju," said Jackson's mother in a voice that fairly reeked with disapproval.

Naturally, my ears pricked at the unusual word. "Juju?"

"Voodoo power," Jackson whispered.

"Who you be, girl?" demanded the voodoo queen. Her voice was deep and rich and reminded me of melted semi-sweet chocolate. Very smooth, her voice.

Deciding I had nothing to lose unless she aimed to cast a spell on me, and I didn't really believe people could do stuff like that, I strode over to her and stuck out my hand for her to shake. "Daisy Gumm Majesty. I've been a friend of your son's for...oh, a long time now."

"That's true, Mama," said Jackson, looking disconcerted at my hand hanging in the air and not being grasped and shaken.

But Mrs. Jackson finally unbent enough to take my hand in hers. Her hand was big and warm. She didn't shake mine, but turned it over and studied my palm. My goodness. I'd never met another person who practiced one of my own personal job skills, but I got the impression Mrs. Jackson was a whole lot more adept at palm-reading than I was.

She stroked my hand with the hand that wasn't holding mine. "You have a gift, child. Sonny told me you did, but I never met no white lady with the gift before."

I wasn't sure what to say, but decided to take her comment as a compliment. So I finally said, "Thank you," even though I wasn't altogether sure I should.

Sam cleared his throat to let us all know it was time to get down to business. Mrs. Jackson, still holding my hand, took something out of a pocket in her voluminous skirt and pressed it into my palm. When I looked, I saw a tiny doll. I guess my eyes bugged or something, because she said, "That's good juju, girl. Don't lose it."

"I won't," I promised. And I wouldn't, although I had no idea what to do with the thing. Jackson's mother solved that problem for me.

"Hang it on this string here and wear it 'round your neck, girl." And darned if she didn't then hand me a long rope-like necklace that looked as if it had been tightly crocheted out of multicolored pieces of string. She must have sensed I was a brainless nitwit, because she snatched the little doll out of my hand, strung it on the rope, and put it on over my head. I blinked at it, dangling there against my chest, and said, "Thank you," again.

She said, "Huh. You take care."

Sam, who had been looking upon us with one of his fiercer scowls, said, "Can we get down to business now?"

Mrs. Jackson gave him a smile I could have sworn was a blend of wickedness and humor and said, "Yes, sir."

"Have a seat, Miss Daisy and Detective. I'll go fetch Henry, my brother."

So we did. I glanced around the small living room of Jackson's home and wondered precisely how many people lived here. Our house on Marengo was larger than this, and there were only the four of us. Jackson had a wife and at least one son. I guess we'd soon meet his brother, Henry, and then we'd know how many children he had. It made me sad to think little kids were being terrorized by a gang of big bullies in white sheets.

Jackson, whose Christian name, I learned, was Joseph, escorted his brother into the living room and made introductions. Henry and Joseph Jackson didn't look much alike, but I don't look much like my brother or sister, either, so there you go.

"I understand you and your family moved to Pasadena from Tulsa, Oklahoma, Mr. Jackson," Sam began. "Can you tell me why you did that?"

Henry Jackson appeared uncomfortable. "The Klan's been makin' life a misery for us black folk there in Tulsa, Detective. I decided to move my family away from the violence and lynchin'."

"I've read about the riots and violence in Tulsa," said Sam. "Did the Klan pick your family in particular to torment?"

The Jackson brothers exchanged a worried glance. I perked up some. The brothers knew something, but would they reveal their knowledge to Sam? Some of whose brothers-in-uniform belonged to the same organization that had driven Henry Jackson's family from its home?

"If you know of any reason you should be singled out for Klan attention, I wish you'd tell me. Your knowledge might help us put a clamp on Klan activities here in Pasadena before things get even worse for you and your family," said Sam, sounding almost gentle, for him.

"I...I seen something," stuttered Henry Jackson. "Back in Oklahoma." Big help.

"What did you see?" asked Sam.

"Well, I ain't real sure—"

"Henry!" came the stentorian voice of Mrs. Jackson. "Tell the man what he needs to know, and do it now."

"Yes, Mama," said Henry meekly. I was impressed. Even if the woman couldn't practice honest-to-goodness magic, she could sure get things done. I approved.

"The truth is that I ain't sure what I saw," said Henry, sounding miserable. "But if I seen what I thought I seen, then I seen a white man kill another white man."

Oh, my goodness!

"In Tulsa?" said Sam.

"Yeah. I didn't know anyone'd seen me, but I reckon someone did, 'cause things started happening to my family. They burned a cross on my property, and somebody tried to shove me down a flight of stairs. I worked the elevator in a law office in Tulsa, and this was at work. Then they put notes in my mailbox saying as to how they was gonna kill my family and my kids and burn my house down."

"And that's when I told him to come here," said my Jackson. "But somehow or t'other, word done spread, and now they's after him here, too."

Sam shook his head, as much in frustration as annoyance, if I were to guess. How do you catch people who run around in white sheets and won't show their faces?

"I'm sorry, Mr. Jackson. This has to be a frightening time for you."

"You can say that again."

Sam didn't bother. "Do you have any idea at all who the men in Tulsa were? The one who killed the other man and the man who was murdered?"

After a short spate of silence, Henry said, "Well, I heard folks talkin' in the elevator the next day, and I heard the name of Bruce McIntyre. He be the dead man. I don't know who the killer was."

"Bruce McIntyre." Sam wrote down the name, and I could envision cable messages flying back and forth between Pasadena, California, and Tulsa, Oklahoma, in the next few days. "Well, that's something, anyway."

"Hope it helps," said Jackson.

"Me, too," said Henry.

"I understand your children have recently been bothered," said Sam of Henry.

"Yes, they been bothered," said Henry, sounding angry about it, and I understood completely. "Some white man in a sheet driving a big ol' Cadillac car tried to run 'em down when they was goin' to school."

"Good Lord!" I cried, horrified.

Sam looked at me, and I vowed to remain silent for the remainder of our sojourn in the Jacksons' home.

"Where do they go to school?" asked Sam.

"Grover Cleveland Elementary School, on Washington," said Henry Jackson. "They was walkin' up Mentone to Hammond. Then they walked to Lincoln and went on up to Washington. When they crossed over to Washington from Lincoln was when they was almost hit. Crossin' the street at Lincoln."

I pictured the intersection in my mind. The area was residential, and most of the people living there were of one color or another, but not white.

"The Cadillac missed 'em by an inch," said Joseph Jackson. I think I'll keep calling him Jackson from now on, because otherwise my brain will develop a cramp.

"I got 'em taken care of," declared the deep, mesmerizing voice from the fireplace.

When we turned to glance at her, she held up another little doll, all dressed up in a tiny white robe and a tiny white dunce cap, and she very deliberately stabbed a pin into the doll's leg. I didn't say anything, keeping to my vow, but I did gasp a trifle. Sam's lips only compressed slightly.

"Mama's got her own ways," said Jackson.

"That she do," said Henry.

"May I speak to your children, Mr. Jackson? Perhaps they saw something else that might help us identify the perpetrator of this deed." Sam.

"I 'spect you can talk to 'em, but they don't much like talkin' to white folk," said Henry.

Don't ask me why, because I don't know, but his comment offended me for about five seconds. Then it occurred to me that if my own children had almost been run down by a Negro in a sheet and dunce cap, they probably wouldn't want to talk to black folk. So I forgave Henry and his children. Not that it matters.

Henry left the room to fetch his kids, and I asked Jackson, "How's Jimmy doing? Is he still playing the cornet?"

"Oh, yeah. He gots himself a good job now, playing in a jazz band for them white folks in Los Angeles. Why, he play at the Coconut Grove at the Ambassador Hotel sometimes. He have to go in through the kitchen, but he makes lots of money."

Very well, my ire rose. Jimmy Jackson was good enough to *play* for the white folks, but he wasn't good enough to walk in through the front door in order to do his job? That wasn't fair, confound it! I refrained from saying so, mainly because Sam pinched my arm, blast the man.

It didn't matter anyhow, because Henry came into the living room again, herding three small black children in front of him. They were a good-looking group of kids, if you discounted their expressions, which ranged from fearful to sullen.

"These here folk are gonna try to help you, Gracie, Steven and Wilbert. Don't be afraid on 'em."

I heard something that might have been a snort from the fireplace, but didn't look to see if Mrs. Jackson had done anything else to the doll she'd just stabbed with the pin. To tell the truth, I was becoming rather ill at ease in her presence. Not, of course, that I believed in her voodoo any more than I believed in my own brand of spiritualism, but there was something about her that grabbed one's attention, if you understand what I mean.

"Good evening, children," said Sam formally. "Will you please tell me what happened when the car almost ran you down?"

Silence ensued. It didn't abate. It stretched out until it became downright nerve-wracking.

That being the case, and because it's hard for me to keep quiet even under normal circumstances, I said, "It's all right, kids. Sam here wants to help find out who's been tormenting your family. He wants to learn who's doing it, arrest him, and lock him in jail."

The three children looked at each other and then up at their father.

It was Jackson who spoke next. "Miss Daisy's tellin' the truth, boys and girls. She be a friend of mine from way back, and she knows what she's talkin' about."

That was nice of him.

So Wilbert finally spoke. He was the oldest of the trio. "It was a white man in a white robe and white pointy hat, an' he drove straight at us when we was in the crosswalk. I had to grab Sissy and Stevie or we'd all be black spots on the pavement on Lincoln."

I presumed Grace was referred to by her brothers as Sissy. And ew. The notion of these three, vibrant, living children, who ranged in age, at my guess, from five to thirteen or thereabouts, being run down in the street made me sick.

"Did you recognize anything about the man driving the car?"

"No, except I saw he was white, 'cause of his hair. It was that kind of reddish color. Not as dark as yours. More orange. I saw the machine, though. It was a Cadillac. Nice car. I think they call them things touring cars. The top was down, and there was two men in it. The one drivin' looked older to me than the other one. Don't know why."

"You can't remember why you got that impression?" pressed Sam.

Wilbert peered at his father, as if asking his permission. Henry Jackson nodded. "If you know anything, son, you tell this man right now."

So Wilbert, after heaving a sigh, said, "The fella drivin' was fat, and he had that orange hair. The one next to him was skinny and...I dunno. He just seemed younger. Spryer. I...I don't think he wanted the old man to run us down, 'cause he hollered somethin' at the older man."

"Do you remember what he hollered?" asked Sam.

Again Wilbert glanced at his father, who nodded and said, "Just tell 'im, son. They ain't your words. They's that bad man's."

Wilbert's lips pressed together for a moment before he blurted out, "That younger feller, he said, 'Christ Jesus, don't do that'. At least that's what it sounded like to me. He hollered it, and slapped his hand onto his pointy hat."

And I, for one, hoped he squashed it flat. I didn't say so.

"But neither man called the other by name?" asked Sam as if he were hoping for more.

"Well..." Wilbert scratched his head. "The fat man, he said somethin', but I don't rightly know what it was."

"Was it a word?" Sam pressed. "A name? Did it remind you of anything?"

"Well, sir, I do know he told the younger one to shaddap. I heard that much."

Sam appeared puzzled, so I said very softly, "Shut up." He shot me a scowl, I rolled my eyes, and he finally caught on. Men. I swear.

"I see," said Sam. "Anything else?"

"Well...I think maybe he called out the other fella's name, but I didn't catch it."

"You didn't hear the name? Did what he say remind you of any other word?"

Appearing frustrated now, Wilbert shook his head and said, "It don't make no sense. It sounded like *eats* or *feets*, but that don't make no sense at all."

"Hmm. Eats or feets. It might have been a name, all right, although it probably wasn't eats or feets. Maybe the name rhymes with one of those words or contains one of those words."

Wilbert shrugged, which made perfect sense to me.

"Thank you, Wilbert. And that's everything you can think of? You didn't see any other people or hear any other words that might have been connected with those two men?"

Wilbert shook his head. "Nothin' but a lot of screamin' from some ladies walking on the street. They all come over to make sure we was all right."

Good for the women. Would that one of them had written down the car's license number and telephoned the police. Oh, well.

Sam sighed. "Thank you very much, Wilbert. If you do think of anything, will you please tell your father or your uncle?"

"Yes, sir." Wilbert seemed relieve his ordeal was over.

"Thanks again. I'll talk to your father and uncle now. You children can go back to...whatever you were doing."

"They was gettin' ready for bed," said Mrs. Jackson from her throne beside the fireplace, shooting a quelling look at the three children, who scurried out of there as if scorched by invisible fire. The woman had power; I'll give her that.

After the children left the room, Sam turned to address Jackson and Henry. "And I don't suppose you saw anyone when they burned the cross on your front lawn." He sounded defeated.

Both men shook their heads, and Jackson said, "Nope. Sorry. Wish we had. I'll tell you in a second if I recognized any of them bastids. Or at least give you a description on 'em."

"Joseph," said Jackson's mother.

Jackson jerked to attention. "Sorry, Mama."

"You don' 'pologize to me. You 'poligize to the young lady."

"Oh, there's no need for that," I hastened to assure everyone. "People say worse things than that in front of me all the time." Especially Sam, although I didn't mention him in particular.

"It's all right, Miss Daisy. I do apologize for using bad language in front of you."

I gave up trying to convince him his language was mild compared to what I was accustomed to. And I thought "bastids" was a rather polite word for the animals who'd burned a cross on his front lawn and tried to kill his kin.

It soon became evident that the two Jackson brothers had nothing more of a significant nature to report to Sam, so we prepared to leave the Jackson home. I first paid a special visit to the regal being beside the fireplace. "Thank you, Mrs. Jackson. I appreciate your juju."

"You jus' be sure to carry it with you, child," she admonished me. "And come back to talk to me one of these here days. Soon."

Oh, my! "I'll be happy to," I told her in all honesty. After all, how often does a fake spiritualist get to compare notes with a semi-famous voodoo mambo? I don't know about New Orleans, Louisiana, but in Pasadena, California, I can tell you from experience: not very darned often.

It was a happy Daisy Gumm Majesty who left the Jacksons' well-kept home on Mentone Avenue and got into Detective Sam Rotondo's Hudson automobile that evening.

NINE

We were almost at my house when Sam spoke again. "You're going to do it, aren't you?"

I'd been fingering my juju, thinking to myself that I'd heard of voodoo dolls before and wondering if this was one, when Sam's question jerked me out of my contemplation. "I'm going to do what?"

"Go back and talk some more with that woman."

"Sure! I've never been given the opportunity to speak with a real, live, honest-to-goodness voodoo queen before. Or voodoo mambo, I guess is the appropriate term."

"Criminy."

"Oh, bother you, Sam. It'll be interesting. I'm always ready to learn more about my line of work."

"If you start making little dolls and sticking pins in them, Daisy Gumm Majesty, I'll...I'll...well, I don't know what I'll do, but it won't be pleasant for you."

"Don't be nonsensical, Sam. I won't do that. For one thing, I don't have that particular skill. I expect you have to know a whole lot of lore about voodoo and what kinds of things to say over the dolls and how to make them look like whoever you want them to look like and stuff like that before mutilating a doll can be effective." Recalling to whom I was speaking, I added hastily, "*If* it can be effective at all, which is highly unlikely. You don't think I *believe* this nonsense, do you?"

"Everyone who hires you thinks you do."

"The only people who hire me have more money than brains. You already know that. Recall Mrs. Pinkerton, if you will."

"I'd rather not," said he as he pulled his machine to a stop next to the curb in front of our house.

Sam came into the house with me, but he didn't linger. He said he had to return to the police department and write down what little he'd learned from our visit to the Jackson family. It wasn't much, and I understood how disappointed he must have been. At least he now knew why Jackson's brother was being persecuted. At least, I thought *I* knew. I figured whoever killed Bruce McIntyre had kin in Pasadena, and they didn't want McIntyre's murderer's name to come out. I wondered if the killer's name was Keats or Dietz or something like that.

I was still pondering the matter when I fell asleep with Spike curled up under the blanket next to me.

The next day, Saturday, the telephone rang just as Pa and I were finishing breakfast. Ma had already gone to her job at the Hotel Marengo, and Vi was on her way to Mrs. Pinkerton's house, where she'd prepare an evening meal and then come home and cook for us, bless her heart.

"Bother," said I, glaring at the telephone on the kitchen wall. Not that its ringing was the 'phone's fault. "I've already told Mrs. Pinkerton I'd be at her house at ten thirty. What the heck does she expect of me, anyway?"

Pa only chuckled and went back to reading the *Pasadena Star News*.

So I shoved myself away from the table and stomped to the telephone. It took a whole lot of self-control to sound spiritualistic and soothing when I said, "Gumm-Majesty residence, Mrs. Majesty speaking."

You could have knocked me over with a spring zephyr when a man's shaky voice said, "Mrs. Majesty? Is your dad there?"

"Why, yes, he is," I said, startled. I didn't recognize the voice.

"This is Charlie Smith, and I need to talk to Joe."

Merciful heavens! What did this mean? Charlie Smith didn't sound happy. At all. "I'll get him for you, Mr. Smith," I said, and carefully allowed the receiver to dangle so it wouldn't hit the wall and knock Charlie Smith's eardrums cockeyed.

Pa had put down his newspaper and was gazing at me quizzically.

"It's Mr. Smith, Pa. He needs to talk to you." And I returned to the table and resumed eating my scrambled egg. Which I'd fixed myself, and which was a trifle leathery. Cooking and I just don't get along, and that's all there is to it.

"Good morning, Charlie," said Pa.

It was only then I realized that I hadn't shooed the party-line neighbors off the wire. Oh, well. If Charlie Smith had something of significance to report, the neighborhood would get a thrill.

I don't know what Mr. Smith said to Pa, but it must have been fascinating, because Pa said, "Stop right there, Charlie. Don't tell me anything else over the telephone. Why don't you come here, and I'll see if Daisy's friend can join us."

Daisy's friend? Did he mean Sam? The detective? Good Lord. Whatever could have happened overnight to Charlie Smith that required Sam's presence?

"All right. See you in a few minutes."

And, with an odd look on his face, Pa hung the receiver gently in the cradle. When he turned to me, his expression was troubled.

"What's the matter, Pa?" I wasn't sure I wanted to know.

Oh, that's a flat lie! I was avidly curious.

"Charlie's next-door neighbor was killed last night."

I know my eyes bugged. Talk about shocked! "Killed? Do you mean...*murdered?*"

"That's what it sounded like to me. Say, Daisy, will you call Sam for me? He should hear this from Charlie's lips. Charlie's afraid someone saw Sam at his house yesterday and that's the reason the poor man was killed."

I thought about that for a split-second. It didn't make sense. "But, Pa, if you think this was a Klan slaying, wouldn't they have killed Charlie himself? Why'd they kill a neighbor?"

With a shrug, Pa said, "I don't know. But if you'll remember, Sam parked his machine in front of Charlie's neighbor's house. Maybe someone saw us and thought we were visiting the neighbor."

"But his Hudson isn't a marked police car or anything."

Pa shrugged again. "Just call Sam, all right?"

"Sure. Was Mr. Smith's neighbor in the Klan, too?" I got up from my place and once again headed to the telephone. I didn't know why Pa couldn't call the Pasadena Police Department for himself, but I didn't argue. Besides, I knew the number by heart. After I'd shooed all the other party-liners off the wire, including the persistent Mrs. Barrow, I dialed it.

When an officer at the police station picked up his receiver, I said, "Detective Rotondo, please." Then it occurred to me that it was Saturday, and Sam might not be at work.

Fortunately for me, he was. There was a pause, during which I presume my call was being transferred, and then came Sam's gruff, "Rotondo here."

"Sam, is it possible for you to come to our house? Mr. Smith is on his way over here, and he has something important to report."

"The—" He didn't finish his sentence, which had sounded as if it was going to be a question. "Cripes. All right." And he hung up. No manners, that man.

Then it occurred to me that, as a member of the homicide squad, or whatever it was called, Sam probably already knew about the murder. Hmm. But he was coming to our house to talk to Charlie Smith, so I could ask him then.

I decided I could discard the remains of my leathery egg. So I did. Then I went to my bedroom and chose a green-checked day dress. I didn't want to be in my robe and slippers when the men showed up at the house.

Poor Spike's walk was late that day. After I'd changed clothes, I washed and dried the few breakfast dishes and put them away. By that time, a knock had sounded on the door.

Pa and Spike opened the door to Charlie Smith. The poor man looked as if someone he loved had just died. Although I know it's irrational, I decided to blame him for his neighbor's death. After all, if he hadn't been stupid enough to join the Klan, his neighbor would probably still be alive.

Of course, I didn't know anything at all at that point, so perhaps I was jumping the gun. An odd but apropos sentiment that morning. I did wonder under what context "jumping the gun" came from, however. Racing? But don't mind me. It was early on a Saturday morning, and my head was still a trifle fuzzy.

"Come on in, Charlie. Sam Rotondo will be here shortly."

Charlie entered, stopped dead in his tracks, looked at Spike with disapproval and said, "Is that a dachshund?"

"Yes," I said, already nettled at Mr. Smith, the Klansman. Criminy, he didn't hate all black dogs, did he?

"That's a German dog," said Smith.

"He's a liberty hound," said I, sniffing with meaning. "Anyhow, aren't *you* of German extraction?"

"My family's Swiss," he said. "But that dog is German."

"He is not. He was born in Altadena." I *really* didn't like Charlie Smith. "And he behaves better than most of the people I know."

"Come with me, Charlie," Pa said, hurriedly guiding his chum into the living room and to an overstuffed armchair.

Charlie Smith sank into the chair as if he carried a great weight and buried his head in his hands. Huh. "God, Joe, I don't know what to do."

"Let's wait and see what Detective Rotondo has to say about this whole thing."

"Are they going to come after me next?" asked an anguished Charlie.

"We don't know who they are or why your neighbor was killed," Pa reminded him. "Detective Rotondo's automobile isn't a marked police car. Perhaps your neighbor had enemies you don't know about."

"Maybe," said Charlie, plainly not reassured.

A knock sounded at the door, and Spike and I hurried to greet Sam, who instantly knelt to pay obeisance to my dog, as was only Spike's due. A German dog, my foot. He creaked a little when he stood again. Sam, not Spike.

"Come into the living room, Sam. Mr. Smith and Pa are there already."

"Right." Sam joined the two men. So did I, although I don't think my presence was appreciated by Sam or Mr. Smith. Phooey on them.

"What is the name of the neighbor who was killed?" Sam asked Charlie.

"Don't you know?" I asked. Not unreasonably, I do believe.

Reasonable or not, all three men turned their heads and frowned at me. I huffed. "Oh, all right. I'll be quiet. In fact, I'll go get some coffee and some of Vi's cookies and bring them here."

"Good," said Sam.

Beast. I listened as hard as I could as I rummaged in the kitchen and fixed a tray. I heard a good deal, too.

"It was Todd Merton. He was shot when he went out to get the newspaper last evening."

"Did you see who shot him?"

"No! I was in the house." His head hit his hands once more. I know, because I peeked. "Lord. I'd just come in from picking up my own paper."

"You didn't see anyone or anything suspicious?" asked Sam.

"No. I was already back in my house. I did hear a car slow down, then a shot, and then the machine squealed away. It left rubber on the street. I ran outside to see what had happened. I couldn't believe my eyes when I saw Todd lying there on his front lawn, bleeding into the grass."

Mercy sakes. Glad I didn't have to see that. I brought the tray into the living room and set it on a table. I'd already poured coffee into three mugs, and the sugar bowl and creamer were on the tray along with spoons if the men wanted either of those things in their coffee.

Pa and Sam each took a mug. Sam, I noticed, drank his coffee black. Pa used cream and sugar. Mr. Smith still had his head in his hands, so I don't even know if he'd seen the tray at that point.

"What time was this?" Sam had put his mug down, taken his notebook out and was writing busily.

"Around seven. Maybe six forty-five."

It was then about eight thirty on the following morning. I was surprised the police weren't still questioning Mr. Smith at the station or his home.

"And you didn't see the automobile you heard?"

"No. I...well, I wasn't looking for it. I was too stunned when I saw Todd lying there."

Lifting his head and pinning Charlie Smith with a look that had withered me once or twice—or maybe more—Sam asked, "Mr. Gumm said you think this killing might be Klan-related. Why do you think that?"

"Because I talked to *you*! I never would have thought of them in connection with a killing until you visited my house. But I guess they really don't like people talking to the police about them."

"They?" Sam said.

"The Klan. I know in the meetings, they tell stories about how the police harass members of the group."

"Do they ever tell stories about the people *they* harass?" I swear to heaven, if I could keep my mouth shut, I would. Honest.

Again the men all shot me nasty looks. I clammed up, even though I believed then, and still believe, my question was pertinent.

"Anyhow, I understand from the few meetings I've attended that the police don't like the Klan. Well, I guess the City of Pasadena doesn't like them, either, for that matter," said Charlie, making me wonder yet again why he'd joined the stupid organization in the first place.

"The members of the Pasadena Police Department have never, to my knowledge, harassed any group of citizens, no matter what their affiliations," declared Sam, sounding as if he didn't appreciate being labeled a harasser of innocent people.

"Well...I don't know," said Charlie. "But all I know is, I talked to you yesterday, and Todd was shot down yesterday evening."

"But that's just it," said Sam. "*You* talked to me. Your neighbor didn't."

"You parked in front of his house."

"In my own personal automobile. I wasn't in a police car, and Daisy and Joe were with me. That doesn't sound police-related to me. Maybe your neighbor had other enemies."

"I can't imagine it. Everyone liked Todd."

Sam shut his notebook. "I don't know, Mr. Smith. The connection between our conversation yesterday and your neighbor's murder last evening seems awfully tenuous. Did you tell Mr. Merton that you spoke with us? Did anyone in your family talk about our meeting?"

"God, no!" cried Mr. Smith. "I didn't want anybody to know about it. Aw, hell, I should have come here, shouldn't I?"

He asked the question of my father, but it was Sam who answered. "So the Klan would have killed Mr. Gumm instead of Mr. Merton?"

Mr. Smith's eyes bulged. "No! No, I didn't mean it that way! It's just that...oh, I don't know. I talked to a policeman about the Klan, and almost instantly my neighbor is murdered. Don't you see a connection?"

"Quite frankly, no," said Sam.

My father said, "You told me the Klan's only purpose in life is to honor Americanism. What's American about murdering someone because he talked to the police?" Good old Pa. He could always get to the heart of any problem.

"Well...I don't know," said Charlie, obviously in great mental distress, which was no more than he deserved.

"I can't see a connection," said Sam. "For one thing, how'd anyone know I was with the police department?"

Charlie shook his head. "I don't know."

As if a lightning bolt had hit my brain, I suddenly knew precisely how someone had known Sam was a detective and had spoken to Charlie Smith. There was a spy in the police department. I didn't dare suggest such a thing to Sam, especially in front of Pa and Mr. Smith, because he'd have exploded. But you tell me: if no one who was involved in the conversation between Charles Smith and Sam Rotondo told anyone about it, who could have known about it? The only logical answer to that question, in my mind, was another member of the police department. Blast! I wish I'd taken down names when I was with all those policemen at Mrs. Pinkerton's house. Maybe one of them had a name that rhymed with feet. Or eats. Well, you know what I mean.

Sam went on, "I think you're worried for nothing, Mr. Smith, although you might consider terminating your Klan membership."

"But I thought you needed him to go to meetings and try to find out stuff." Me. Again.

Sam turned a surly frown upon me. "I did, but not if it's going to cost people their lives."

"Oh, God," muttered Charlie. Huh.

"In any case, I'll look into the Merton matter and see what the investigators have discovered so far. If you're worried about someone coming back to murder you, perhaps you ought to go visit a relative in another town for a few days or something."

Oh, boy, Sam was doing great. I wished I knew shorthand and could have written down this conversation to savor later.

Charlie Smith slumped. "I'm probably worrying too much."

Pa patted him on the back. "You might well be, Charlie. But if you really think your fellow Klan members might have killed Mr. Merton, why did you join the Klan in the first place?"

And Pa was doing great, too.

"Oh, the Klan's not bad. I don't know why I...Listen, just forget I said anything, all right?"

"Sorry," said Sam. "It's too late for that. But keep your eyes open and report to Mr. Gumm if you see anything you think might be pertinent to the Merton case." Rather snidely, he added, "Since you don't want to be seen speaking to the police."

"Yes," said Charlie. "I'll do that. I...I'd rather quit the Klan."

"But then you wouldn't be able to help the police solve Mr. Merton's murder," I said, figuring it would be all right to speak now.

"But Detective Rotondo doesn't think the murder's connected to the Klan," Charlie said.

"You seem to," I said.

"Oh, I don't know." Charlie Smith had started whining.

"Well, if you do decide to quit, just tell them the truth. You don't want to lose your job. Several policemen working for the city have been suspended because of their Klan affiliation. So your fellow white-sheeters know what'll happen to you, as a city employee, if your membership in the Klan is discovered." And I aimed to make sure it was. I decided to tell him that. "And it will be, because, after the murder of your neighbor is solved, if you still belong to that organization, I'm going to telephone the water department and make sure they know you're a Klansman."

"Daisy!" said Pa, appalled.

"Daisy!" said Sam, exasperated.

"That's blackmail!" said Charlie, furious.

"Blackmail isn't anywhere near as bad as murder," I pointed out. "And you yourself suspect your precious Klan of murdering poor Mr. Merton. And *he* isn't even the one who talked to the police! *You* are!" Then I picked up the tray and returned it to the kitchen. I heard the front door close, and Sam and Pa entered the kitchen as I was washing up the extra mugs and spoons.

"That went well," said Sam. He was being sarcastic.

"He deserved it," I said, angry on behalf of Mr. Merton, whom I hadn't even known.

"These cookies are great," said Sam. I guess he thought it would be wise to change the topic under discussion.

I turned to see him holding one of Aunt Vi's masterpieces. "Those are called Swedish cream-filled cookies. Vi got the recipe from one of her friends back East, and she's been making them ever since she was a girl."

"Delicious," said Sam.

"They should be. According to Vi there's nothing in them except butter, flour, and sugar. Well, I think she adds a little vanilla extract. What's not to like?"

Pa remained mute and looked somber. I feared his demeanor boded ill for yours truly. Oh, well.

Sam left, and I got my sweater and Spike's leash, and Pa and I and a rapturous Spike took a walk.

Pa was silent for the first part of our walk, which took us south along Marengo Avenue. I knew he was either annoyed or disappointed with me, but I felt defiant.

"You weren't very polite to Mr. Smith, Daisy," he said at last.

"Well, he's a blazing fool," said I. "Anyhow, you didn't see the three Jackson children describe how two men in white sheets and dunce caps tried to run them down on the street the other day. The Klan is an evil institution, and your buddy Charlie is either stupid, pretending to be stupid, or too naïve for his own good. Not to mention the good of any person of color living in Pasadena. Or any Catholics. Or any Indians. Or any Jews. Or, evidently, any neighbor of his."

"Yes, yes. You've made your point. Still, Charlie's your elder, and you should show some respect."

"Why?" I stopped walking and glared at my father, allowing

Spike to sniff and piddle at will on the sidewalk. "Just because he's older than I am?"

"Well...yes. I guess so. I don't want him to think my daughter's a hoyden."

"Piffle. If he thinks I'm a hoyden because I don't approve of grown men bullying little children, burning crosses on people's lawns, blowing up people's mailboxes, or murdering other people, let him. I don't care, and quite frankly, my feelings are a little hurt that you *do* care." I didn't generally speak so frankly to my father, whom I love above all other earthly males. I still loved Billy best of all, but he wasn't around anymore.

Pa gazed at me sadly for a moment or two, then said, "The modern world is too much for me, I reckon. I guess I agree with you about Charlie and the Klan, but I'm sure not used to children talking back to their elders."

"I'm not a child any longer, Pa," I reminded him gently. "And Charlie Smith is too old to belong to a little boys' club, especially one that's so darned dangerous. I don't believe I was disrespectful in pointing out that salient fact to him."

Pa only sighed. I felt kind of crummy for the rest of the day. But I didn't regret speaking my mind to Charlie Smith. Well, not much, anyway.

TEN

The telephone rang just as I was hanging up my sweater in the bedroom. Nuts. The 'phone was entirely too busy that morning to suit me.

"Who can that be?" asked Pa, staring at the ringing telephone as if it were some kind of evil entity. I couldn't entirely fault him.

"Beats me," said I, exiting the bedroom and heading for the 'phone. "I'm already booked to see Mrs. Pinkerton in forty-five minutes, darn it."

Lifting the receiver, I said, "Gumm-Majesty residence, Mrs. Majesty speaking," same as usual.

A hesitant female voice at the other end of the wire said, "Daisy?" in a not-quite-sure tone of voice.

For pity's sake, I'd just told the caller who I was. Rather than snapping, as I felt like doing, I said sweetly, "Yes. This is Mrs. Majesty." For all I knew, this was a prospective client wanting to give me boocoo bucks for holding a séance, so I was polite.

"Daisy, this is Laura Hastings."

Good Lord! Laura Hastings was Mrs. Stephen Hastings. Or Mrs. Exalted Cyclops, if you prefer, although I don't know why you would. I still couldn't imagine Mr. Stephen Hastings, Esq., being in charge of anything so menial as a chapter of the KKK. I vowed I'd look into the matter further when I could. Admirably hiding my surprise, I said in my soothing spiritualist's voice, "Good morning, Mrs. Hastings. I hope you're feeling better these days."

And that was a stupid thing to say. Her only son, Edward, had been murdered several months prior to that morning, and how any mother could even survive an ordeal like that, much less feel better about her life again, ever, mystified me.

"Well, I do feel better in a way. At least now we all know Eddie didn't kill himself, and the men who did it are behind bars."

"And they'll be staying behind bars for a long time, too," I said firmly, hoping I was correct.

"It...it was a shock to discover Mr. Hastings' partner was involved in Eddie's demise," said Laura Hastings.

"I'm sure it was." It had definitely shocked me. But that wasn't the point. "Did you need me to do something for you, Mrs. Hastings?" I had to get dressed and hie myself over to Mrs. Pinkerton's house, bless it, and this telephone call was eating up precious time. On a Saturday, when I was supposed to be lolling around reading or, at most, doing some gardening.

"Yes. Yes, I wondered if you could come to my house some time soon. I need to speak to you about something that's...something that's been bothering me."

Oh, yeah? And precisely what was I? An alienist? I didn't think so. "You need my services as a spiritualist?" I asked, syrup fairly dripping from my words.

I heard a sigh whiz over the wire. "Well...not so much a spiritualist as a sensible woman who might be able to help me decide what to do about a...particular problem."

Oh. Well, that was nice of her. I mean, it was nice that she considered me a sensible woman, especially considering my line of work. "I'll be happy to do that, Mrs. Hastings," I fibbed. "When would you like me to come over?"

"Not today," she said.

I darned near heaved a sigh of my own in relief.

"Stephen is here today, and he's holding a meeting in the house this evening."

A meeting, eh? What the heck; I decided to ask. "What kind of meeting?" Not that it was technically any of my business.

"That's what I need to talk to you about, actually."

Great. I was probably wrong, and Sam was probably right, and Stephen Hastings probably *was* Pasadena's exalted cyclops, and Mrs. Hastings was probably going to ask me to persuade her husband to quit the Klan. As if Mr. Stephen Hastings, who had once banned me from his law offices on Colorado Boulevard, would ever listen to a word I said about anything at all.

"Very well. Shall I come over on Monday? I'm busy all day tomorrow." Thinking fast, I said, "Would ten thirty on Monday be all right with you?" I figured Mrs. Pinkerton was going to beg me to attend her every day until whoever was dogging Jackson's footsteps and her own gatehouse had been stopped, but perhaps I could at least set my own times for sessions with her. Sessions with Mrs. Pinkerton were always trying to my nerves.

"That would be perfect. Thank you so much, Daisy."

"Happy to help," I said, fibbing again.

Actually, it wasn't a big fib. I did want to understand what the allure, if there was one, of the Ku Klux Klan was to so big a wig in Pasadena society as Mr. Stephen Hastings, Esq. He was head of the most prestigious law firm in the city, even after the scandal that had erupted a few months prior, thanks to me. I hadn't intended to precipitate a scandal. Things had just worked out that way.

"You're such a kind person, Daisy."

"Nonsense. I'm only doing my job."

Which was the truth. But, as I said farewell to Mrs. Hastings and hung the receiver on the cradle, it did cross my mind that she might gift me with more orchids. She'd given me approximately a thousand orchid sprays the last time I'd visited her. They were not merely pretty, but they lasted a long, long time.

As I decided what to wear to Mrs. Pinkerton's, I wondered if orchids and chrysanthemums would look good together in a bouquet.

When I drove up to Mrs. Pinkerton's mansion at about ten twenty-five that day, I slammed on the Chevrolet's brakes and gaped at what had once been the intact gatehouse and the tall black iron gate. And the approximately sixty uniformed policemen gathered around it. Very well, that's an exaggeration, but there were a whole lot of coppers there.

Harold had called in workmen to repair damage from the bomb and the paint-throwing, but now bullet holes riddled the gatehouse. My heart almost stopped until Jackson stepped out from behind a bricked-up barricade to greet me.

"Jackson! I'm so glad you weren't shot! Are you all right? What in the name of God is going on here?"

"Wish I could tell you, Miss Daisy."

"Ma'am, please move along," said a uniform. "We're investigating this scene."

"Miss Daisy has a 'pointment with Mrs. Pinkerton, sir," said Jackson to the copper.

"Aw, crap. Is that you, Daisy?"

And Sam stomped up to my machine. The uniform frowned, but stepped away. I glanced at his badge to see what his name was. It wasn't anything that rhymed with eats or feets. I remembered him as one of the uniforms who'd exchanged what I now believe was a guilty glance with another uniform the day of the bomb. And I also remembered his name was Petrie, which reminded me I needed to go to the library.

"Good morning again to you, too, Detective Rotondo," I said, irked with Sam, which was entirely normal. "More Klan trouble, I see."

"You don't know it's Klan trouble," Sam growled.

"Huh." I craned my neck to see around Sam, who's an immovable object when he wants to be, to find Jackson. "Have you or your brother had any more trouble lately, Jackson?"

"No, ma'am, Miss Daisy. Thanks for askin'."

"I'm glad to hear it." I sniffed. "If you'll be kind enough to move, Detective, I can get to my appointment with Mrs. Pinkerton on time."

Sam rolled his eyes, which was also normal. "Go on." He stepped aside. I squinted at the other officers milling about, wishing I could see their badges clearly.

Featherstone led me to the drawing room after I'd clunked the knocker on the huge front door, and I was pleased to see Harold in the room, attempting to soothe his mother, which wasn't possible, but Harold was a good son.

"Good morning," I said to the both of them. Harold, bless him, held his mother in her seat on the sofa so she didn't run me down. He was a good friend as well as a good son.

"Not much good about it," said Harold. "You saw the bullet holes, I'm sure."

"Yes, I did."

"*Oooooooh!*" wailed Mrs. Pinkerton.

Harold winced. She'd screeched directly into his ear. "It's all right, Mother. Daisy is here now, and she'll soon set things to rights."

I would, would I? I didn't know how I was supposed to do that, but I gave it my best shot, using the Ouija board and the tarot cards.

Harold left the drawing room with me an hour or so later. He'd sat quietly in the room whilst I'd spewed fake spiritualistic nonsense for Mrs. Pinkerton. She claimed my efforts made her feel better, which made one of us.

"She's going crazy with everything that's been happening in and around the gatehouse," Harold muttered as we walked down the hallway toward the kitchen. "Which is bad, since she's not stable under the best circumstances."

"I guess that's true, but I don't blame her for being upset this time. What happened? That's a whole lot of bullet holes."

"They think whoever did it used a Thompson submachine gun."

"Good Lord! A Tommy gun?" I'd read about Tommy guns in the newspaper, but never in connection with my fair city of Pasadena, California. Things were getting really ugly around town, and I didn't approve. "Did the police already talk to her before I got here?"

"Oh, yes. They've been toddling around the property since around three thirty this morning, when the gunfire erupted."

"Good heavens! I'm so sorry. Of all the people in the world for this sort of thing to happen to...Well, I don't know why whoever's doing this is picking on your mother."

"They're not. They're picking on Jackson, poor fellow. Fortunately, the Klan doesn't seem to know about Del and me yet. At least I haven't received any threatening letters. Mother has, though." Harold's frown was a masterpiece that almost equaled one of Sam's. "She got another one today, after the police got here. The police have taken it into evidence."

"Oh, dear, I'm surprised she didn't cry to me about the letter."

"I think the gunfire put it out of her mind."

I could have said something about Mrs. Pinkerton being out of her mind in general, but I didn't. "I'm glad she had sense enough to give it to the police."

"She didn't. I did."

That came as no surprise. "Did this latest letter again recommend she get rid of Jackson?"

"No. It threatened her that if she didn't get rid of Jackson, more disasters would strike her. Poor Jackson offered to quit, but your buddy Rotondo wouldn't let him. I think the rest of the force would have been happy to see the back of Jackson, but not Sam."

"Well, he knows an injustice when he sees one," said I, hoping it was the truth.

"Either that, or he has sense enough not to let Jackson wander around loose. When he's here, the police can keep an eye on him."

"Wish they'd keep an eye on the rest of his family," I muttered, thinking the police were discriminatory in their surveillance tactics.

"We are keeping an eye on the rest of his family," a familiar voice growled from behind us.

I twirled around. "Sam!" Taking a better squint at him, I said," Have you been working all through the night? You look terrible."

My comment was only the truth, but I probably could have phrased it more tactfully. Sam gave me a glorious frown. "Yes, I've been working all night and, so far, all day. Christ, I was at Merton's place until almost midnight. I was still at the station when the call came in about the Pinkertons' place being shot up, and then you called and I went to your place, and now I'm here again."

"I'm sorry, Sam. You should go home and take a nap or something."

"Criminy. I'm a cop, Daisy. I can't just *go home and take a nap*."

"Oh. Well, I'm glad you talked Jackson into staying at his job, even if you didn't do it out of compassion."

"Cripes," muttered Sam.

For some reason, that reminded me of something. "Say, Sam, do you know any policemen named Keats or Dietz or...well, anything else that rhymes with feets or eats?"

"No," he said. I got the distinct impression he wouldn't say more about policemen's names if I tortured him.

"Why were you at Daisy's house?"

Since Sam didn't seem inclined to open his mouth, I answered Harold's question for him. "Oh, Harold, it was awful. The Klan killed my father's friend's neighbor. We think they did it because Sam went over there to talk to Pa's friend yesterday."

Both men eyed me strangely. Well, Harold did, anyway. Sam only scowled at me.

"You don't know who did the killing or why," Sam more or less growled.

"They *murdered* someone?"

I nodded. "Shot him when he was picking up the evening newspaper on his front lawn."

"You don't know who killed him or why," said Sam, repeating himself. I guess he had a point, although it wasn't one I bought.

"Who else could have done it?" I asked him.

"Anybody in the world."

"Hmm. Well, maybe, but my money's on the Klan."

"I know."

At that moment, we were interrupted by another policeman, who came running down the hallway after us. Sam turned and trained his scowl on the uniformed officer, who was the same Officer Doan I'd met before.

"Yes?" Sam snapped.

"It's Petrie," said Doan, panting slightly. "He was taking measurements on the guardhouse and fell off. I think he broke his leg. Andrews is using his police radio to call for an ambulance."

"Aw, shit," grumbled Sam, and he turned and followed Doan back to the front door. Before he got there, he turned to me once more, "And don't go telling me *this* was Klan-related!"

"Oh, for pity's sake, Sam Rotondo. If you aren't—" But he was gone out the front door. Featherstone, who had stood beside the door as Doan fetched Sam, shut it calmly behind the two coppers' retreating forms. Nothing *ever* ruffled Featherstone.

"Well," said Harold. "That's too bad."

Petrie had broken his leg, had he? Naturally, my mind had instantly reverted to Jackson's living room, and my mind's eye distinctly saw Mrs. Jackson stick that pin in that white-sheeted juju's leg.

I turned again to Harold. "Is the library open today, do you know?"

His mouth fell open for a second. Then he said, "The *library?*"

"Yes. I need to go there."

"Hell, Daisy, I don't know. You're the one who's always hanging out in the library."

"Oh, bother. Well, never mind. I'll go see if Vi is ready to come home, and then I'll find out if the library's open or not."

"Why do you have to go to the library all of a sudden?"

I pondered Harold's question for only a moment before I said only, "Research." No sense in having two men laugh at me just because I wanted to find out if my Miss Petrie was related to broken-legged policeman Petrie. Who might or might not belong to the Klan, and who might or might not have had some voodoo juju justice enacted upon him.

Our lovely Pasadena Public Library was open two Saturdays every month, but I couldn't offhand remember which two Saturdays those were. Harold and I continued on to the kitchen, and Vi was so happy to see us, she fed us lunch. She was also glad to have a ride home.

ELEVEN

I was in luck. The library was open from noon to six on that particular Saturday. I could have telephoned to find out if Miss Petrie was working that day, but I already knew from experience how little librarians enjoyed having the peace of their surroundings disturbed by ringing telephones, screaming children, etc. So I just left Vi at home, scooped up the books waiting on the table next to the front door to be returned to the library, and went back out to the Chevrolet. After, naturally, telling Spike what a wonderful boy he was. I could tell he didn't believe me when I left him again, because his big, brown doggie eyes called me names. I vowed I'd make it up to him when I got back from the library.

My luck held. I had no sooner walked through the sacred library doors when I saw Miss Petrie, sitting behind the check-out desk, reading a book. The library was almost empty that day. So, after putting my books on the return table, I walked over to Miss Petrie, who looked up from her book with reluctance. When she saw it was me, she smiled.

"Mrs. Majesty! You don't usually grace us with your presence on Saturday, but I have two books I've been holding for you."

"Thank you!" I really liked the books she picked out for my family and me.

"They're both British, and they're both wonderful. And we *just* got them in. Here's *Whose Body*, by a woman named Dorothy L. Sayers, and this is another book by Mrs. Christie."

"Oh, I loved *The Mysterious Affair at Styles*."

"I think you'll love this one, too. It's called *Murder on the Links*."

"Thank you!" I tried to refrain from grabbing the books out of her hands, but if you're as much of a reader as I am, you know how greedy one can get for good new books.

"You're most welcome. I like picking out books for you, because we share the same tastes."

"I know, and I can't tell you how much I appreciate your help." However, I was at the library on a mission not book-related that day, so I figured I'd best get to it. "Oh, say, Miss Petrie," said I, trying to sound as if I'd just that moment thought of what I wanted to ask her. "I recently met a policeman named Petrie, and I wondered if the two of you were related."

Her mouth pursed and her eyebrows lowered over her thick eyeglasses. Miss Petrie wasn't what you'd call a natural beauty. In truth, she was a rather plain woman, but until that moment, I didn't realize she could approximate the demeanor of a wicked witch. The effect startled me.

"That," said she, snarling slightly, "is my cousin Roland. As far as I'm concerned, he's a discredit to the family."

Interesting. "Because he's a policeman?"

"Good heavens, no. Law enforcement is an honorable profession. It's the things he gets up to in his off hours that have the family in a state."

They were in a state, were they? Promising start. "Golly, what kinds of things does he get up to in his off hours?"

"Well..." Miss Petrie stole a glance around the library as though she didn't want anyone else to hear what she was about to tell me. As we were alone as far as I could see, I didn't think she had anything to worry about. "He's begun joining so-called 'patriotic' organizations. *I* think they're a lot of hooey. And I can't vouch for his strength of character. I do believe he's become involved in some kind of shady dealings with a coterie of his so-called friends."

"My goodness." There were a couple of "so-called" things in Miss Petrie's explanation. I wanted specifics. "What kinds of patriotic organizations?" I asked, keeping my voice at a whisper.

Miss Petrie leaned forward over her desk and beckoned me to do likewise, so I did, only I had to bend a bit to achieve the position. "I truly believe he's violating a city ordinance, but I'm almost certain he's joined that misspelled clan you did research on the other day, Mrs. Majesty, and I'm sick that his involvement will get out and disgrace the family name."

"Oh, dear," I said, since I could think of nothing more cogent to say.

"And I also know he's borrowed and invested some money in a real-estate scheme that sounds to me as though it's built on sinking sand."

Merciful heavens, I didn't know the woman could be so poetic. "Do you know anything else about the real-estate scheme?" While I couldn't quite feature Mr. Stephen Hastings as an exalted cyclops of the Ku Klux Klan, I could definitely see him finagling people out of their money via a phony real-estate deal.

"No. I wish I did. I'd tell somebody in a hurry, you can bet. All I know is that he intends to buy property with a bunch of other men in some southern state and build on it. I think the deal sounds mighty shaky. I also know that Roland borrowed the money from his mother and father, my aunt and uncle, and they can ill afford to lose it. But they've always given Roland anything he's ever wanted, which is probably why he's the way he is now. He's a leech on society, that boy."

"I'm so sorry," I said, meaning it. "It must be tough to have someone like that in the family, although I'm sure you're not alone. I was appalled when I learned that the Ku Klux Klan actually had a group in Pasadena, so there must be other people besides your cousin who have joined it."

Miss Petrie sniffed. "Well, you can be certain that if there's something rotten going on, Roland will be in the thick of it. I was surprised when he joined the police force, since police work seems such an honorable profession. In fact, I'd rather hoped he'd changed his wicked ways, but alas, it was not to be." Her lips flattened into a wrinkly line for a second before she burst out—if one can burst out in a whisper—"I'm tempted to telephone the police station and tell someone about Roland's affiliation. He's a blot on the family name."

"I think you should," I said. My back was beginning to ache from bending over, so I stood and stretched. I continued whispering, however, when I said, "If it'll make you feel any better, your cousin broke his leg this morning when he was investigating a Klan shooting."

"A *shooting!*"

Miss Petrie forgot to whisper, and I felt guilty. A quick glance around the room reassured me that we were still alone, however. I hastened to amend my stark statement. "No one was hurt. I think— the police have yet to confirm this—that Klan members used a Thompson submachine gun to shoot up Mr. and Mrs. Pinkerton's gatehouse. The Klan has been harassing their gatekeeper, Joseph Jackson, ever since Mr. Jackson's brother, Henry, moved here from Tulsa, Oklahoma. They're a Negro family, and the Klan went so far as to burn a cross on their lawn last Monday night."

Slapping a hand to her probably palpitating heart, Miss Petrie said, "Oh, no!" She appeared harried for a moment, then said, "His side of the family is from Tulsa."

"Good heavens!"

"The rest of my family is perfectly fine, but Roland's side is iffy. Roland himself is a cad. I wouldn't be surprised if he's the culprit who's been harassing that poor family." Then she sat up straight in her chair. "I'm glad he broke his stupid leg. I'm sorry it wasn't his neck."

"Now that you've told me about him, I am, too."

We stood gazing into the distance for a moment before Miss Petrie broke the silence. "Um, Mrs. Majesty, I know you are friends with a detective on the Pasadena police force." She licked her lips and swallowed. I got a sinking feeling in my innards. "I know, because I've read the newspapers, that twice in the past couple of years, you've received a commendation from the police chief for assisting them in their investigations."

It was a good thing Sam wasn't with us. He'd have set her straight in a split-second about my "assistance" in his cases—although I *had* been instrumental in helping the police department in both of those incidents. I murmured a tentative, "Yes?"

"I don't suppose you could ask your friend to look into the real-estate deal Roland's involved with, could you, as well as his Klan membership? I know I don't have much information, but perhaps I can get more. I just am so afraid he's going to lose the last of my aunt and uncle's savings. They don't have much, you know, and the economy has been so hard on people these past few years."

It sure had been. It seemed to me, back in those days, that there were maybe ten Mrs. Pinkertons who had more money than was good for them, in the good old USA, to every ten thousand of us just plain folks, who struggled every day to put food on the table. Mind you, I'm not including my family among the latter, mainly because Ma, Vi and I were gainfully employed, and I made scads of money through the few of Mrs. Pinkerton's type extant in the City of Pasadena. Still, things weren't fair, and I knew it as well as did Miss Petrie.

But could I enlist Sam Rotondo to help me smash a phony real-estate ring? Much less turn on one of his own?

I'd have laughed sardonically if I weren't ensconced in the severe silence of the Pasadena Public Library.

Nevertheless, I felt sorry for the good side of Miss Petrie's family, so I said, "I'll see what I can do. If you can gather any more particulars, it would certainly help. At this point, I fear my detective friend would only be annoyed if I told him there was some kind of criminal real-estate bunco crime going on in Pasadena. If you see what I mean."

"Of course, I do," said Miss Petrie, who was sharp as a needle. "Men seldom believe anything women tell them. I'll see what I can find out. Roland loves to boast, so I might be in luck."

Until that moment in time, I never would have believed Miss Petrie could produce such an evil smile, but she sure produced one that day.

"In fact, I do believe I'll visit the poor boy in the hospital. They did take him to the hospital, didn't they?"

"I truly don't know. The last I heard, he'd just that minute broken his leg. I expect they'll take him to the Castleton, since that's the hospital nearest where the accident happened." If it was an accident, thought I, and not a voodoo curse come to life.

"If it was an accident," said Miss Petrie, startling me. "I wouldn't hold it against Mr. Jackson to shove him off a roof, given what Roland's been up to lately."

Merciful heavens! "Oh, but Mr. Jackson would never do anything like that."

"Pity, that," said Miss Petrie with a sniff.

It was then I decided to forego separating iris bulbs for another day or two and pay a visit to Mrs. Jackson, voodoo mambo extraordinaire, and tell her what had happened as a result of her sticking a pin in that Klan juju's leg. Maybe I could get her to stick some pins in a Stephen Hastings juju or an exalted cyclops juju. I'd probably need the name of the cyclops, and I still doubted it was Mr. Hastings, but perhaps she could put a general, all-around hex on the entire Klan. Of course, I knew only the bits and pieces of voodoo lore Jackson had told me about, so I didn't know if a hex had to be specific in nature. I fingered the juju hanging around my neck through the fabric of my dress.

One more good reason to visit Mrs. Jackson, by gum. So I did.

Mentone Avenue wasn't far from the library, which was on the corner of Raymond Avenue and Walnut Street, so it only took about ten minutes for me to drive there. When I arrived, I saw no children playing, but that ugly black burn mark on Jackson's front lawn was definitely noticeable. I shook my head in disgust as I exited the Chevrolet.

Mrs. Jackson, the voodoo mambo herself, answered my knock at the door. Her face held not a single hint of an expression for the first several seconds of our meeting. We just stood there and gazed at each other. Then a slow smile creased her face.

"Come in, child. Tell me what's happened. You still got your juju?"

Once more I fingered the little doll hanging on its string beneath my day dress. "Oh, yes. I never go anywhere without it."

She nodded. "Good thing. Keep wearin' it. You's gonna need it."

I was? I swallowed the lump that had formed in my throat. "I will? What's going to happen that I'll need it?"

"Oh, you just never know about them things," said she. Big help. "But you got news to impart, so you jest go on and impart it. Come into the kitchen with me, and I'll fetch us some tea and beignets."

I wondered what a beignet was when it was in Pasadena but didn't ask, figuring I'd learn soon enough.

And, boy, did I! I carried the tray Mrs. Jackson had loaded with tea and a plate of beignets into the living room and set it on a table between two chairs. Mrs. Jackson took one chair and I took another, and she waved at the plate of pastries, so I took one and bit into it. In case you don't know, beignets (I think that's a French word) are the sweetest, most delicate and delicious doughnut-type pastries I've ever eaten.

"This is wonderful," I told Mrs. Jackson after I'd swallowed my first bite.

"They's from New Orleans, child. The recipe is, I mean." She pronounced the city's name "Nawlins" just like Jackson.

"Um, I don't suppose you'd care to give me the recipe? My aunt is a wonderful cook, and she collects recipes."

"I knows who your auntie is, child. Jackson's been tellin' me 'bout her good cookin' since I moved to this here city."

It made me proud that Jackson had bragged about my aunt's cooking skills to his mother, who clearly had magical skills in the kitchen herself.

"And I'll be glad to give her my receipt. 'Course, it's rightly not mine, but my great-grannie's, but that don't make no difference."

"Thank you very much."

"Pshaw, child. Now you go on an' tell me what's happened. I 'spect somebody got his leg broke." She gifted me with a knowing smile.

"You're precisely right. A policeman named Roland Petrie fell off Jackson's guardhouse and broke his leg. I don't know how bad a break it is, but it's going to hurt for quite a while, I expect."

"Amen," said Mrs. Jackson, and she took a bite of her own *beignet*. They weren't particularly easy to eat, being covered with powdered sugar, which dripped all over one's front, but Mrs. Jackson had provided napkins for us. "And now you're gonna tell me who gets the next juju, am I right?"

"Well, as to that, I'm not quite sure yet. I'm sure there are probably other police officers who belong to the Klan, but who aren't telling anyone. But there's something else going on. Miss Petrie, who's a librarian friend of mine and Roland Petrie's cousin, is worried that he's involved in some sort of real-estate swindle."

"The boy be a grifter, do he? He gots a black heart, that young man."

I wasn't sure what a grifter was, but I was pretty sure Roland Petrie qualified if it was something slimy. Therefore, I said, "Yes." I thought for a moment how to phrase my next question.

Mrs. Jackson beat me to the punch. "You thinks you knows something else 'bout the swindle, don't you, girl?"

"Well, I'm not sure. But Mrs. Stephen Hastings telephoned me yesterday and wants me to meet with her. Her husband's a big cheese in Pasadena. He's a rich attorney, and she's worried about something he's involved with."

"No doubt," muttered Mrs. Jackson. "Them lawyers is all made of the same dirty linen."

Not sure about that, but unwilling to argue with my hostess, I only said, "If he is involved in the real-estate deal, I might find out on Monday, and then I can tell you more."

She nodded. "In the meantime, I'll just get some of my jujus ready. You know more 'bout who's doin' the KKK things to the Pinkertons' gatehouse and my poor Henry and his babies?"

"Not yet, but I'm working on it," I said. It was a feeble admission, since I really had nothing to work on yet. Then I thought of Charles Smith. "However, a friend of my father's is in the Klan, and Detective Rotondo, Pa and I went to talk to him the other day. That very evening, his neighbor was shot and killed as he went outside to collect his newspaper."

"Gotta stick another pin in that bad boy's juju," said Mrs. Jackson darkly.

"Well, nobody knows for sure if the shooting had anything to do with—"

"I do."

"Oh." She sounded certain, and who was I to gainsay her? She knew a whole lot more about voodoo juju—and the workings of the Ku Klux Klan, for that matter—than I did. "Have your grandchildren suffered any more near misses or anything?"

"No, but that's because Henry's took 'em to my daughter's home in Los Angeles. This here Klan don't know where they be. And it's goin' to stay like that. I don't want nothin' to happen to my boy or my grandbabies."

"I can certainly understand that." Curious, I asked, "Do you know precisely why the Klan in Pasadena is after Henry and his kids? I mean, he said he saw something, but even he said he isn't sure what it was."

"He saw a Klansman murder another Klansman," Mrs. Jackson

said as if she knew whereof she spoke. "Henry, he don't like to admit it, but it's the truth. And the murderin' Klansman's got relations here in Pasadena. He saw Henry see him."

"But Henry—I mean Mr. Jackson—told me he wasn't sure what he saw."

"Huh. That boy always done been a fence-sitter. He tol' me what he seen, and I know what it was, if he don't. He ain't the brightest candle in the box, my Henry. And he's got a good heart, but when you fightin' people with no hearts at all, you gotta be firm."

"That's a fact," I said, meaning it. Still, I couldn't help but wonder if Mrs. Jackson hadn't interpolated her own meaning onto what her son told her.

"And don't you go doubtin' me, neither, girl. I know them people, and I know what one of 'em done to the other."

Shoot, the woman could read minds. "It's not that I doubt you—"

"Yeah, it is. But you got no reason to. I know what Henry seen."

"Do you know the names of anyone involved? Wasn't the murdered man's name McIntyre?"

"It was. And the killer was another one of your Petries." Mrs. Jackson gave me a smug smile.

"Another one?" Flabbergasted might be an appropriate word to use to describe my sensation at that moment, but there's probably a better one somewhere that I can't think of offhand. "How do you know that if Henry doesn't?"

"I knew them people," she said. "Ask your librarian friend. Ask her if her family done come from Tulsa."

Thinking back to the conversation I'd recently had with Miss Petrie, I said, "You're right. Miss Petrie told me they did."

"Told you so. *I* know they did the killin'. And so does Henry, but he's afeared."

"For good reason."

"Maybe." Mrs. Jackson sniffed as if she didn't approve of her son's state of fear. I didn't blame Henry one bit for being afraid.

I thought of something else. "Mrs. Jackson, do you have any idea who the exalted cyclops of the Pasadena Klan is? Someone told me he's the same wealthy Pasadena lawyer who might be involved in the real-estate scheme, but I know a good deal about the man, and I can't see him heading an organization like the Klan."

"Exalted cyclops." Mrs. Jackson gave a wicked chortle. "The top man in this here city ain't no rich lawyer. He be an ordinary, every-day sort of man, only with a bad heart. He be a small man wantin' to be a big one, only he don't have the talents to rise by his own merits."

My thoughts precisely. "I don't suppose you know his name," I asked, not expecting much. Which is exactly what I got.

"Naw, but I know good and well he's good at pretendin' he ain't what he is."

"Yes. He must be. Well, thank you, Mrs. Jackson."

"You're welcome. And don't forget your juju, and next time you visit, I'll have that receipt all writ out."

"Thank you very much."

I left Jackson's place with my head spinning. *Another* bad Petrie in the wood pile? Or maybe it was the same Petrie. Only Roland Petrie looked so young. And Miss Petrie had said most of the rest of his family wasn't bad, like he was. Good Lord. Life could get awfully complicated while one wasn't looking, couldn't it?

TWELVE

After all my meanderings and consultations that Saturday, it was an exhausted Daisy Gumm Majesty who greeted her ecstatic dog, said good-day to her father, and then went to her bedroom to lie down and take a nap with Spike. Vi was napping, too, so I didn't feel guilty.

However, after I woke up, I took Spike for a walk *sans* Pa, who'd gone to a friend's house to help him work on his motorcar. When I got home again, Spike and I separated a whole bed full of irises, and I decided to ask Jackson if his mother might like to plant some of them. See? I don't spent all my time snooping.

During Spike's walk, and as I separated iris bulbs, I pondered the many questions swirling in the air in Pasadena recently. Was Petrie a member of the Klan? Had he or another member of his family murdered Mr. McIntyre in Tulsa, Oklahoma? Was he involved in a phony real-estate scheme?

The Jackson children had heard someone—I believe they'd said it was the villainous driver of the Cadillac—call out something that sounded like eats or feets. Could the driver have called out the name

Petrie? Definitely a possibility, although I don't know where the S at the end of the word came from.

And then there was the exalted cyclops. If Mr. Hastings wasn't the exalted cyclops of Pasadena's Klan, who was? If he was one of the men in the Cadillac, he was chubby. "Fat" was the word the Jackson children used, but how much could they have seen, really, as they raced to get out of the Cadillac's way? How the heck could I know? Anyhow, if the man in the car was the exalted cyclops, he wasn't Stephen Hastings, who wasn't fat. Maybe the exalted cyclops had minions to run down kids for him, but I still couldn't quite feature Hastings in the position. He didn't mingle with the riffraff, and I think he considered policemen and people like Charlie Smith, who worked at the water department, riffraff.

Then there was Charlie Smith's dead neighbor. Who had shot him and why? Could he have been a member of the Klan, too? If so, why hadn't Mr. Smith told us so? If he wasn't in the Klan, who'd want to shoot him? Had they shot him when they'd meant to be aiming at Mr. Smith? Why would they want to kill Mr. Smith?

Oh, bother.

It was getting close to dinnertime, so Spike and I went indoors, I removed my gardening gloves and apron, washed my hands, and noticed dirt clinging to the hem of my ratty old day dress. So I changed into another ratty old day dress and asked Aunt Vi if I could help her with anything in the kitchen. I don't know why I always did that, because the kitchen and I are mortal enemies, but I did it anyway.

"You can set the table, sweetheart," said she. "Set an extra plate. Sam's coming to dinner this evening."

"Oh." He was, was he? I swear, Sam might as well live at our place. But I didn't mind. "What's for dinner?"

"Nothing very exotic. Chicken fricassee with peas and carrots and onions. The butcher at Jorgenson's gave me an extra chicken when I ordered for the Pinkertons. He's a nice man, Mr. Putnam."

"Mr. Putnam's the butcher?"

"Yes, indeed. He's nice about giving me bargains and extra chickens and suchlike when he has meat he needs to get rid of. You know. Before it spoils."

Hmm. Looking closely at my darling aunt's face, I didn't see a trace of pink, but I wondered if there might be a romance brewing there, between her and Mr. Putnam. They'd make a perfect couple, a butcher and the best cook in Pasadena. I didn't ask, not particularly wanting to annoy Aunt Vi.

Then it dawned upon me why Mr. Putnam gave Vi meat, and I hoped he didn't allow whatever he gave her to hang around his butcher's counter *too* long. None of us had died of ptomaine yet, so I guess he didn't.

"So I should set out bowls instead of plates?" I asked, which was a nice, neutral question.

"Probably. And little plates for the biscuits."

"No dumplings?" I wasn't really disappointed. I loved Aunt Vi's biscuits as much as, or more than, I loved her dumplings.

"No. I decided to have biscuits. You can split a biscuit, put it in your bowl and spoon fricassee over it if you want to."

"No, thanks. I'll have my biscuits with butter." Needless to say, Vi made the best biscuits in the world. Then I remembered the *beignets*. "Oh! I forgot to mention that I stopped by the Jacksons' house this afternoon. Mrs. Jackson is going to give me a recipe for *beignets*."

Vi beamed at me. "Oh, my! I've wanted a recipe for *beignets* for the longest time!"

"You have?" Boy, among the other imponderables in life, you never knew what would make people happy, did you?

"Indeed, I have. Ever since Mr. Jackson told me about his mother's powdered doughnuts. I'm assuming that's what a *beignet* is." She lifted her eyebrows at me.

"Well, yes. Maybe a little flakier."

"Better and better," said Vi, with a dreamy look in her eyes.

I got a dreamy look in my eyes when I watched a Rudolph

Valentino movie. Which just proves my point about imponderables, I guess.

Anyhow, I finished setting the table and took a detour to my room to check myself out in the cheval mirror, wishing I'd put on a more becoming frock since Sam was coming to dine with us.

But no. I wasn't going to primp for Sam Rotondo. This was especially true since I wanted to ask him about Roland Petrie's leg, and ask him if Petrie might have been the name the Jackson children heard called out that dismal day. That would probably make him really mad, so I'd wait to ask him about Charlie Smith's dead neighbor and Stephen Hastings running a real-estate swindle until I had more information. *One temper fit at a time*, I told myself.

Ma roamed into the dining room—she'd been napping, too—about the time Pa got home from his friend's house.

"Something smells good," said Pa, rubbing his hands together as if they were cold, which they probably were, the weather being a bit brisk.

"Chicken fricassee with biscuits," I told him promptly.

"Go and wash your hands, Joe," said Ma, frowning at my father's greasy hands. "You might want to use turpentine to get that muck off."

Pa kissed her on the cheek and headed to the back of the house, where he kept turpentine, gasoline and all his tools left over from his chauffeuring days. Hmm. Turpentine and gasoline. Both were extremely flammable. I wondered if either of those substances had been used to burn that cross or explode that mailbox. I added that to the list of questions I had for Sam.

Speaking of Sam, Spike announced his arrival promptly at the stroke of six o'clock, which is when we Gumms and the last remaining Majesty had our dinner. I opened the door for him. He still looked pretty rugged around the edges.

"I don't suppose you got any sleep today," I said in greeting.

"No. What with the Pinkertons getting their gatehouse machine-gunned and Todd Merton's murder, I've been kept busy. Thanks for your concern."

That was supposed to be sarcastic, but I didn't mind. I got grumpy when I didn't get enough sleep, too.

"Well, come on in and dine on chicken fricassee with us, and then you can go home and go to bed." I thought about his job for a second, then stopped and gazed up at him. "You *can* go home and go to bed after dinner, can't you?"

He heaved a massive sigh. "Yeah."

"That's good. It's not fair that you have to work day *and* night."

"It's my job," he grumbled, hanging his hat and overcoat on the tree beside the door and clumping to the dining room. "Good evening, all," he said to Vi and my parents in a much more civil tone than he'd used on me. I was accustomed to it.

"Merciful heavens, Sam Rotondo, you don't look as if you've had an easy day," said Ma, who was honestly concerned.

"My job," said Sam.

"He had to investigate the murder of Charlie Smith's neighbor and the Tommy-gunning of the Pinkertons' gatehouse, and he hasn't had any sleep since yesterday sometime," I informed my family.

"*Murder!*" Ma was shocked, although I don't know why she should have been. She knew what Sam's job was. We all did.

With a pretty darned mean scowl at me, Sam said, "We don't have to talk about it."

"Dear me, no," said Vi. "Poor Mrs. Pinkerton was in a state all day today. I don't know how Daisy manages to cope with her sometimes."

I didn't, either.

Sam said, "Huh."

Vi went on, "But Mrs. Pinkerton is always more at ease after Daisy does her magic, so I'm glad she's willing to do it."

"Thanks, Vi." I wrinkled my nose at Sam as a sort-of "so there" gesture. Childish, I know. I fingered my juju and hoped Sam would be willing to answer a couple of pertinent questions after dinner.

Good Lord, was I beginning to use that silly juju as a prayer wheel, or whatever those Tibetan monks use? As a talisman upon which to pray for help? Good thing the next day was Sunday. I think I needed a dose of normality and good, old religion.

Dinner was, of course, delicious. What's more, I discovered that a buttered biscuit laid in a bowl and then covered with chicken fricassee was every bit as delicious as chicken fricassee and dumplings. I think everything tasted even better because the chicken had been given us and not bought. We Gumms are a thrifty lot. Anyhow, Vi gave us apple crisp with vanilla ice cream for dessert, and we all left the table feeling liked stuffed Thanksgiving turkeys. At least I did.

I was cleaning the table and taking dishes to the kitchen sink when I heard Pa ask Sam, "Do you feel like a game of gin rummy tonight?"

"I'm sorry, Joe. I'm so beat, I'm going to have to go home and fall into bed." He turned to Aunt Vi. "If you hadn't fed me, Mrs. Gumm, I'd have gone to bed hungry as well. I'm all in."

Blast! As a rule, as soon as dinner is finished, I wash up the dishes and put them away and then join the family in the living room. But Sam didn't aim to stick around. Therefore, I heaped dishes in the sink and ran after him.

"I'll see you to your car, Sam," I said, smiling brightly at him.

"Good idea," said Pa.

"Wonderful idea," said Ma.

Vi only gave Sam and me a sweet smile, as if she knew a budding romance when she saw one. Ha. If she only knew.

Sam knew, though. He eyed me as he might eye a squishy bug crawling across his dinner plate. He didn't say anything until we stood beside the driver's side of his Hudson. "All right, what is it?" he asked, sounding about as weary as I'd ever heard him.

I prevaricated a trifle. "Mrs. Hastings called me this morning. She thinks her husband is at the head of a real-estate swindle." Maybe that was more of a big, fat lie. She hadn't told me what she thought her husband was involved with; I'd figured out the real-estate swindle part on my own, using information given to me by others.

"She what?"

"You heard me. She asked me to drop by on Monday morning, because she's worried and wants to talk to me about whatever it is her husband is doing."

Sam sagged a bit. "Why the devil is it that people call *you* instead of the police when they suspect others of wrongdoing?"

"We've been over this before, Sam," I told him—and I was being honest, too. "I'm nicer than the police, and the Mrs. Hastings and the Mrs. Pinkertons of the world don't want to get involved in police matters."

"Hell. So you're going to do some more snooping around Stephen Hastings, are you?"

"I'm not going to snoop!" I answered indignantly. "Mrs. Hastings asked me to go to her house so we could chat, and I'm going to go to her house and I'll chat with her. That's all. If I learn about anything illegal going on, I'll tell you, and I'll also try to find out if Hastings is the Klan's exalted cyclops, which I don't believe for a minute. I'm *not* merely snooping. I'm helping out a friend. Friends." Sort of.

"I just bet you are."

Oh, piddle on Sam Rotondo. However, since he seemed too exhausted to roar, I decided to go on to another sore subject. "And do you think Roland Petrie belongs to the Klan? His cousin, Miss Petrie at the library, thinks so."

It wasn't awfully bright out there on Marengo Avenue under all the pepper trees, but I saw Sam close his eyes and shake his head. "I don't know. I'll look in to the matter."

"Thank you. I think he's also involved in the real-estate swindle. That is to say, Miss Petrie thinks so."

"Christ."

"And it was a Petrie whom Mr. Henry Jackson saw murdering that guy in Tulsa."

"*What?*"

Very well, so that was a moderate roar. His eyes sure opened quickly. I nodded. "Mrs. Jackson told me so."

"Why the devil didn't someone tell *me* that when we were talking to the Jacksons at their house?" I opened my mouth to speak, but Sam didn't let me. "I know, I know. You're nicer than I am."

I sniffed. "I actually don't think that's the reason they didn't tell you at the time. According to Mrs. Jackson, Henry is too kind to tell a tale on another person."

"Even if it involves a coldblooded murder?"

"Apparently. Anyhow, I don't imagine, if Roland Petrie belongs to the Klan, the Jacksons are too fond of the police. They're probably scared of retaliation if they name names. Heck, they're being retaliated against anyway. I don't blame them for keeping mum."

"God," muttered Sam, closing his eyes and bowing his head again. He sounded defeated, which made me feel kind of sorry for him, but not a whole lot.

Then I bethought me of something else. "What did Todd Merton look like?"

Sam lifted his head and opened his eyes enough to squint at me. "What the hell do you want to know *that* for?"

"It should be obvious to a police detective," I told him. "The driver of the Cadillac that almost ran down the Jackson children was fat and had gingery hair. Was Todd Merton fat, and did he have gingery hair? I wouldn't put it past Mr. Charlie Smith to get his neighbor to join the Klan and then lie like a rug about it. In fact," said I, having just had an intriguing thought, "it wouldn't surprise me to know that Charlie Smith is the exalted cyclops! He makes more sense to me in the role than Stephen Hastings."

Sam stared at me for what seemed like a little more than eternity, but probably wasn't. "Todd Merton was...plump and had brown hair. I don't know about his Klan affiliation, if he had one."

"Ha. And do you suppose he might have called out 'Petrie!' to his fellow passenger rather than feets or eats?" I had a brilliant idea. Or maybe not. Sometimes it takes a while to know if an idea is brilliant or not. "Maybe people call Petrie Pete!"

Another eternity or three passed. Then Sam said, "I'm going home. I'm too tired for this right now."

"But you'll think about all those things, won't you? I'll get Vi to make you some *beignets*, if you do." It was the strongest inducement I could think of at the moment.

Sam only said, "Whatever they are," and got into his car.

"I'll let you know what I learn!" I called after him.

His hand came out the window and he waved at me. Hmm. Well, I'd done my best.

So I went back indoors and washed the dishes and put them away.

THIRTEEN

On Sunday, September reverted to its usual state of being, and the air was quite warm. Therefore, I dressed in a pretty sleeveless dress in a printed dark green I'd found on sale at Nash's Dry Goods and Department Store. It was a straight up-and-down number, with just a hint of a belt at about hip level. Before Billy died, I'd have had lots of unseemly lumps and bumps to spoil the tubular effect of the dress, but I was still slimmer than I'd been a year ago.

Lucille Spinks and I sang our little hearts out during our duet and did a smashing job during the fifth verse of "Amazing Grace." I even heard a couple of discreet "Amens" from the congregation after we were through singing. We Methodists don't go in for a lot of calling out or clapping during our church services. I've heard that the Baptists really go to town when it comes to that sort of thing.

Several people came up to Lucy and me after we'd taken off our choir robes and headed to the Fellowship Hall to tell us we'd sounded lovely. That made both of us happy.

Mr. Zollinger was waiting beside the coffee pot for Lucy, so she veered off in his direction and I looked for my family. When I spied them in the crowd, my heart gave a little lurch. For years and years on

Sundays after church, Billy had been among them. Even before we were married, Billy and his family attended this same First Methodist-Episcopal Church. But there was no more Billy and no more of the rest of his family. My heart ached a little when I joined my own family.

"You girls sounded wonderful, Daisy," said my mother, giving me a peck on the cheek.

"Thanks, Ma. I think our voices blend pretty well together."

"They blend great together," said Pa.

"Indeed. Why, I had tears in my eyes after your duet," said Vi.

It was so nice to be appreciated.

Since Vi had a pork roast in the oven cooking away as we were in church, we didn't eat any cookies or have any coffee, but merely greeted our friends and left the church to walk home. When we hit the house, the telephone was ringing. Ominous, that. But I didn't run to answer it. Rather, as I greeted Spike, who was thrilled that his humans had returned, I silently prayed this particular telephone call wasn't from Mrs. Pinkerton.

Silly me. Of *course* it was from Mrs. Pinkerton.

"Oh, Daisy!" she wailed. I was used to it. "Some awful person shot Jackson!"

My jaw dropped and I stood there, speechless, for several moments, my mind trying to grapple with what I'd just heard.

"Daisy?" she said, as if she thought we'd been disconnected by some inept operator at the telephone exchange.

"I'm sorry," I said, my heart leaping about in my chest like one of those Mexican jumping beans you can find in downtown Los Angeles sometimes. "You say Jackson was *shot*? He isn't...he isn't...*dead*, is he?" No, no, no. Jackson couldn't be dead.

Actually, Jackson *could* be dead. My heart continued to pound like a drum.

"No. But he's in the hospital."

"Which hospital?" I asked, forgetting to sound like a spiritualist.

"The Castleton. But Daisy, I *need* you!"

She needed me! What about Jackson?

"I'm terribly sorry, Mrs. Pinkerton, but I can't come over today. I can come over tomorrow in the late morning. Perhaps eleven thirty?" I hoped that would give me enough time for Mrs. Hastings. But what the heck. If I was late to Mrs. Pinkerton's, I didn't care. Someone had shot *Jackson*. I could scarcely take it in.

"You can't come today?" She sniffled pathetically.

"I'm awfully sorry, but I have family commitments today." And I aimed to visit Jackson in the hospital, too. And telephone Sam Rotondo.

"Very well," said Mrs. P in a woebegone voice. "Tomorrow at eleven thirty. Thank you, Daisy."

"Do you know where Jackson was shot? I mean, what body part? Is he badly hurt?" This entire Jackson situation was getting totally out of hand. Damn it, I was going to hunt Sam Rotondo down and *force* him to take action. Somehow. Oh, Lord. Poor Jackson.

"I don't know. I don't believe he's too seriously wounded, although he's going to be in the hospital for some time. Naturally, I'm paying for his care."

"That's very kind of you, Mrs. Pinkerton."

"Fiddlesticks," she said, sounding firm, for her. "This shooting and letter-writing nonsense has to stop. You'll tell your policeman friend about Jackson, won't you?"

"Yes. I certainly will."

"Thank you, Daisy."

"You're welcome." I hung the receiver on the hook in something of a daze. When I turned around, the whole family was staring at me.

"Jackson was *shot*?" Vi asked.

"Yes. He's at the Castleton. Mrs. Pinkerton is paying for his medical care."

"As well she should," said Vi somewhat belligerently. "After all, he's worked for her for years and years, and done a good job. Daisy, I think you should telephone Sam about this, don't you?"

"Yes, I do."

"Is this more of that outrageous Klan's nonsense?" asked Ma.

"I suspect it is."

"I wonder if Charlie Smith is as innocent as he claims to be," said Pa, surprising me. I'd been wondering the same thing, but I figured Pa, who was so nice and loyal, would stick up for his friend come hell, high water, the Klan, or the devil himself. I should have known better. Pa's smarter than that.

"Me, too," I said, picking up the receiver once more. No one on our party line was speaking, so the line was clear. To be safe, I said, "If anyone else is on the wire, please hang up. I have an emergency." Very well, so it wasn't precisely my emergency. It got three clicks, so my fib was worth it.

Thinking Sam might have been called in already regarding the Jackson situation, I dialed the Pasadena Police Department. When the officer at the front desk answered, I said, "Detective Rotondo, please."

"He isn't here at the moment. May I help you?"

It was nice that he said "may" instead of "can", but it didn't help me. "This is Mrs. Majesty, and I'm telephoning about the shooting of a friend. Joseph Jackson. Do you know anything about that?"

A short spate of silence ensued, and I heard papers shuffling on the desk at the police station. At last the officer spoke again. "I have a note here from Detective Rotondo. It says he's at the Castleton Hospital regarding the Jackson matter."

"Thank you very much," said I, and I replaced the receiver on the hook.

"Sam wasn't there?" asked Vi, madly mashing potatoes and calling to me over her shoulder from the stove.

"He's already at the Castleton. I guess he's talking to Jackson and his kin about what happened."

"Well, before you go haring off to the hospital, eat some dinner," said Ma. "We don't want you wasting away again."

"Very well, but I'm not going to change clothes or anything. I hope you don't mind if I eat quickly."

"Tosh," said Vi. "Eat as fast as you like. In fact, you fix your plate from the stove before I dish up everything."

"We don't want you getting skinny again," added Ma.

"Yeah. You need to find out what's going on," said Pa. "I swear, if Charlie Smith is involved in any of this...Well, I just don't know."

I picked up a plate and headed stove-wards. "What made you rethink the Charlie situation, Pa? You were sure he was innocent as a newborn lamb the other day."

"I've just been thinking about him and the Klan and the bad things that have been happening. That's all. I don't buy his 'the Klan's a patriotic organization' reasoning."

I'd have guffawed if I hadn't been forking a piece of pork from the fragrant roast Vi had fixed for us. It was so tender, I didn't even have to use a knife, and I made sure to get a crusty piece. Then I scooped some potatoes and gravy onto my plate and asked, "Are the carrots ready yet?"

"No. You can eat your carrots when you come home."

"Good deal."

You see? There are many very good reasons I love my family so much. They had their priorities in the right place, unlike a lot of other people I could mention but won't.

I didn't do justice to Aunt Vi's delicious roast pork, but I gobbled it down as if I were starving. Then I kissed each remaining member of my family, including Spike, and headed out to the Chevrolet. I didn't break any land speed records, but I drove pretty fast down to the Castleton, which wasn't awfully far from our house.

An elderly lady sat at the information table in the front lobby, so I asked her in which room Jackson had been housed. She shuffled through some papers on the table and then looked up to me, a surprised expression on her face. "Mr. Joseph Jackson?"

"Yes. He's the one."

"He's a Negro."

"I know he is. He's also a dear friend of mine." I glared at the woman, and she swallowed and said, "Room two thirty-six. I believe there are some policemen with him at the moment."

If she'd said that to make a point, it didn't work with me. "I'm sure there *are* policemen with him. Some idiots in the Ku Klux Klan shot the poor man!"

"Oh, my!" I heard her whisper as I stumped off.

The hospital didn't have an elevator for visitors, so I walked up the stairs to the second floor and didn't have any trouble finding room 236. A uniformed officer stood at attention outside the door. Huh. They were finally taking Jackson's problems seriously, were they? Well, it was past time.

And who should the guard be but the ubiquitous Officer Doan. He saw me coming and frowned. He usually frowned when he saw me coming.

I didn't even bother with a greeting. "Is Detective Rotondo in there?"

"Yes, but you can't—"

"Pooh. Jackson is my friend, and he'll be glad to see me." And I pushed right on past Officer Doan. I wouldn't have been surprised to learn *he* was a Klan member, too.

Rotondo loomed over Jackson's bed, and Mrs. Jackson had more or less taken a throne at her son's bedside. Both of them looked toward the door and watched me enter, Rotondo with a scowl, and Mrs. Jackson with a smile. I fingered my juju for the heck of it, and felt Doan at my back.

"How is he?" I asked without preliminary greetings.

"He done been shot," said Mrs. Jackson.

"He's going to be all right," said Sam. To Doan he said, "It's all right, Doan. Family friend."

That was nice of him. And totally unexpected.

"Is that Miss Daisy?" came a feeble voice from the bed.

"Yes, it is, Mr. Jackson. How are you feeling?" I really had to come up with some better lines to use on people who are grieving or wounded.

"Not too good. Thanks for comin' by."

"You bet I came by." I turned to Sam. "So, what do you think, Detective? Will the police department finally do something about that vicious Klan now that two people have been shot?"

Sam looked a little healthier that Sunday afternoon than he had the last time I'd seen him. I presume he got a good night's sleep after he left our house on Saturday evening. He sure didn't appear pleased to see me, however, no matter what he'd said to Officer Doan.

"I'm here gathering information from Mr. Jackson, for God's sake. We need facts and information before we can arrest anyone. Even you should know that," barked Sam.

"Don't you be gruff with the girl, Detective," said Mrs. Jackson. "You's the police. You need facts. The rest of us only need to use our common sense to know what's what."

I wondered if I could adopt Mrs. Jackson as an honorary aunt or something. I walked to the bed and winced when I looked down upon poor Jackson, whose dark complexion had a distinct grayish cast to it. "Oh, Jackson, I'm so sorry this happened!" And darned if I didn't start to cry. I swear, sometimes I think I should be chained up somewhere. It always embarrasses me to cry in front of people. I snatched my hankie out of my handbag and wiped away my tears, feeling foolish.

A huge hand descended on my shoulder, and when I looked to see whose it was, I was shocked to discover it belonged to Sam. Was he trying to comfort me or get rid of me?

"The doctor was just here, Daisy. He really did say Mr. Jackson will be all right." He even sounded sympathetic. Good heavens.

I sniffled. "I'm so glad. Where were you hit, Mr. Jackson?"

"M'leg," said Jackson. "Hurts somethin' awful."

"Can't they give you anything for the pain?" Sniffles vanished and I began to get indignant again.

"They just give him some drugs," said Mrs. Jackson, who didn't sound as though she quite approved of this. "He'll feel better soon. But take a seat, gal, and sit by me."

Easier said than done. There was another chair in the room, but it was on the other side of it, and Sam was in the way. To my shock, he lifted the chair, hoisted it over Jackson's form on the bed, and set it down beside Mrs. Jackson's chair. I said, "Thanks, Sam," and sat.

Mrs. Jackson patted my hand. "It'll all be all right, girl. Joseph, he a strong man. And this here policeman seems to care what happens to him."

"I care a lot," said Sam in a gruff voice. I believed him.

"Did you see who did it?" I asked Jackson.

"Daisy," said Sam, sounding as if his patience was nearing the end of its tether. "Why don't you just sit there and be still while I chat with Mr. Jackson about what happened."

I felt a trifle mulish but decided it would do no good to argue, especially with Officer Doan standing outside ready and, I'm sure, more than willing to remove me should Sam request him to do so.

"But *did* you see who shot you?" asked Sam of Jackson.

"No, sir. It was goin' on toward night, and I was walkin' from the bus stop to get home. Corner of Lincoln and Washington, it was. A feller come out from behind a building and shot me, slam, in the leg. Then I fell down, and heard the feller come closer, but then other folks began runnin' up, and he took off."

"Who came running up? Do you know if any of them saw the man?"

"I don't know, Detective. I was in a lot of pain and tryin' not to shout or cry. Then somebody wrapped my leg in a towel and some-body else opened the door to an automobile, and two men hauled me into the car and drove me here. I think the one who owned the car was Carl Simmons. I know Carl was there, but by that time, I...well, I guess I was bleedin' a lot, 'cause I passed out. Next thing I know, I'm in this here room with my leg in a big bandage and Mama sittin' at my bedside."

"Huh," said Jackson's mother. I don't know why.

"Carl Simmons, you say?" Sam was diligently writing everything down in his little policeman's notebook.

"Yes, sir. He the chauffeur for some rich folks in Altadena, but he live on Mentone close to our house."

"Do you know the name of the people he works for?"

"The Greys. You know that writer feller, Zane Grey? That's the one."

Holy jumping cats. I knew Zane Grey, the famous writer of western fiction, owned a huge estate at the top of Lake Avenue in Altadena, but I didn't know anyone who'd actually *met* the man or his family. And Jackson knew his chauffeur! I felt kind of like I was visiting royalty, which was silly. I was only visiting a friend of a person who worked for royalty. If you know what I mean.

"Zane Grey, eh?" Sam didn't appear noticeably gratified to learn this bit of information, perhaps because Altadena was in the county sheriff's venue, or perhaps because he didn't fancy getting involved with any more rich folks. I think the Pinkertons had cured him of any envy he might once have entertained in regard to having great wealth.

"That's the one," said Jackson.

We heard a scuffle outside in the hallway and turned toward the door to see a harassed-looking Doan trying to fend off a very large Negro woman, who held a box in her arms.

"Vera!" exclaimed Mrs. Jackson.

I think I heard Jackson moan a little.

"This man won't let me come in, Mama Jackson. Tell him I needs to see Jackson!"

Sam and I exchanged a quick glance. Sam sighed. "Let her come in, Doan. Might as well."

So Vera came in, along with a delightful aroma of cinnamon, which I presumed emanated from something in the box she carried.

As you might imagine, that hospital room was becoming *really* crowded. And hot. And stuffy. But oh, well. The cinnamon scent helped a trifle.

FOURTEEN

It turned out that Vera Armistead, the friend of Jackson's mama, worked as a cook for a family named Walsh. The Walshes were fabulously wealthy, having made their fortune manufacturing chewing gum, and they lived not far from the Pinkertons. It also turned out that Vera Armistead was a fount of information about darned near every rich family in Pasadena and Altadena.

Not that she spent her time in the hospital room gossiping. Rather, after she maneuvered her bulk around Mrs. Jackson and me, she bent over Jackson's bed, gave him a big smack on the cheek, and said, "You take and eat this here cinnamon cake, Joseph Jackson. Cinnamon's good for what ails you."

"Even a gunshot?" I asked, very softly. I wasn't arguing with the woman; I was honestly curious.

Mrs. Armistead turned her head and gave me an appraising, not-awfully-friendly look. "Cinnamon cures everything, young woman. Who you be, anyhow?"

"Vera," said Mrs. Jackson in her most regal tones, "this is Missus Majesty. Her and me, we share the gift."

Mrs. Armistead's eyes grew huge. "You mean *she* be a mambo, too? But she's white!"

"She a white mambo. They's different from us black mambos, but this one still has the gift."

I definitely heard Sam grinding his teeth.

"Glory be," said Mrs. Armistead. I think she'd have sunk onto a chair in shock, but there wasn't a vacant one handy.

I leapt out of mine and said, "Here. Have a seat." Then I scooted over closer to Sam, just in case the woman fainted. I didn't want her to faint on me, because she'd probably have smothered me. She was even bigger than Mrs. Jackson.

"All right, let's have a little order in here," said Sam, sounding extremely official. "Mrs. Armistead, did you happen to be in the vicinity when Mr. Jackson was shot?"

"No. My son, Marshall, him and Carl Simmons is friends, and Carl come over and told us what happened."

"Did he happen to mention who held the gun and shot Jackson?"

"No, but he described that bad man, whose soul is cursed forever more."

Mrs. Jackson nodded, and I believed them both.

Sam brightened a trifle. "Can you remember what he said the man looked like?"

"Plump. Not fat like me, but plump. Brown hair. He weren't wearin' a sheet, but he one of them Klan folks."

"How do you know that?"

"Because he done shot Joseph!" said Mrs. Armistead as if Sam should already have known that. "Ain't no white men come around that part of town after the sun sets unless they be bent on mischief, and that man, he was bent on mischief."

"He was bent on murder," muttered Mrs. Jackson.

I noticed she'd taken out another juju from somewhere or other on her person, and she very deliberately broke one of its arms. I winced in spite of myself. I then told myself I didn't believe in voodoo mambos anymore than I believed in the fluff I spewed forth in my career, but I winced again anyway.

"That he was. Marshall said Carl said that the man was walkin' up to Joseph and looked like he was goin' to finish the job, but folks rushed out, and he got scared and run off."

"Wish somebody'd tackled him," mumbled Sam.

So did I.

"I done told Marshall that Carl was a fool not to of done just that," Mrs. Armistead said to Sam, "but Marshall told me Carl was more worried about gettin' Joseph to the hospital than in tacklin' no gun-totin' villain."

Well, when she put it like that, I guess he'd been wise not to try to tackle the shooter.

Mrs. Armistead continued, "Anyhow, when a couple of the fellows looked, the man was long gone. Don't know where he went, 'cause that street's a long one, and they's nothin' around except for some businesses, and they was closed for the night."

Sam sighed and said, "Yes, I understand. Do you know the names of anyone else who might have seen the shooting or the shooter?"

Mrs. Armistead tapped one or two of her chins as she thought. I began to wish I'd changed from my Sunday church shoes into more sensible walking shoes because my feet ached as I stood there. "You might want to talk to Georgia Akers. She works for a couple of families in Pasadena as a maid. Not an everyday maid, but a once-a-week maid. I think she knows which folks have joined that stupid Klan."

"Georgia Akers, you say?"

For the first time in a long time, Sam seemed happy about something. Probably because people were finally beginning to spill what they knew about local Klansmen. Past time, perhaps, but I understood the unwillingness of some of the Negro families in the city to talk to the local coppers. After all, several of the local coppers were members of the Klan. The Jacksons and their like were in one of those a damned-if-you-do and damned-if-you-don't predictions. I'd been in several of them myself, and I knew firsthand how uncomfortable they could be.

"Georgia Akers. Yes. That's the one," agreed Mrs. Armistead.

"Georgia, her and her husband and kids live near us on Mentone," added Mrs. Jackson.

Sam, scribbling like crazy, asked, "Address?"

So Mrs. Jackson gave the Akers' address, which sounded like it might be across the street from the Jacksons. I began to wonder if Mrs. Jackson wasn't so much a voodoo mambo as she was a collector of really fascinating gossip, with maybe a bit of magic thrown into the pot to make people pay attention. I fingered my own juju until I saw Mrs. Jackson smiling at me.

"My son, Marshall," went on Mrs. Armistead, "he's a photographer. He takes pictures of most everything. Want he should take a picture of where Joseph got hisself shot? Too bad he wasn't there at the time, 'cause he'd've caught the villain with his Kodak."

"In the dark?" There I went again, talking when I shouldn't.

"T'weren't that dark," said Mrs. Armistead.

"Oh," said I for want of anything more cogent so say. Jackson had said it was going on towards night, but I didn't want to argue.

"He's a photographer, is he?" said Sam—loudly, in order to get our attention.

"That he be," said the proud Mrs. Armistead.

"It might be helpful if he could take pictures of where the shooting took place. By the time we were told about it at the police station, no one could tell us exactly where it happened, or we'd have sent our own photographers to take pictures."

"Uh-huh," said Mrs. Armistead.

"Yeah," said Mrs. Jackson.

Poor Sam. His department really didn't have a very good reputation among the non-white population of Pasadena. I almost felt sorry for the poor lug, mainly because I knew Sam didn't harbor a prejudice against anyone in the world unless they committed crimes. And me. He had a prejudice against me, but I think that was based on personality and profession. Race didn't enter into the equation.

"I'll get him to do that today," said Mrs. Armistead.

"Thank you." He shuffled through his notebook for a few seconds. "Can you think of anyone else who might have seen the shooting?"

I saw Jackson's head wag back and forth on his pillow. The poor man looked awfully tired. I'm sure he wished we'd all go away and let him alone.

"It's time for us to leave my boy to hisself," said Mrs. Jackson, echoing my own thoughts. "The boy needs to rest." She shot a piercing glance at Sam. "You goin' to post a policeman at the door to his room so that white man can't come back and shoot him dead in the hospital?"

Jackson uttered a pitiful squeak. I gasped.

But it was sure something to think about. "I'll see what I can do," said Sam, sounding doubtful.

Mrs. Jackson heaved herself to her feet. "Don't bother. *I'll* get some folks to guard my boy. He don' need no Klan policemen makin' his life uglier than it already is."

"Mrs. Jackson—"

But Sam didn't get to finish his sentence, because Mrs. Jackson stepped on his words and squashed them flat. "I know where us black folk stand in this here community, and it's at the bottom of the ladder. But we can take care of our own. So you don't need bother, Mr. Detective."

"Very well." Sam both sounded and looked defeated. "That would probably be a good idea. I'll make arrangements with the hospital staff so they'll know there will be people posted at Mr. Jackson's door."

"Big black people," said Mrs. Jackson, giving Sam her most evil grin.

"Heh," said Mrs. Armistead. She heaved herself up from her seat and said, "You eat every crumb of that there cake, Joseph Jackson. Cinnamon is good for what ails you, no matter what it is."

I decided I'd search for books on medicinal uses for spices next time I went to the library. And that would be...Lordy, not tomorrow. Tomorrow I had to deal with two rich women, one of whom might have answers to some of my questions. Or not. I'd see.

Mrs. Jackson bent to give her son a kiss on the cheek and told him to rest up. Then she and Mrs. Armistead left the hospital room. I went up to Jackson's bedside and said, "I'm so sorry this happened, Mr. Jackson, but you'll get better, and Sam really *will* find out who's doing these awful things." I took his hand and squeezed it, not too tightly since he was already in pain.

"Thank you, Miss Daisy. You're a good girl."

"Thanks for the information, Mr. Jackson," said Sam. He neither kissed the cheek of nor shook hands with Jackson, but said, "Daisy's right. We're taking this seriously, and we *will* catch whoever's responsible for this."

"Thank you, Detective."

I could tell Jackson was fading fast, because his eyes kept closing and his words to Sam were somewhat slurred. The drugs were kicking in, no doubt.

Before he could escape, I grabbed Sam by his arm and hauled him to the door. There I whispered, "You're not going to leave Jackson unguarded until Mrs. Jackson's guards show up, are you?"

Sam opened the door and shoved me out into the hall, then closed the door quietly after he left Jackson's room, too. "We don't have the manpower to post a guard at his door, Daisy. Cripes!"

"Then I'll stay here until Jackson's guards show up," I said, feeling defiant and angry. They simply *couldn't* leave Jackson without a guard; not with someone out there, probably quite nearby, bound and determined to kill him. It was one thing—and a bad one— to burn a cross on the man's lawn, but to go so far as to *shoot* him... well, it was too much. Besides, the Klan would probably be swarming all over the hospital because Petrie was there with his stupid broken leg. Or he probably was. I should have asked at the front desk. Pooh.

Without responding to my...what? Threat? Well, whatever it was, Sam turned to Doan. "Stay here until Mrs. Jackson can organize a couple of fellows to stand guard at this door, Doan." Then he stopped and squinted at Doan, whose eyes opened wide with what looked a whole lot like alarm. "You don't belong to that damned Klan, do you?"

"*Me?* Good God, no! I think the KKK is a work of the devil."

For goodness' sakes. "Are you a religious man, Officer Doan?" I asked out of honest curiosity.

"I am, ma'am. My wife and I attend St. Andrew's Catholic Church every Sunday of our lives."

"Good. Glad to hear it." Especially since the Klan hated Catholics almost as much as they hated Negroes. "I'm sure Mrs. Jackson will have reinforcements here soon."

Sam heaved a big sigh. "Yeah. Well, if no one shows up within the hour, give the station a call, Doan. I'll telephone to have a uniform come here to relieve you."

"Yes, sir." He seemed troubled for a moment, then said, "If I have to telephone the station, sir, I'll have to leave this door unguarded while I do it."

Sam hung his head and muttered, "Shit."

"Tell you what," I said, having come up with a brilliant notion. Well, maybe not, but you already know my experience with brilliant notions. "I'll stay with Officer Doan, and then if one of us has to telephone you, someone will still be posted at the door."

Neither Sam nor Officer Doan seemed particularly taken with this idea, but they didn't object. All Sam said was, "I have to talk to the hospital administration folks and then get in touch with someone at the station." So he left to do so.

And it all worked out all right, considering Officer Doan and I didn't have a lot to say to each other, and every time I looked into Jackson's room, he seemed to be sound asleep. Perhaps thirty or forty minutes after Sam left, four extremely large black men cleared the top of the staircase and moved like a freight train toward Jackson's door. Officer Doan seemed a trifle intimidated, so it was I who walked up to the men.

"Are you here to guard Mr. Jackson?" I asked the man who appeared to be the oldest of the bunch. His curly black hair was streaked with silver in spots.

"Yes, ma'am," said he, appearing rather standoffish. Guess he wasn't accustomed to white ladies accosting him in hospital corridors.

I held out my hand. "I'm Mrs. Majesty. Daisy Majesty. I've been a friend to Mr. Jackson for years now, ever since I started working for Mrs. Pinkerton. Well, when she was Mrs. Kincaid and now that she's Mrs. Pinkerton. Both. For more than ten years, anyway." Bother. I was getting all confused.

Fortunately, the man smiled, took my hand and shook it, thus redeeming the situation of my idiocy.

"Carl Simmons, Mrs. Majesty."

"Oh, you're the one who drove Jackson to the hospital! Thank you *so* much for doing that. Poor Mr. Jackson has been going through so much lately, and this is just...horrible."

"Yes, ma'am." Mr. Simmons let go of my hand and tilted his head to his companions. "These here guys are Jackie Jones, Ron Griffith and Alvin Lee, ma'am."

"I'm so glad you fellows are here. I was afraid that awful man who shot Jackson might come back here and finish the job before you arrived, so Officer Doan and I stood outside his door until you got here."

"That was right kind of you, ma'am."

The glance he shot at Doan wasn't quite as friendly as the one he gave me. I wanted to tell these men that Doan was a Catholic and, therefore, as much of a target of the Klan as they were, but I held my tongue, something I too seldom did.

But the four men planted themselves on either side of Jackson's door, and Doan and I left our posts and walked together to the staircase.

"Thank you for staying with me, Officer Doan."

"Just doing my job, ma'am," said Officer Doan fairly stiffly.

"Well, thank you anyway. I've come to understand, since Jackson's family has incurred the wrath of the Klan, that most Negro families don't expect much by way of help and protection from the police. Unfortunately, I believe they have a good reason for their expectations. I think you've proved yourself to be one of the good men on the job." Did I sound pompous or did I not sound pompous? I didn't mean to. I meant what I said.

There was a noticeable pause before Officer Doan said, "Thank you."

"You're welcome."

And that was it as far a conversation between the officer and me went. I went down the stairs before him, he clunked along behind me in his big policemanly shoes, and he held the front door of the hospital open for me to exit, and I exited. Then we parted ways, and I went home.

Where Sam was. I ought to have known he would be.

FIFTEEN

"S am!" I said as soon as I stepped into the house and before I knelt to greet Spike. "Have you interviewed anyone or learned anything else yet?"

Aggrieved, Sam said, "I only just got here, for Pete's sake. I had to go to the station and make arrangements for someone to relieve Doan if he called. Since you're here, I guess he didn't need anyone to come rescue him."

"Four of Mr. Jackson's friends showed up just a few minutes ago. They're huge, Sam. If anyone tries anything funny, I expect one of them will just pick him up and throw him down the stairs or something. Or maybe sit on him until he suffocates. Or—"

"I get the picture," said Sam, grumpy as usual.

Pa chuckled, bless the man. Neither Ma nor Aunt Vi was anywhere in sight—this was in the dining room, since I'd come through the side door. Sam and Pa had each taken a seat at the table. I presume Ma and Aunt Vi were napping, which was what I aimed to do as soon as I could. It had been an eventful day, and I wanted to rest a while. After, of course, I ate my carrots like a good girl.

Too bad for me Sam had other ideas. "Would you be willing to go with me to interview Mrs. Georgia Akers?"

That woke me up in a hurry. I stood abruptly and stared at the man. "You want *me* to help you?"

He heaved a huge sigh. "Yeah. These people don't seem to dislike talking to you as much as they dislike talking to police personnel."

I smiled at him. "Told you so. Over and over again. I'm nicer than you are. That's why people talk to me."

"Daisy, that's not fair," said Pa, not awfully forcefully.

"It might not be fair, but you don't understand what some segments of Pasadena's populace have endured via the police of our fair city."

"You don't know that they've endured anything," said Sam, thundering slightly.

I sniffed. "How many policemen have been suspended because they're members of the Ku Klux Klan?"

"Dammit. Six. But they've been suspended, which means the city fathers of Pasadena won't put up with that sort of nonsense."

"Officer Petrie is a member of the Klan, and he hasn't been suspended." Although he did break his leg, a circumstance that made me smile.

"He will be. I visited him after I left Jackson's room. He was pretty mad about my questioning him, but he owned up to being a Klan member, so I told him to quit either the Klan or the police department. I'll tell the chief tomorrow. Don't want to bother him on a Sunday."

"Was Miss Petrie there with him?"

"I don't know Miss Petrie," Sam grumbled. "A woman was in his room when I entered it. She didn't speak while I was there."

"Medium height, skinny, mouse-brown hair, limp—her hair, not her—big glasses. Looks intellectual. Actually, I think she'd be pretty if she fixed her hair and wore a touch or rouge. Wears boring clothes."

After eyeing me for an appreciable second or two, Sam said, "Yeah, I think that must have been the one."

I grinned. "She said she was going to visit him. She hates his guts because he's a disgrace to the family. She's the one who told me he was a Klansman."

"And she thinks he's involved in some shaky real-estate deal. Yes, I remember quite well."

I sniffed again. "Well, he's a louse. By the way, I'll probably know more about the real-estate thing after I see Mrs. Hastings tomorrow."

With a roll of his eyes, Sam let the real-estate question slide. "Well? Will you come with me to interview Mrs. Akers?"

"Sure! Let me change my shoes. My feet are aching like mad because I didn't change into sensible shoes after church and before I drove down to visit Jackson. In fact, I think I'll change my dress, too."

"I want to see the woman today, Daisy."

"You needn't be sarcastic, Sam Rotondo. It'll only take me a minute."

Very well, so it took me about five minutes to change out of my church clothes and into regular, but suitable for visiting strangers, clothes. It was then around three in the afternoon and still warm, so I chose a blue-and-white checked dress and low-heeled black shoes. It occurred to me that I was wearing this very same dress the day Sam tracked me down on a motion-picture set to tell me that my Billy had finally drunk all the morphine syrup he'd had stashed away in our closet, and my heart took to aching again. I didn't tell it not to, because that would have been stupid. I missed my husband still. Probably always would. With a sigh, I gave my stylish straw hat a pat and went back into the dining room, where Pa and Sam awaited me.

"The Hudson's out front," said Sam, rising.

"I saw it," said I, tucking my handbag under my arm and giving my father a peck on the cheek. "Be back soon, Pa."

"Probably," said Sam.

"Probably," I amended.

"Take your time. Nothing's going on today that I know about," said Pa with a big smile.

I hoped it wasn't as obvious to Sam as it was to me that my family wanted a romance to spark between the two of us.

"By the way," I said as we bade Spike farewell—Spike was quite unhappy with me for deserting him so much that day—and went out onto the front porch, "Carl Simmons, the fellow who drove Jackson to the hospital, is one of his door guardians."

"Guardians," Sam repeated in a disgusted-sounding voice. "You make it sound as if a gang of hoodlums is after him."

"A gang of hoodlums *is* after him," I said, my own tone acidic.

"Maybe. We still don't have proof of anything or anyone. I did talk to Petrie, but he said he hasn't had anything to do with the Jacksons and their troubles."

"Well, he would say that, wouldn't he?"

"I guess. But let's concentrate on Mrs. Akers now."

"Very well." I think I sniffed again. But I held my tongue and didn't tell Sam what I thought of him or his police Klan cohorts or say anything else of an incendiary nature.

The Akers' home was a little north of the Jacksons', on the other side of the street. I waited for Sam to open my door for me, even though I'm quite good at opening doors for myself. But I didn't want to goad the bear, if you know what I mean. This home, too, was small and neat and had lots of flowers around it. In fact, it looked to me as if someone in the Akers family was particularly fond of roses, because there were scads of them, most of them still blooming, even on this warm September day.

I'd read a book about roses once. Don't ask me why. I didn't intend to, but I saw it lying on a table at the library, picked it up, and learned that roses truly are interesting flowers with a very long history. Until I read that book, I didn't know how much trouble horticulturists have taken over the years to invent varieties of roses. I really wanted to get my hands on a climbing rose called Zephrine Drouhin, which is supposed to be fantastically fragrant and has no thorns! I'd like a rosebush with no thorns, mainly because I always managed to gouge myself several times every January when I prune our paltry ten rosebushes at home. Not that Zephrine Drouhin has anything to do with this story; I only mention it. Her. Whatever it is. Probably her. Zephrine sounds like a woman's name, doesn't it? Oh, never mind.

Anyway, I was admiring the lovely rose garden someone in the Akers' household had cultivated when Sam and I walked up the porch stairs, and Sam knocked at the door. A moment or two later the door opened a crack, and a small black face peered out at us. I smiled at the face.

Sam held out his police badge. I don't know about you, but having a policeman show up at my door, spang, on a Sunday afternoon, without previous knowledge of his intent, would make me very nervous. I could have clipped Sam on the ear for frightening this person. But I didn't.

"We're here to speak with Mrs. Georgia Akers, if she's available. My name is Detective Rotondo, and this is Mrs. Majesty. We're investigating the injury sustained by Mr. Joseph Jackson."

As soon as the face heard my name, its eyes widened, the door opened a little more, and I could tell that it belonged to a small, spare woman, who looked as though she were still dressed in her Sunday best. Mrs. Akers? I didn't know, but I smiled harder.

Without looking at Sam, the woman said to me, "You the Mrs. Majesty Joseph Jackson knows from the Pinkerton place?"

"Yes, indeed."

"You the white mambo?"

The question brought me up short. I hesitated for a second and then decided what the heck. "Yes, indeed. That's me, all right."

"Huh." She finally turned her head and looked way, way up—she was a small woman—at Sam. "And you're the detective friend of the white mambo, right?"

Sam, who was a good deal quicker on his feet than I, didn't skip a beat. "Right."

"Well, you all come on in, then. I'm Mrs. Akers, all right. My children are cleaning up after dinner, so I can chat with you in the parlor."

She didn't have the New Orleans accent Mrs. Jackson and her son did, nor did she talk like Mrs. Armistead. I wondered where she'd come from originally. Well, she might have been born right here in Pasadena, just like me, for all I knew.

"Thank you," I said, walking into the house.

"Thank you," said Sam, following me.

Mrs. Akers led us straight into the front parlor of the little house. It was as neat as a pin, with crocheted doilies covering all bare surfaces and the backs of chairs and sofas. I wondered if Mrs. Akers was the crocheter. I couldn't imagine her having a whole lot of time, if she cleaned other people's houses every day.

"You can take that chair, Detective," said Mrs. Akers, pointing to an overstuffed chair with doilies on both arms and its back. "And you can set on the sofa with me, Mrs. Majesty."

"Thank you." I took one end of the sofa, and Mrs. Akers took the other. She sat on the edge of her seat, as if she were ready to run if she had to. I noticed a framed picture of a Negro family that looked as if it had been taken in the late 1800s. My family had a couple of framed pictures of our family from before we moved West from Massachusetts taken around the same time period.

Mrs. Akers must have noticed my looking at the picture, because she said, "That's my grandmother and grandfather. Their name was Stoddard, and they were free Negroes from their first day in the United States. Lived in Hartland, Maine. I think my first Stoddard ancestor landed in seventeen sixty-nine or thereabouts. That was before Hartland was incorporated, but they were farmers in the area."

"My family is from Auburn, Massachusetts. I'm not sure when they arrived, but it must have been around the same time. Are you from Revolutionary stock?"

Her chin lifting slightly, Mrs. Akers said, "Yes, ma'am."

"So are we!" I beamed at her. She appeared a bit taken aback. Oh, dear. I think I was trying too hard. I shut up and let Sam take over the conversation.

He did so instantly, after shooting me a withering glance. I probably deserved it.

"Mrs. Jackson and Mrs. Armistead said you work for several families in Pasadena, Mrs. Akers. They also said you might know if any of them are connected with or belong to the Ku Klux Klan. We're looking into the harassment suffered by the Jackson family recently. The family seems to think the Klan is the cause of their troubles."

"So do I," I said, unable to keep still as usual.

Mrs. Akers sat there, her mouth twisted a trifle, looking to me as if she wasn't sure she wanted to confide in a police officer. Couldn't blame her for that, knowing what I knew about the police and the darker-skinned population of Pasadena. I felt ashamed of my race at that moment, even though I'd never done anything awful to a person because of his or her skin tone.

Silence prevailed while Mrs. Akers decided how—or perhaps whether—to answer Sam's question.

After the pause had stretched to the nerve-wracking stage, Sam broke it. "Your name will never come up in any reports. No one will ever know you talked to me. Us," he amended, probably because he feared I would if he didn't.

"You sure about that?" asked Mrs. Akers, her skepticism plain.

"Absolutely."

More silence, during which Mrs. Akers seemed to take Sam's measure and then mine. I felt like squirming, but didn't.

"I can't afford to lose any of my jobs. And I sure don't want my kids run down, or my husband shot, or a cross burned on my lawn. Mr. Akers takes care of those roses, and I don't want 'em ruined."

"I love your roses," I plopped irrelevantly into the conversation.

"Well..." Again Mrs. Akers stopped speaking. "You got a notebook in your hand. How do I know my name won't pop up somewhere in your records."

"I'll make sure it doesn't," said Sam.

"I don't know..."

I decided what the heck. "Please, Mrs. Akers. We've got Mrs.

Armistead's son photographing the area where Mr. Jackson was shot, but we really need more help in identifying possible members of the Klan. Both Mrs. Jackson and Mrs. Armistead told us you know pretty much everything about everyone in Pasadena."

Turning her attention to me, Mrs. Akers said, "It was those two ladies gave you my name and address?"

I nodded and Sam said, "Yes. At the hospital."

"Detective Rotondo was there trying to find out who shot Mr. Jackson," I added.

"Hmmm. Well, I don't know." Another silence ensued, during which I felt like twitching or shouting or grabbing the woman and shaking information out of her. I didn't.

"All right," she said at last, upon a long and heart-felt sigh. "I can tell you what I know. I work for the Mertons on Friday afternoons."

I started slightly in my chair but didn't speak.

"The Mr. Todd Mertons?" Sam asked, his dark eyes round.

"Them's the ones. I was walking to the bus stop when Mr. Merton was shot."

Good heavens! Practically an eye witness! Had we struck gold or had we not struck gold?

"Did you hear or see the killing?" asked Sam, who was quite poised. Guess he was used to this sort of thing, unlike yours truly.

"I heard it," said Mrs. Akers.

"We were told by another neighbor that an automobile drove down the street and slowed right before the shot was fired. Can you confirm that?"

More silence. Mrs. Akers frowned at Sam. "I didn't see or hear an automobile on the street at the time that shot was fired."

"You neither saw nor heard a car before you heard the shot?" Sam had stopped writing, and was pinning Mrs. Akers with an intense stare.

She repeated, "I didn't see or hear an automobile on that street at the time that shot was fired. No, sir."

Definite. She sounded absolutely definite.

"So...you didn't see an automobile."

"No, sir. There wasn't one. That there's a quiet street. You can hear cars when they drive up and back. I didn't hear an automobile when I walked down the street that day."

So had Charlie Smith lied to us? Mercy sakes, what did this mean? Was he protecting his Klan kin? Or could he be the shooter? Oh, dear. I didn't like that idea at all, especially since Mr. Smith had been treated to my opinions about the Klan several times so far. If he was a mad gunman, what were my chances of eluding him? I felt a chill on my arms and rubbed them with my hands.

"I see," said Sam, as composed as ever. "Do you work for anyone else on that street, and do you know which people there belong to the Klan."

"Mr. Merton did," said Mrs. Akers. "And Mr. Smith, across the street from him, does. I don't work for anybody else on Madison, so I can't tell you about anyone else there. But I know a family called Petrie is in thick with the Klan. Not all of 'em, but a few of 'em."

Aha! Miss Petrie was correct!

"Petrie, you say?" Sam again.

"Yes, sir. Petrie's the name. One of 'em's a policeman."

Huh. Confirmation, if Sam needed it, which he didn't since Petrie himself had confessed. Or bragged.

"Do you know the names of any other Klan members, Mrs. Akers?" Sam went on doggedly.

"What about rich people?" I said, unable to keep quiet another second. "Do you know the names of any rich folks in Pasadena who belong to the Klan?"

Mrs. Akers' gaze left Sam's face and settled on mine. Goodness, but she had an intimidating stare. I swallowed and fingered my juju before I realized what I was doing, and I dropped my hand to my lap instantly.

"Rich folks? I don't work for no rich folks. Not like the Pinkertons, if that's what you mean. Not like Jackson does. I clean houses for some folks in Pasadena who like to have a lady come in for a few hours a week. In fact, I work for Mrs. Longnecker, near where you live, Mrs. Majesty."

I swallowed again. "You know where I live?"

"I work for Mrs. Longnecker. Thursday mornings. I've seen you several times. You live in that nice bungalow up the street two houses. You have that sausage dog."

The mention of Spike relaxed me. "I don't know why I've never seen you, but isn't Spike a darling doggie?"

"He's...cute," said Mrs. Akers. She didn't sound as though she were overwhelmingly fond of dogs, but what the heck.

"I think so," I said.

Sam cleared his throat rather loudly, and I shut my mouth. Shouldn't have opened it in the first place, I know.

"So, do you know any other Klan members among those folks for whom you work, Mrs. Akers?"

After a moment or two of silence—the woman seemed completely unaffected by spaces of silence in conversations, if this could be considered a conversation—she said, "Mr. Merton and Mr. Smith are the only two I can think of. And I know about that Petrie boy, because word gets around. Especially among us black folk when it comes to the police."

Ow. That must have hurt Sam on his pride. I sneaked a peek at him, and didn't see him flinch. But then, the man might as well have been a marble monument as a human male when he was on the job. I guess that meant he was good at it.

"I'm sorry if any of the officers in the Pasadena Police Department have given you grief, Mrs. Akers," Sam said woodenly. "All police officers who are known to belong to the Klan have been suspended."

"Most of 'em," said she.

Sam went so far as to tilt his head in interest. "Can you name any others?"

"The names I know of in the police are Grubbs, Petrie, Bailey and Allen. Them's all last names. I don't know their first names."

"How do you know their names at all?" asked Sam. Not unreasonably, I believe.

"Because they stopped my friends for no reason. Lots of times."

"For no reason?"

"Not unless you think a Negro going to work or coming home from work is a good reason. You ain't black, Detective. If you was, you wouldn't be surprised. Mr. Akers, he works for Mr. Zane Grey as one of his gardeners. He was stopped every day for two weeks solid when he walked to the red-line stop from Mr. Grey's house, for no good reason. 'Less you think a black man working in Alta-falutin-dena's a crook for bein' there."

"That's terrible," I said, thinking about how it would be if I, for example, were to be pulled over by the coppers every day for two weeks when I went about my business. And my business was fake! Poor Mr. Akers was gainfully employed as a gardener by an important man.

To my surprise, Sam said, "Yes, it is. I'll look into the matter."

"You will?" Clearly, Mrs. Akers was surprised, too.

"Yes, I will," said Sam, closing his notebook. "But you can't think of any other names of Klan members?"

After another silence, during which, I suppose, Mrs. Akers thought hard, she said, "No. Those are the only names I know of."

"Thank you very much for your time, Mrs. Akers."

"I hope you find whoever shot Joseph Jackson," she said as she led us to the front door. "He's a good man, even if he isn't white."

"Yes, he is," I concurred, feeling out of place and uncomfortable. Shoot, if I felt uncomfortable being a white woman in a Negro woman's house because she seemed to hold a legitimate grudge against some white people, I can't imagine what Pasadena's Negro population felt like every day of their lives, if they were harassed by the police for absolutely no reason at all.

Sam and I didn't speak as we walked back to his Hudson.

SIXTEEN

In fact, we didn't speak until we were almost back to the Gumm-Majesty residence on Marengo Avenue. Then it was I who broke the silence. How typical of me, huh?

"Well, what do you think?"

"About what?"

If he'd been looking at me instead of the road, I'd have rolled my eyes, but it didn't seem worth the effort since he wasn't. "About the names Mrs. Akers gave you. Do you believe her about the policemen?"

"Yeah. Except for Petrie, the others have all been suspended. And Petrie will be as soon as I tell the chief about him."

"Good. What about the police stopping Mr. Akers every single day for two whole weeks when he was going home from work. And, oh, boy, I'd *love* to see that estate!"

Sam heaved a gusty sigh. "Yeah, I expect that's true, too."

"You mean you *knew* about stuff like that going on?"

With a squint-eyed glance at me, Sam said, "Some of my fellow officers think they're doing the population of Pasadena a good deed when they stop what they consider to be suspicious characters walking the streets in the evening or at night."

"*Suspicious?* What's suspicious about a man going to and from work?"

"Nothing. Some of my fellow officers are dumb bozos, and some of them do stuff like that to make themselves feel like big eggs. Not all of them. Some of them. But every one of them who does stuff like that makes all of us look bad."

Wow, that was the worst thing I'd ever heard Sam say about his co-coppers. "Yes. I suppose they do. That's not fair to the good guys."

"Right. So I'm going to see what I can do about it."

"I'm so glad! Maybe we can find Jackson's harassers, the shooter, and the coppers who harass Negroes for no reason."

"Ambitious plans you have for the department," said Sam with a wry edge to his voice.

"Well, it would be nice if you could do all those things."

But we were home, and Sam didn't seem inclined to talk anymore. He parked his Hudson in front of our house, walked around to open my door for me, and we toddled up the walkway to our house. As we did so, I scanned the yard, trying to decide where to put all the rosebushes I aimed to plant. I hadn't made up my mind when we got to the front door. We didn't need a knocker. Spike was making enough of a racket to raise the dead.

Therefore, as soon as I was in the house, I knelt and allowed my poor abandoned hound to leap upon me and kiss my face. I returned the favor until I noticed an immovable object standing and looming over the two of us. Naturally, the object was Sam. I said, "Well, he missed me! I left him for almost the whole day today, and usually I'm home all day on Sunday after church."

"I didn't say anything."

"You were thinking something," I said.

"Huh."

Typical conversation between Sam Rotondo and my own

personal self. I just hugged Spike another time or two and rose to my feet. I creaked again. Shoot, was this what happened when a person got old? But I was only twenty-three. That wasn't old. Was it?

"So how'd it go, you two?" said Pa, joining us in the front entryway—well, the door led into the living room, but the furniture was to your left as you entered the house, the door itself being to the right of the room. The only thing in this vicinity was the book table and the hat stand. Pa had on his specs and was holding a Zane Grey novel, so I guess he'd been reading.

"Oh! Pa, you'll never guess! Today Sam and I met two people who actually *work* for Mr. Zane Grey!"

"Oh?" Pa blinked at me. "I thought you were on the trail of a gunman."

"Well, we are, but—"

"*I'm* interviewing folks who know Mr. Jackson, Joe," said Sam, stamping on my sentence. "She went with me to Mrs. Akers' house because I figured Mrs. Akers might talk to me more easily if I brought a friend of Jackson's along with me."

"Makes sense," said Pa. "Who works for Zane Grey? That's kind of exciting."

I shot Sam a *so there* glare and said, "Oh, it is! Mrs. Armistead, whom we met at the hospital—she'd brought Jackson a cinnamon cake because she said cinnamon cures all ills—"

"Even gunshot wounds?" asked Pa. We were a lot alike, Pa and me.

"That's what she said. Anyway, she cooks for the Greys, and then Mrs. Akers' husband helps tend the Greys' gardens. Oh, and the Akers have *such* a beautiful rose garden, Pa! I really want to plant a rose garden in our—"

"I'd better be going now," Sam said, again interrupting me. Darn him, anyhow!

"Want to stick around for a couple of hands of rummy?" asked Pa hopefully. Guess he was no more interested in roses than was Sam. Very well. Fine. I'd study roses on my own.

"Better not. We've got a murder and a couple of attempted murders to solve, and I can't do that playing cards. Wish I could." Sam sounded wistful.

Phooey on him. On the other hand, I felt as though I should, so I said, "Say, Sam, before you go, want a sandwich? I'm going to make one for myself. Leftover roast pork, which makes scrumptious sandwiches. And I have to eat my carrots, too, since I didn't have time to eat them before I went to the hospital to see Jackson."

"You're going to eat cold carrots?" asked Sam, his mouth twisting in a grimace of distaste.

"There's nothing wrong with cold carrots. They aren't as good as they are when you eat them hot and dripping with butter, but carrots are carrots."

"Thanks. I'll take a sandwich. Think I'll pass on the carrots, though."

"You need your vegetables, Sam Rotondo. Everyone needs their vegetables."

"Maybe Sam could eat an apple with his sandwich," said Pa before all-out war could prevail. "I know apples aren't vegetables, but I'm sure he needs fruit, too."

I sniffed, but said, "Good idea. Thanks Pa."

"*Very* good idea," said Sam. "And I appreciate you making me a sandwich, Daisy."

"You'd probably have gone to bed hungry if I didn't."

"Well, I have crackers and cheese at home. And even some apples."

Which made me think of something. "Where *do* you live, Sam? I've always wondered."

"Little apartment on Los Robles. Actually, it's a tiny house in a court. You'd like my landlady. She believes in ghosts."

I ignored the ghost snipe, since Sam knew good and well *I* didn't believe in ghosts, no matter my line of work. "Is the court on North Los Robles or South Los Robles."

"South. Way south. Almost to San Marino."

I'd taken the leftover roast, which Vi had thoughtfully sliced and wrapped in waxed paper, from the Frigidaire and set on the counter. As I reached into the breadbox to fetch a loaf of her wonderful bread, I remembered the last time I drove down Los Robles Avenue. Swinging around with the bread in one hand and the bread knife in the other, I said, "Do you live in that darling little court a little south of Glenarm? On the"—I had to think about whether right was west or east as one drove south on Los Robles —"on the east side of the street? The one with the ivy and the roses?"

"Hey! Watch that knife!"

I looked at the knife. Very well, so it was kind of pointed at Sam. He knew I wouldn't use it on him. "Don't be ridiculous, Sam Rotondo. I'm going to cut the bread with the knife." I thrust the bread at him, and he jumped back a little. I tutted. "Well? Is that the court where you live?"

"Yeah. That's the one. The landlady takes care of the yards."

"I remember. Each one of those little cottages has a tiny yard, doesn't it?"

"Yes. I mow the back, which isn't very big, but Mrs. Johnson likes to care for the flowers herself. Good thing. If I had to do it, they'd all die. I don't have time to cultivate flowers."

"You lead a hard life, Detective Rotondo," I said with mock sympathy. Then I turned, got out the cutting board and cut four slices of bread. I looked over my shoulder. "Want a sandwich, Pa?"

"No, thanks. Your mother and I already had one. So did Vi."

It was by that time around eight o'clock Sunday night, later by far than I generally took a meal. No wonder I was hungry. "All right. Just Sam and me then."

"You might make Sam two of those things, Daisy. He's a big man."

Hmmm. I glanced at Sam, who was trying to pull his stomach in. Not that Sam was fat or flabby. But Pa was right: he was a big man. "Don't want him to get too big," I said in order to rile him.

"One sandwich will be plenty," said Sam, sounding a trifle grouchy.

"There's devil's-food cake for dessert."

"Oh, yum! Thanks, Pa."

"You should thank Vi."

"I would if she were here. Did she and Ma go to bed already?"

"Yep. They have to be up early to go to work. I feel like a shirker."

"Nuts. You do a lot of things for a lot of people, and you can't drive any longer, so just shush about that, Pa."

"She's right, Joe," said Sam, for once agreeing with me.

I slathered the bread with Vi's home-made mayonnaise and some mustard, plopped a couple of slices of pork on each bottom, topped each sandwich with another piece of bread, sliced each sandwich in half, making two triangles out of each, got out two plates, and put a sandwich on each plate. I added some cold buttered carrots to my plate and sliced an apple (I even cored it for the big galoot) and laid it out artistically on Sam's plate. I may not be able to *cook*-cook, but my presentation was quite pretty.

Shoving the plates in Sam's direction, I said, "Here. Take these to the dining room table. I'll get napkins and silverware. Want a glass of milk?"

"I think I can eat my sandwich and apple with my fingers," said Sam. "But I'll take a glass of milk. Thanks."

"I need a fork for my carrots," I reminded him.

"Huh."

Still, we ate together amicably enough—and cold buttered carrots, while not quite as tasty as hot buttered carrots, are nothing to sneeze at—while Pa asked questions about the various interviews we'd conducted that day. Or *Sam* had conducted. According to him.

"Do you think that lad's photographs will help you any?" asked Pa after Sam told him about Mrs. Armistead's son.

"I don't know. Can't hurt. It was too dark by the time the police got there to take any decent photographs."

"And Mrs. Armistead is the one who cooks for the Greys?"

"Yes, and she looks like it, too. She's as big as a house, just about."

"That's not kind, Daisy," said Pa in a reproving voice.

"Well, I know it isn't, but she is large. She's at least as large as Mrs. Bissel. Isn't she, Sam?"

Chewing on a bite of his sandwich, Sam only nodded.

"Guess cooks have to sample their wares," said Pa.

"Aunt Vi isn't very fat. She's just a wee bit plump."

"Guess so," said Pa. "So do you have any idea who the fellows were who drove the automobile that almost ran down the Jackson children?"

"I have a pretty good idea," I said after I swallowed a bite of sandwich and washed it down with a sip of milk. "But Sam says he needs evidence."

"I *do* need evidence," snarled Sam.

"Who do you think did it?" asked Pa. "And, yes, Sam does need evidence. He can make all the hunches he wants, but a court of law will demand proof."

"I know it," said I after swallowing a couple of carrot slices. "But *I* think the driver of the machine was Todd Merton. And I think the man with him was a policeman named Roland Petrie." I shot Sam a peek to see if he was going to object, but he was crunching on his apple and only appeared resigned to listen to my theories. "I don't have a clue who shot Todd Merton, although I wouldn't put it past your friend Charlie Smith. Mrs. Akers said she heard no car on the street when Mr. Merton was killed, and she'd just left his house after cleaning it."

"Charlie?" came, squeakily, from my father's mouth. "You think *Charlie* shot his neighbor?"

"They were both Klan members. If Mr. Merton objected to the mean things the Klan's been doing in town, maybe Charlie shot him for his efforts."

Shaking his head, Pa said, "I can't believe Charlie is a cold-blooded murderer."

"He's a coldblooded hater of everyone in the world who isn't him. He. Whatever it's supposed to be."

"And I still need evidence," said Sam, grouchy. He'd finished half of his sandwich and took a vicious bite out of the second half.

"I know you do. What a shame." If everyone would only listen to me and do what I wanted them to do, life would be so easy. For me, anyway. "At least I might be able to give you some information about the real-estate swindle Mr. Hastings is hawking after I see Mrs. Hastings tomorrow."

"There you go again," said Sam. "You don't know Hastings is involved in anything at all, much less a phony real-estate scheme. For all you know, Mr. Pinkerton was right, and he's the sainted cyclops of the lousy Klan."

"Exalted," I said, musing about Mr. Stephen Hastings. Nope. I still couldn't picture him in a sheet and a pointy hat.

"What?" said Sam, eyeing me with disfavor. Nothing unusual there.

"It's the *exalted* cyclops, not the sainted cyclops."

"Huh." Sam chewed some more sandwich.

"Those people sure give themselves some funny names," said Pa.

We'd all said much the same thing before, so I didn't agree with him again. Rather, I polished off my carrots and started the second half of my own sandwich. It was *so* good. If I didn't know there was devils-food cake for dessert, I might just have fixed myself another sandwich.

"Oh, and, Pa, Mrs. Akers works for the Longneckers!" I'd forgotten all about that. "She said she's worked for Mrs. Longnecker for years and years, and has seen me several times. Funny that I never noticed her before."

"You weren't looking at your neighbors' servants," said Sam. "People don't tend to notice irrelevancies."

"Mrs. Akers isn't an irrelevancy!" I said, shocked by his words.

He only squinted at me and said, "Yet she's seen you, and you haven't seen her. People's servants are invisible for the most part."

I set my almost-eaten sandwich back onto my plate and stared at Sam in dismay. I'd always thought of myself as a kind, if sometimes rash, individual, yet Sam was right. Servants, unless you were one, were invisible. Of course, if Mrs. Longnecker had ever hired me to perform a séance, I'm sure I'd have met Mrs. Akers long since. "That's kind of depressing, Sam."

He shrugged. "I guess."

"I don't envy Mrs. Akers," said Pa. "I have a feeling Mrs. Long-necker isn't the easiest person in the world to get along with."

"Boy, you're right about that. And she's a terrible gossip, too." Which gave me an idea. "Say, Sam, do you think I ought to talk to Mrs. Longnecker about what's going on with the Jacksons? Maybe she knows something Mrs. Akers didn't tell us."

"I'd just as soon you didn't spread the case all over Pasadena," said Sam with a pretty good frown. "The fewer people who know we have Klan problems here, the better."

"But they've been written about in the newspapers," I pointed out. "Anyone who takes the daily *Star News* or the *Pasadena Herald* or even the *Los Angeles Times* already knows about the Klan taking up residence in Pasadena."

"Maybe, but I'd rather you stay out of it."

"Stay *out* of it! How can I stay out of it when you keep dragging me along on your precious interviews? Darn you, Sam Rotondo. If you aren't the most illogical—"

"How about some cake?" asked Pa in a rather loud voice.

Steaming, I subsided in my rant, rose from my chair, picking up my plate and Sam's, and the last of my sandwich. "I'll get it." I stuffed the remaining bite of sandwich in my mouth as I stomped into the kitchen. The dining room was right off the kitchen. In fact, it sat between the living room and the kitchen, if anyone cares.

"Thanks. I'd like a piece of cake." Sam. Mildly. Well, he'd won. Why wouldn't he be mild?

Nuts. I got the cake out of the pie safe, cut two fairly large slices and, since our sandwich plates were relatively clean, plopped a slice

of cake on each and brought them back to the kitchen. I even remembered to bring Sam a fork, although he didn't deserve one.

He left us shortly thereafter, and I discovered that, after such a
full day, I was exhausted. So I said good-night to Pa, and Spike and I
went to bed. Tomorrow might prove to be another long day, and I
needed my rest.

SEVENTEEN

Monday morning dawned warm and sunny, two characteristics I didn't share with it. I was chilly and grumpy, probably because Sam had annoyed me so much the night before. Or maybe not. Maybe all the loose ends in the Jackson-Pinkerton-Merton-Hastings cases were frustrating me.

I decided that must be the case when I threw on a robe, let Spike out onto the deck outside my bedroom so he could do his own morning duty, and made my way to the kitchen. Where sat Pa, looking at the Monday morning edition of the *Pasadena Star News*.

"Hey, Pa," I muttered, heading to the coffee pot on the stove top. "Did Vi make anything good for breakfast?"

"Bacon and eggs. There's an article about Mr. Jackson on page three, Daisy. About him being shot."

Pa's news perked me up a trifle. Not much. I mean, Jackson was a good friend of mine. I was, however, glad to know the local newspaper had taken interest in his case, even if it were relegated to the third page. "There is? You mean the newspaper actually reported a crime committed against a Negro citizen of our fair city?"

I heard the newspaper crinkle as Pa laid it on the table before himself. Uh-oh. Guess I'd been a trifle sarcastic.

"Yes, and I don't know why you sound so savage this morning." Pa wasn't generally so blunt. Guess I'd riled him. Oh, dear.

"Sorry, Pa. I guess this Jackson case is really getting under my skin. Everything just seems so unfair. And how the Ku Klux Klan could induce *anybody* with half a brain to join it has dimmed my faith in my fellow man." Not that I'd possessed much to begin with. Shoot, I made my living fleecing so-called intelligent members of my species.

"I guess I can understand that. But listen to this: 'On Saturday evening, at about seven p.m., Joseph Jackson, a member of Pasadena's Negro community, was gunned down on the corner of Lincoln Avenue and Washington Boulevard. Mr. Jackson is recuperating at the Castleton Hospital. His shooter's identity remains unknown at this time.'"

"Hmm. Well, at least they reported it," I said, contemplating the bacon Vi had left to keep warm on the stove. Did I want to scramble myself an egg? More to the point, *could* I scramble myself an egg. The last time I'd tried, the egg had turned all leathery on me.

At that very moment, my darling aunt walked into the kitchen, carrying her handbag and wearing her hat. She was ready to take on preparing the Pinkertons' meals for another day. She must have seen me looking glum, because she said, "Let me scramble you an egg, Daisy."

God bless the woman as a saint. Nevertheless, I didn't want to make her late for work. "No, Vi. I can do it. You go on to work. You shouldn't have to fix eggs for me. You cook everything else."

She shook her head. "It'll only take me a second. It would probably take you ten minutes and five eggs to scramble an edible egg."

While that was true, it didn't make my mood any brighter. Hanging my head, I said, "Thanks, Vi."

She patted my shoulder. "Nonsense. We all have our gifts. Yours isn't in the kitchen."

"You can say that again."

She didn't, for which I was grateful. I stuck a piece of bread on a fork and held it over a burner on the stove. We had an electrical toaster, but I was feeling a trifle martyred that Monday morning, so I toasted my bread the old-fashioned way. What's more, I only singed one side of it.

Vi was right. It took her approximately thirty seconds to scramble and cook an egg for me. I noticed she cooked it in a small cast-iron skillet, used butter on the skillet's bottom so the egg wouldn't stick, and had the gas flame turned to a moderate heat. Hmm. Maybe I could cook an egg after all. I think I'd tried to use higher heat the last time I'd scorched one of them.

She scooped the perfectly scrambled egg onto a plate, I added my singed toast and two pieces of bacon, and I said, "Thanks, Vi. You're a blessing to us all."

"Pshaw," said she as she turned and marched to the front door. From there, she'd walk north on Marengo to Colorado, catch a red car going west, transfer on Fair Oaks to a northbound red car, get off at Orange Grove, and walk the rest of the way to Mrs. Pinkerton's house.

Pa was through with the newspaper when I sat at the table, so I took a peek at it. Some clever devil had invented a word game called the crossword puzzle, and the *Star News* had begun publishing one of them every Monday. Thinking solving the puzzle might cheer me up, I found it and a pencil and saw that Pa had already started filling in the little squares. Blast!

I'm almost sure I didn't frown at my father, but he said, "I remembered too late that you love to do the word puzzle, Daisy. You can finish it for me. Sorry I spoiled your fun."

So I felt guilty along with frustrated and grumpy. "Don't be silly, Pa," I told him, mad at him for spoiling the puzzle for me. And it was only Monday morning.

However, I did finish the puzzle. I also ate my breakfast, washed the dishes and put them away, and went into my room to put on a cool day dress in which I aimed to take my dog for a walk. With my father, if he hadn't usurped that pleasure, too.

But I'd wronged the man. When I left the bedroom, he'd already put on his hat and had Spike on his leash. "Ready?" he said, trying a little too hard to be cheerful.

"Sure am," said I, doing the same thing.

Spike didn't have any trouble at all being cheerful, which is one of the very best things about dogs. We strolled down Marengo, and when we passed the Longneckers' house, I squinted to see if I could detect Mrs. Longnecker in the garden. No luck. I wondered if she'd think it strange if I decided to pay a call on her. Probably. I wasn't on visiting terms with the Longneckers. Not that we were enemies or anything; it's just that we didn't walk in and out of each other's houses as some folks did.

Which made me think that we weren't on visiting terms with any of our neighbors. Not like that, anyway. When I thought about it, I came to the conclusion this was because all the ladies in our house worked away from home. Well, except for me sometimes. Occasionally, I'd make appointments to read cards or manipulate the Ouija board for a paying client in the dining room of our home. Generally, however, it was Pa who was the neighborhood gadabout.

"Say, Pa, are you friends with Mr. Longnecker? I mean do you chat over the back fence and stuff like that?"

"It would be difficult to chat over the back fence when there are two other houses separating our house from his. But no, I don't chat with him on a regular basis. He's a good deal older than I am, for one thing, and I'm a car man. He's a philatelist."

I knew what that was, by gum. "Collects stamps, does he?"

"By the thousands. I'm sure he'll be glad to bore you to death if you want to chat with him about philately. He cornered me one day, and I didn't think I'd ever get out of his clutches."

"So he's a fanatical philatelist." I was kind of proud of that sentence.

Pa chuckled, so I guess he liked it, too. "You might say that."

"Drat. I wish Mrs. Longnecker was interested in spiritualism or something."

"Why? You don't think the Longneckers have anything to do with the Jacksons, do you?"

"I guess not. I suppose I just feel guilty because I never noticed Mrs. Akers on our street before."

"Nuts. Lots and lots of folks have people who come in and work for them one morning or afternoon a week. You can't notice them all."

"I guess not," I repeated, still feeling guilty. Oh, well.

When we got back home, it was time for me to dress and drive to Mrs. Hastings' house in the San Rafael area of Pasadena. San Rafael was home to the massively rich. I mean, lots of folks in Pasadena were wealthy in those days, but San Rafael was special. It had gigantic, multi-acre estates that went on forever and that were virtually lost in a forest of greenery. I loved it. Fortunately for me, I remembered how to get to the Hastings' estate, and drove up the miles and miles and miles of road from their gatehouse to the house without getting lost. Because Mr. Hastings had ties with Hong Kong—the family had even lived there for several years—all of their servants were Chinese. Probably if Mrs. Akers had been Chinese or Japanese, I'd have noticed her. Well, maybe. Oh, probably not. Bother.

The same Chinese girl who'd opened the door for me the very first time I'd visited Mrs. Hastings again opened the door for me that day. I smiled at her. She smiled back, which was the second good thing to happen that day.

"Good morning, Mrs. Majesty. Mrs. Hastings is expecting you. She's in the conservatory."

Oh, boy! The conservatory was where Mrs. Hastings grew her orchids. I foresaw orchids in my future, spiritualist medium that I was.

Sure enough, Mrs. Hastings was on her knees with the secateurs in her hands and dirt on her apron when Li, the Chinese girl, opened the conservatory door for me. Mrs. Hastings looked up at me and smiled. "Oh, Daisy, come here. I have the most gorgeous oncidium orchid just starting to bloom! This is the first oncidium I've had any luck with." She looked from me to Li. "Li, will you please bring us some tea."

"Yes, ma'am." And Li disappeared as silently as a wraith.

I strolled over to where she knelt, my gaze bouncing from orchid plant to orchid plant, feeling almost overwhelmed by the beauty of the waxy flowers. I didn't know beans about orchids, but I praised the orchid of which Mrs. Hastings was so proud. It didn't hold a candle to some of the others she had in the conservatory, but I didn't say so.

"Oh, my, it's lovely."

"Don't you love the color? It's kind of a...what would you call it? A peach color?"

Sounded about right to me. "Yes. Or apricot." At least it wasn't purple, a color of which I wasn't fond, although I don't know why. Lots of her other orchids were various shades of purple. And they were pretty. But I liked the yellow, white and green ones best. Although...very well, so there were some perfectly *gorgeous* purple, lilac and lavender orchids in Mrs. Hastings' conservatory. The woman possessed a green thumb when it came to orchid cultivation, for certain.

But I hadn't come there that day to discuss orchids. "Did you wish to speak with me about something, Mrs. Hastings? I love your orchids, but..."

She heaved a sigh and rose from her pampered oncidium. "Yes. I'm glad you could visit me today, Daisy. I have a bad feeling about something Mr. Hastings is up to, and I'm worried that it might even be...illegal." She whispered the last word.

As I'd already suspected, although I didn't let on. In fact, I allowed my eyes to widen and my mouth to form a shocked O. "Goodness!" I said. "Whatever is he doing?"

She took off her gloves and apron, laid them on a table, and washed her hands in a sink she must have had installed especially for her use in the conservatory. Wiping her hands on a little embroidered towel, she joined me at a table and two chairs in a corner of the room.

The room was pretty much all windows, and from it you could see the extensive grounds of the Hastings' estate. The woman was surrounded by a mile and a half of beauty, although it didn't seem to make her awfully happy. On the other hand, her only son had been murdered a few months prior, so that absolutely colored her outlook on life. Even such an astonishingly lovely outlook as she had before her eyes every day.

"Please sit down," she told me, so I did. She went on, "I'm not sure it's illegal, but I'm afraid it's not quite right. Stephen—Mr. Hastings—has joined a consortium of his friends and another man whom he only met recently in order to buy land and develop it in Florida."

"*Florida?*" I fear the word squeaked slightly as it left my lips. But...*Florida?* What did Florida contain besides swamps and crocodiles? Or were they alligators? I think crocs lived in Africa and gators in the USA, but I wasn't sure.

She shook her head. "I know. But Stephen—Mr. Hastings—claims Florida is the next California, and that there are millions of dollars to be made in land there. But I don't trust the fellow who's heading the scheme. I think he's a shady character, and he's only recently come to town. He's...oily." She shuddered slightly.

Oily, eh? That didn't sound good. "What's his name? Do you know?"

"Billingsgate. Enoch Billingsgate. He's evidently a wildly wealthy real-estate developer in Florida. Have you ever heard of him?"

"Me? No, but I don't know many people who deal in high finances. Maybe Mr. Pinkerton, but no one else."

She nearly leapt on the name. "Mr. Pinkerton is one of the members of the consortium!"

"He is?" Oh, dear.

"Yes. I've spoken to Madeline"—Madeline being Mrs. Pinkerton's first name—"about the Florida deal, but she...well, she didn't know anything about it. Actually..." Mrs. Hastings paused, but finally went on, "In fact, she doesn't seem to have much of a head for business of any kind."

Boy, wasn't *that* the truth! She had a head filled with cotton fluff, did Mrs. Pinkerton. Naturally, I didn't say that. "Yes. I do believe you're correct there."

"She was quite bewildered when I asked her if she knew anything about the scheme Mr. Hastings and Mr. Pinkerton were planning with Mr. Billingsgate. Then again, I doubt Mr. Pinkerton talks to her about his various business interests. But, Daisy, I know you know the Pinkertons. In fact, don't you visit them often?"

"Yes. In fact, I'm going to visit Mrs. Pinkerton right after I leave you. They've been having some trouble regarding their gatekeeper." I wasn't sure how much to tell her, but what the heck. Maybe I could discover once and for all whether or not Mr. Hastings belonged to the Klan. "Um...Mr. Jackson, their gatekeeper, is a Negro man, and he's being harassed by the Ku Klux Klan. In fact, he was shot on Saturday night, and *I* think it was a Klansman who pulled the trigger."

At the mention of the word Klan, Mrs. Hastings put her hand to her mouth. "Good heavens! The Klan? In Pasadena?"

"Yes, ma'am. I was surprised to know they've gained a foothold here, too."

"Dreadful organization! How awful for those people. That poor man. Is he going to be all right?"

"Yes. I visited him in the hospital yesterday. He has guards on his door so whoever shot him can't come back and finish him off." That wasn't elegantly put, but there you go.

"Oh, my Lord. And to think of these things happening in Pasadena."

"My sentiments exactly."

Li brought in the tea and cookies just then, and I pondered the Klan problem as Mrs. Hastings poured tea and asked if I wanted lemon or milk.

"I'll take a little milk, thank you. Um, Mrs. Hastings, I don't want to alarm you, but Mr. Hastings' name has been mentioned in connection with Pasadena's branch of the Klan."

"Mr. *Hastings*! Good Lord, Daisy, Stephen would never belong to such an organization! In fact, he deplores the fact that they even exist. He's told me so more than once. He was frightfully offended when he read in the newspaper that some policemen were members of that ghastly Klan. I didn't realize those were Pasadena policemen." She handed me my cup, frowning up a storm. "In fact, I can't imagine who could have told you Stephen is involved in so evil an organization. My husband may be many things, some of which I don't much like, but he's never discriminated against a person because of his color. None of us do. We learned that much in China. A person's skin color has nothing to do with his character."

Ha. I'd thought as much. So much for Mr. Pinkerton's belief in Stephen Hastings as the exalted cyclops.

"Perhaps Mr. Pinkerton was mistaken when he told Detective Rotondo he believed Mr. Hastings to be the Klan's leader in Pasadena." I didn't want to go through the exalted cyclops nonsense again. The title was just too stupid.

"Mr. *Pinkerton* told Detective Rotondo that?" Clearly shocked, Mrs. Hastings' hand shook, and she carefully set her cup and saucer on the table between us. It was a pretty little table, with curly wrought-iron legs and a glass top. "I can assure you, Daisy, that he was mistaken. For all of Stephen's faults, he'd *never* belong to, much less lead, a chapter of the Ku Klux Klan."

I believed her. At least I believed she believed what she said. I was interested to see her eyebrows tilt until they made a frowning V over her eyes. "But I wouldn't put such a dastardly thing past Mr. Enoch Billingsgate. *If* that's his name. I'm sure there's something wrong with that man, Daisy. He's just too...too...slimy."

Hmm. Interesting. My brain began sorting through various threads and trying to tie them together. "What does Mr. Billingsgate look like, Mrs. Hastings?"

"Oh, call me Laura, please. He's fat. And he has red hair. And he smiles and smiles. And you know what Shakespeare said about people like him."

"Yes. A man might 'smile and smile and be a villain.'"

"Precisely. And I swear to you that Enoch Billingsgate is a villain. Only I don't know how to prove it."

One of the thought-strings in my head tied itself into a neat little bow. "I think I know how to find out. Mr. Harold Kincaid—Mrs. Pinkerton's son by that awful first husband of hers—has a good friend who's a banker in the Kincaids' bank. In fact, I think he runs the place. If anyone can get the goods on a phony financial scheme, it's Del Farrington."

I could almost see the burden of worry lift from Mrs. Hastings' shoulders. "Oh, would you ask him to check into it, Daisy? I'd *so* appreciate it. If Enoch Billingsgate is a legitimate businessman, I'll eat my hat."

She wasn't wearing one, but I didn't point it out to her. "I'll be happy to do it, Mrs.—er, Laura."

"I feel better already. I'm not going to tell Stephen we had this chat."

"Thank you. He's probably still angry with me for invading his offices last June."

She gave me the friendliest smile I'd ever yet seen on her face. "Yes, he is. But I'm so grateful to you, I don't even know how to thank you."

"You've already thanked me," I told her sincerely. She's also given me a heap of money, bless the woman.

"Not enough. But perhaps you'll take some sprays of orchids. I'm afraid I can't give you any of the oncidiums yet, because there's only the one spray beginning to bloom, but I have several pretty cymbidiums and cattleyas and dendrobiums that are blooming up a storm."

"Thank you!"

So I left the Hastings home armed not merely with interesting information and a new name to investigate, but an entire car seat full of spectacular orchid blossoms.

EIGHTEEN

Because my visit with Mrs. Hastings hadn't taken very long, I had time to go home and put the orchid blossoms into various vases and pots before I left to see Mrs. Pinkerton. Pa was most impressed with the orchids.

"Holy cats, Daisy, where'd you get all those flowers?"

"They're orchids from Mrs. Stephen Hastings' conservatory. She cultivates them."

"I remember you brought home a bundle of them the last time you did business with Mrs. Hastings."

He was right about that, bless the woman as a flowery saint. By the time I'd found containers for all the orchid sprays, and even had a lovely bouquet of yellow and white ones for my own personal bedroom, I was ready to wash my hands, powder my nose, and pay my next call of the day.

I hied myself to Mrs. Pinkerton's house, armed with a name and a request for Harold, whom I hoped would be there. He often was, although he also often wasn't, since he did have a legitimate job as a costumier for a motion-picture studio in Los Angeles.

Workmen had made rapid and splendid repairs to the black iron gate and the gatehouse, which was back to being in one piece and gleaming with new white paint. The gate stood open, baring the twin rows of deodars lining the drive for all to see from the street. I presume the gate hadn't been latched because Mr. Jackson was still recuperating from his gunshot wound, poor man. "Oh, Harold, please be there," I whispered as I parked the Chevrolet in the circular drive in front of the Pinkertons' gigantic front porch.

I was in luck. In fact, when I whacked the knocker growing out of the lion's head on the massive double front door, it was Harold himself who opened the door to me.

"Harold!" cried I. "I'm *so* glad to see you! I have some detective work for you and Del. It involves a phony financial scheme your step-father is involved with and may very well also involve a man who might—or might not—be the head of the Ku Klux Klan in Pasadena."

Blinking a bit at my flood of words, Harold swung wide the door and let me into the house.

"I've already got Del investigating the Florida baloney. The development is supposed to be in Dade County, which, I presume, is in Florida. Somewhere. My stepfather is a really nice guy, but he's got feathers in his head sometimes. Kind of like my mother, actually."

"Have you and Del already looked into a man named Enoch Billingsgate?"

"No, is that the shyster who's in charge of the scheme?"

"Yes, it is. Mrs. Hastings doesn't trust him. Also, Mr. Pinkerton told Sam that Mr. Hastings was the Pasadena Klan's exalted cyclops, but I don't believe it, and Mrs. Hastings just told me he definitely isn't. So maybe Billingsgate is."

Shaking his head, Harold muttered, "The names these guys give themselves continue to amaze me."

"You and me both. The person who goes out and recruits for the Klan is called a kleagle."

"Good God."

"Precisely."

We were almost to the drawing room, so I tugged on Harold's arm and whispered urgently, "Please have Del check out Enoch Billingsgate, the Florida scheme, and anything else he can learn. I'll ask Sam to find out if Enoch Billingsgate even exists, or if this fellow annexed the name in order to fool folks." Of course, Sam might pay no attention to my pleas, but I'd oerleap—to continue the Shakespearean theme—that problem when I came to it.

"Will do. But you'd better prepare yourself. Mother is in a *state*." He emphasized the word state.

"Oh, boy. Well, I don't suppose this state is any worse than the others I've seen her in."

"It might be. Stacy was here earlier, and now Mother's all atwitter because Stacy told her Jackson's getting shot was her fault."

I squinted at him. "How can it be her fault? It was a man who shot him."

"You know Stacy," said Harold with unsubtle emphasis. "And Mother."

"Yes," I said, heaving a sigh. "I do know the both of them. I sometimes wish your sister would go on a missionary trip to the wilds of Africa and get herself eaten by cannibals."

"You and me both," said Stacy's brother. We were of a single mind, Harold and me, about his stinky sister.

Sure enough, when I entered the drawing room—I guess Harold had taken enough from his mother for one morning, because he didn't join me—she was mopping her tears with a soggy hankie. She looked up as I walked in and straightened a trifle in her chair. "Daisy!" she said in a choked and water-soaked voice. "Thank you *so* much for coming. I...well, I just don't know. Stacy was just here, and...well, I'm upset."

"I can see that," I said in my mellifluous spiritualist's voice. "And I'm so sorry. Harold told me Stacy believes you're responsible for what happened to Jackson, and I can tell you truthfully that you're not. Not in any way whatsoever." I walked over to her and took the chair next to hers. I thought about taking her hand, but feared it might be as soggy as her handkerchief, so I didn't.

"You don't think it's my fault that Jackson got shot?" Her red-rimmed, drippy eyes sought me over her hankie.

"I certainly do not. Mr. Jackson was shot by some evil man by the evil man's own volition. You've been only kind to Jackson. If you recall, Stacy also wanted you to fire the poor man because other people were harassing him. *You're* not responsible for any of Jackson's problems. If you'd followed Stacy's advice, you'd have done him a great disservice."

She sniffled pathetically. "Thank you, Daisy. You're always such a comfort for me."

"Happy to help," I fibbed. Well, it wasn't much of a fib. Anyhow, as long as I was in her good graces, I figured it wouldn't hurt to ask her something else. "Is Mr. Pinkerton here, by any chance?"

"Algie? No, I think he's at his club." She gave her eyes one last good swipe, patted her now-powderless cheeks, squished her handkerchief into her two hands, which she then laid in her lap. "Do you need to talk to him?"

"Not really. But I kept an appointment with Mrs. Stephen Hastings earlier today—"

"Is *she* why you couldn't come to me earlier?" she demanded.

Oh, dear. "She called me several days ago to make the appointment." I tried to sound apologetic. "My meeting with her was set up before you called. I came to you as soon as I could." I didn't want Mrs. P to get annoyed with me. She was, after all, my best client. Heck, she'd all but supported my family for a couple of years when things were really bad after Pa had his heart attack and Billy came home from that cursed war. "I try to treat all my clients fairly, Mrs. Pinkerton, but you'll always be my main priority."

With another sniffle, she said, "Thank you, dear. I don't mean to sound selfish."

"Not at all," said I. Where had I been before she'd interrupted me? Oh, yes. I remembered. "But Mrs. Hastings is very worried about a Florida real-estate scheme both Mr. Pinkerton and Mr. Hastings are involved with."

"Florida? Why would...? Oh. Yes, I do believe Laura asked me about that. I don't know anything about Algie's business dealings. She told me she doesn't trust some fellow whose name I can't remember, and who's in charge of the financial...whatever you call those things. A consortium?"

"I guess that's the right word." I didn't know any more about financial matters than did Mrs. Pinkerton. Dismal thought.

"Yes. Laura said she doesn't trust that man." She shrugged. "I've never met him, and Algie never talks about business at home."

"I believe his name is Enoch Billingsgate," I muttered, thinking I'd wasted my time, and that Mrs. Pinkerton wasn't going to be able to give me any information at all.

But Mrs. Pinkerton's nose wrinkled, and she surprised me. "*That* man! Algie invited him to dine with us last Thursday. I thought he was a most unpleasant fellow. Whether he's a villain or not, I can't say."

Hmmm. It was unusual for Mrs. Pinkerton to take a dislike to a person. Heck, she still loved her horrible daughter. Curious, I asked, "Why didn't you care for him, Mrs. Pinkerton?"

She thought for a moment, then said, "I'm not sure."

Typical.

"You can't pinpoint any particular thing about him that struck you as being unpleasant?"

"Oh, I can pinpoint many things. He dressed like a fellow in a vaudeville show, he smiled too much, he wore stinky hair oil, and he was fat."

Mrs. P herself was...well, plump. But she was none of those other things. "I see. I'm surprised Mr. Pinkerton and Mr. Hastings seem so enthralled with his Florida scheme. Mrs. Hastings is sure it's a fake business deal, but it's difficult to imagine both Mr. Pinkerton and Mr. Hastings being drawn into a fraudulent scheme."

"Ha! That, my dear, is not difficult to imagine at all. Why, just

look at that ex-partner of Mr. Hastings. Why, he and Eustace"—
Eustace was Mrs. Pinkerton's first, and evil, husband—"actually
killed Laura's son. And Algie himself, while having a first-class financial mind, is rather less than brilliant about people and has lost money
on phony financial schemes before now. Men. Always so sure of
themselves."

"Oh, dear. Well, I hope either the Florida thing is legitimate or
that Del Farrington will sort it all out before anyone loses any
money."

"Darling Del," said Mrs. P upon a deep and heartfelt sigh. "*Such
a fine young man. Why, he's the one who saved the bank after
Eustace stole all those bearer bonds, you know.*"

"Yes, indeed. He worked very hard to get the bank up and
running again."

"Yes, he did. And none of the bank's customers lost a dime. The
man's a saint."

I wondered if she'd think Del was a saint if she knew he was
Harold's lover. Naturally I didn't ask. "He's definitely that."

"Oh, but Daisy, did you bring your board? I need to talk to Rolly.
I'm just so upset about Jackson and all the awful things that have
been happening lately. And then Stacy told me it's all my own fault.
Well, I just don't *know!*"

Before she could get to wailing again—Mrs. P was a first-class
wailer—I hurriedly removed the Ouija board from its splendid star-
dappled wrapper (sewn by my very own hands and the White side-
pedal sewing machine I gave to Ma one year) and set it on the table
next to Mrs. Pinkerton's chair. I pulled up one of the beautiful Louis-
the-Whateverth chairs in the room and sat across from her, and we
began conversing, via the board, with good old Rolly.

Rolly told Mrs. Pinkerton everything she wanted to hear, bless
his nonexistent heart, and Mrs. Pinkerton was in a much better mood
when I left her than when I'd arrived. I managed to scram out of her
drawing room not too long after twelve thirty or thereabouts. I looked
around for Harold for a few minutes, but didn't see him. Deducing

from this that he was either gone or in the kitchen, wheedling my aunt out of food, I walked to the kitchen, where I saw neither Harold nor Aunt Vi. Huh. Although I wondered where Vi was—she was generally firmly ensconced in Mrs. P's kitchen—I didn't bother looking for her, but left the house in something of a dilemma.

As I drove down Mrs. P's drive toward the open gate, I pondered whether or not to visit the police station and see if Sam was there. He might not be. Or he might be. Whether he was or wasn't, he might not want to hear anything about anyone named Enoch Billingsgate.

And besides all that, I was starving to death. Not literally, but it was my lunch time, and I was hungry. But what the heck. I owed both Mrs. Hastings and Mrs. Pinkerton a good deal, and I didn't mind martyring myself in a good cause. So I drove to the police station on Fair Oaks and Union, parked, and pushed through the double swing doors. The uniformed officer sitting behind the reception desk was a fellow I recognized, although I didn't know his name.

"I need to speak with Detective Sam Rotondo if he's here," I said in my most formal voice. I'd kind of created a scene a couple of months prior in this very room, so I wore my dignity around me rather like a cloak for this visit. The man didn't snicker, so I guess my pose worked.

"He's here," said the policeman, whose name tag said he was Officer Crabtree. Boy, I wouldn't want to be named Crabtree. Gumm had been hard enough on me as I was growing up. "Do you want to just go to his room?"

"Yes, thank you."

So the officer rose from his chair, walked to the door leading to the various offices in the police station, and unlocked the door. I walked in, went up the staircase and headed for Sam's room. When I opened the door, Sam was there along with two of his fellow detectives. They all turned to look at me, which they always did, and which always embarrassed me. Naturally, Sam scowled.

I walked to his desk and sat in the chair beside it. "Good afternoon, Sam."

"What's good about it?" he asked, which was typical of him.

"For one thing, I have the name of a crook I think you need to investigate. According to my sources, he's in charge of a fake financial consortium dealing with real estate in Dade County, Florida."

Sam just stared at me for a second or three. It felt like eternity. Then he said, "Florida?"

"Florida."

"Criminy."

"Yes, precisely. He might—or he might not—also be in the Klan." Nobody'd said word one about Mr. Billingsgate and the Klan, but there couldn't be *that* many fat, red-headed villains running around Pasadena. Could there? It would be nice if he were a crook and a cyclops, because then Sam could arrest him and kill two birds with one stone, so to speak.

He suddenly rose from his chair, which skreaked across the floor. "Let's go to lunch. You can explain it all to me over noodles at the chop suey place."

Sounded like a good idea to me. My stomach, which growled loudly at that moment, appreciated it as well. So I rose, too, and we both headed to the door. Sam called to his cohorts over his shoulder, "Out to lunch. Back soon." He spoke like a sign hanging on a doorknob. But at least he seemed willing to listen to me. He grabbed his coat from the stand beside the door, plopped his hat on his head, and shrugged into his coat as we descended the stairs.

It was a short walk to the Crown Chop Suey Parlor on Fair Oaks Avenue. Sam and I had dined there several times before. The place had good food, and I was more than ready for it.

When we were inside the restaurant, Sam greeted several other men, some uniformed and some not, who sat at various tables. I gathered the place was regularly populated by lunching policemen. It was close to the station, so that made sense.

A Chinese waiter led us to a table in a corner, which was good, because I didn't want anyone else overhearing our conversation. I

179

smiled at him, said, "Thank you," and sat in the chair he pulled out for me, hoping my stomach wouldn't make any more rude noises.

Sam sat, too, and the waiter handed us each a menu. Before I could impart my information to him, he spoke.

"Officer Petrie was murdered last night in the Castleton Hospital."

NINETEEN

My jaw dropped, and my thoughts scattered like so much chaff in the wind.

Sam nodded and said, "Somebody held a pillow over his head. The poor guy was pretty doped up, and his leg's in a cast, so he couldn't struggle very much. A nurse found him about an hour or so after he was killed. The doctor said he'd been asphyxiated, and the pillow pretty much bore him out."

Attempting to get my wits under my control, and having no luck at all, I stared at Sam.

With a pretty nasty sneer, he said, "Well? Happy now?"

That jerked me to full attention. "Happy? Why should I be happy about another man being murdered?"

"You and your librarian friend thought he was a bad guy."

"Well...yes. According to everything I've heard about him, he *was* a bad guy. I didn't necessarily want anyone to kill him, for pity's sake."

"Huh. Well, he's dead. And that means he can't tell us anything about anyone in the Klan who might have been harassing the Jackson family."

"Oh, dear. That's right." Darn it, anyhow! Petrie might well have given Sam all sorts of information about whoever had tried to run down Henry Jackson's children or who'd shot Joseph Jackson, but he was now out of Sam's—and everyone else's—reach. "Blast it. That's awful, Sam."

"Yeah. I thought so, too." He eyed me sternly, and it suddenly occurred to me what he might be thinking.

"Sam Rotondo! You're not thinking that anyone connected with the Jacksons did away with Petrie, are you?"

He shrugged. "Don't know. Jackson's in the same hospital Petrie was in, and he's got round-the-clock guards at his door who aren't any too fond of the Ku Klux Klan *or* the Pasadena Police Department."

"It wasn't them!" I started when I realized how loud my voice was and lowered it. "It wasn't them, Sam. They're just trying to stay alive themselves. But I know someone who might have done it."

Very well, I was reaching at straws and constructing theories out of whole cloth. But, darn it, I preferred to think of Mr. Enoch Billingsgate as a murderer than anyone connected with the Jacksons. Or maybe Charlie Smith! That was a good idea.

"Have you spoken with Charlie Smith? He lives directly across the street from a fellow who was murdered, and Mrs. Akers claimed there was no creeping car on the street when Mr. Merton was killed. Maybe Charlie Smith did them both in."

"Maybe. I'll definitely talk to him. But who's this other fellow you wanted to tell me about?"

The waiter appeared at our table at that moment, so we ordered and waited for him to depart before I said another word. Then I told Sam what both Mrs. Hastings and Mrs. Pinkerton had told me about Mr. Enoch Billingsgate. I also told him that Del Farrington was looking into the Florida real-estate scheme.

Sam pulled out a note pad from his inside jacket pocket. "Billingsgate, you say?"

"Yes."

"Enos?"

"Enoch."

"Got it. Now, what's he got to do with the Klan?"

I shrugged, feeling helpless and lost. "I don't know that he has anything to do with the Klan. I was just...well, kind of hoping. He's fat and he has red hair, so he might have been in the machine with Officer Petrie when they tried to run down the Jackson kids."

"You don't know Petrie was in the car at all."

Sam Rotondo was forever flinging facts in my face, darn him! "Well, I think he was. And Petrie was definitely a crook. I think this Billingsgate fellow is, too. He wants to bilk people out of their money."

"How do you know that?"

Darn him! "His scheme sounds phony to me. And it does to Harold, too. And Del Farrington. And Mrs. Pinkerton and Mrs. Hastings both say he's slimy and not to be trusted."

"And how do they know."

"Darn you, Sam Rotondo, can't you just look into the man's background and try to find out if he's legitimate or not? Del's working the financial angle. I think you should see if he has a criminal history. You can do that, can't you?"

"Not without knowing more about him than I know now."

"Nuts." Stumped, I sat there and glowered for a second or two.

Fortunately, the waiter returned to our table with our lunches, so I got to chew on fried shrimp and Chinese noodles as I thought things over. At last I looked up and saw Sam contentedly munching on a sparerib. "I'll see if I can find out something about his background. If I can determine where he came from, maybe that would give you a starting place."

"Sounds like a good idea to me. Offhand, I can't say I've ever heard of Enos—"

"Enoch."

"Whoever. I've never heard of the gent before. If he's got rich men like Stephen Hastings and Algernon Pinkerton believing he's got a legitimate financial scheme going...well, they probably know more about high finance than I do."

"Not necessarily. Both Harold and Mrs. Pinkerton told me that, while Mr. Pinkerton is great with banking matters, he isn't always too bright about the people he trusts, and that he's lost money before on crooked schemes. And Mr. Hastings' long-time law partner was the head of a drug ring, and Mr. Hastings didn't know beans about it until after his son was murdered."

Tilting his head, Sam acknowledged the truth of my speech. "Yeah. I guess that's so. Even rich folks can be fooled."

"You betcha." Heck, I earned my living fooling rich folks. "So you'll see what you can find out about Enoch Billingsgate? I'll try to find out more about him, too."

"Just be careful, will you? If this Billingsgate character is a criminal, you don't want to get close to him. You do tend to jump in where angels fear to tread, you know."

"I don't, either!" I said, stung. "It's not my fault that I have to deal with people who get themselves into trouble. Anyhow, both Mrs. Pinkerton and Mrs. Hastings are good women. They don't deserve to have to suffer because their husbands are idiots." That was a bit harsh, so I attempted to tone down my assessment. "Well, they might not be idiots, but if they're involved in a fake Florida real-estate deal, they're clearly not the geniuses they probably think they are." Nuts. That was just as harsh as my prior comment. I decided to leave it alone. Sam knew what I meant.

"I don't suppose your librarian friend disliked her cousin enough to do him in."

I almost dropped another shrimp. "Miss *Petrie*? Good heavens, no. She's as mild-mannered and nonviolent as a human being can be."

"As far as you know," said Sam, perennially determined to think the worst of people.

However, with a sigh, I acknowledged the truth of his statement. "Yes. As far as I know. But if Miss Petrie is guilty of anything worse than reading steamy novels, I'll be very much surprised. And I doubt she even does that."

To my utter astonishment, Sam chuckled. He wasn't generally good-humored when we were together. He was more apt to bark and rage at me than laugh at anything I said. I felt a little squishy inside.

"Are you going to visit the library any time soon?" he asked.

"I can go there this afternoon, although if her cousin died last night, Miss Petrie might not be there. Family feelings and all that."

"I thought she didn't like the guy."

"She didn't, but she's not the only member of her family. But I'll stop by the library on my way home and ask her if she knows anything. Shouldn't you be the one to question her?"

"I will. But I have a whole lot of other irons in the fire at the moment. For one thing, I have to return to the hospital and find out if any of Jackson's guards left his door last night."

Shaking my head, I said, "I'm sure nobody connected with the Jacksons had anything to do with Petrie's death."

"We'll see."

I had an idea. "Maybe Miss Petrie will recall the name Enoch Billingsgate in connection with the financial dealings Officer Petrie borrowed money from his parents for." What a screwy sentence *that* was.

Nevertheless, Sam understood it. "She told you *Petrie* was involved in the Florida thing?"

I looked up from my plate to find Sam frowning at me again. Oh, well. His good mood was nice while it lasted—a whole fifteen seconds or so. "Didn't I tell you that?"

"No, you didn't tell me that. You told me that Mr. Hastings and Mr. Pinkerton were involved in what you think is a phony real-estate scheme run by a fellow named Enos—"

"*Enoch!*"

"Enoch Billingsgate. Whatever the hell his name is. This is the first time you've bothered telling me Petrie was involved in it, too."

"Oh. I thought I had. Actually, I don't think Miss Petrie

mentioned Florida specifically." I attempted to recall the conversation I'd had with her. "No. She only said the scheme involved Officer Petrie and some other fellows buying land and developing it in some southern state. Bet it was Florida. But I thought I'd mentioned it to you."

"No. You didn't."

"Oh. Well, I know I talked to somebody about it. Maybe it was Mrs. Jackson."

"She and I look so much alike," said Sam; sarcastically, I'm sure I need not say.

"Don't be ridiculous. Anyhow, I'll go to the library and see if Miss Petrie's there. And you're going to visit the hospital?"

"I've already been there this morning, but that visit had to do with the crime scene. I didn't have a chance to question anyone except a few nurses and a doctor or two." He heaved a sigh. "So now I get to tackle the Jacksons. They're going to be thrilled to be questioned about a murder, I'm sure."

"They're probably used to being considered guilty of any number of crimes because of the color of their skin."

Sam glared at me from across the table for about a second before he sighed again and said, "Yes. They probably are. But I pretty much have to talk to them. It's my duty."

"Better you than me," I muttered. I sure wouldn't want to question a Jackson about the murder of a Petrie, given the relationship status of the Jacksons and the Petries in Tulsa. And here, for that matter.

Sam paid for our lunch, which I thought was nice of him, and we walked back to the police station together. He opened my Chevrolet's door for me, and I thanked him. Then I said, "Want to come over tonight to compare notes? You can tell me about the Jacksons, and I can tell you about Miss Petrie."

"Does this offer include dinner?"

"Sure. Why not? Vi always cooks enough for an army."

"Well, please tell her I'm coming. I don't want to just barge in."

"I will. Thanks, Sam."

Sam walked into the station, and I pressed the starter button—it was *so* wonderful not to have to crank a car anymore—and tootled along to the library, which was only a block or so from the station. Miss Petrie or no Miss Petrie, I had to use the facilities.

But she was there! Sitting behind the reference desk, she appeared to be assisting a young woman with a research problem or something. I was glad, because I could make a dash to the restroom before she spotted me.

Much relieved after a few minutes, I strolled out into the main room of the library and was pleased to note that Miss Petrie was free once more. She smiled when she saw me, and I wondered if she knew about her murdered cousin.

"Good afternoon, Miss Petrie."

She gave me a huge smile. "Good afternoon, Mrs. Majesty. You'll *never* believe what happened to Roland!"

Mercy sakes, she looked downright jolly. I guess she truly had despised her awful cousin. "Actually, I will believe it, because I just spoke with Detective Rotondo from the police department. I'm sorry about your cousin."

"I'm not," she said roundly. "He was evil, he was a cheat, a bigot and a liar, and now he can't drain his parents' life savings to put into that ridiculous Florida land deal."

"Aha. So it was Florida."

"I thought I told you that."

"You mentioned a southern state. But now that I've done some more snooping, I discovered that several other men in Pasadena—some of them wildly rich and some not—are in a consortium headed by a man named Enoch Billingsgate—"

"*That* horrid man!" exclaimed Miss Petrie. Then she covered her mouth with her hand and glanced nervously around the library. So did I. Didn't look to me as if she'd disturbed anyone.

"You know him?"

"I've met him. He's fat and oily, and I wouldn't trust him to walk my cat, much less give him money. I told Roland that he aimed to take everyone's money and run. Roland, of course, thought he was superior to all other human beings and only scoffed at me. But I think I'm right. That man gave me the shivers." To prove it, she shivered.

"All the people I've spoken to have told me the same thing about him. Although," I added, "I've only spoken to women whose husbands or relations are in the consortium with Billingsgate."

"There you go," said Miss Petrie. "*Women* can tell a scoundrel when they see one. Well, most of the time. If they could do it all the time, I'm sure my cousin Marge would never have married her ghastly husband."

"Yes. I've known a couple of marriages like that, too."

"If you ask me, it's too bad divorce is considered so scandalous. *And* that women can't earn as much money as men. So poor Marge is stuck with her dreadful husband because she has no way out. She couldn't support herself and the children if she left the bounder. Oh, but Mrs. Majesty, he's *so* awful to her."

"That's a shame." Mind you, my own marriage hadn't been one of unmitigated bliss, but that wasn't Billy's or my fault. It had been the war that had ruined our chances of marital happiness. I was, however, a trifle surprised to hear Miss Petrie voice such firm feminist principles. Not that I didn't agree with her. I told her so. "I absolutely agree with you. Women are treated so unfairly."

She sniffed. "At least we don't have to wear those hideous black burkas and hide our faces from the world like those poor creatures in Arabia have to wear."

"That's true. I saw a lot of women dressed like that when I went to Egypt and Turkey. Although the Turkish costumes were more colorful than those the Egyptian women had to wear. Why, do you know Turkey gave women the vote in nineteen eighteen? That's two whole years before we females here in the United States were declared the equals of men."

"You don't honestly think men believe we're equal to them, do you?"

Goodness, I hadn't realized how...what's the word? Disaffected? Cynical? Disenchanted? I guess any of those would work...Miss Petrie was. "No. I don't suppose they do."

"How many female congresspersons do you know of?" she asked. She sounded belligerent, too.

"Um...none."

"Precisely. Well, there is one, but only one. It's going to take another hundred years or more before we achieve true equality."

"Oh, my, do you really think so?" That was a depressing thought.

"Yes, I do. And it's not fair."

"No, it's not."

Very well, so I now had Miss Petrie's opinion on the death of her cousin, and I'd learned that she was an ardent, if repressed, feminist, but I wasn't sure what to say next. Fortunately for me, Miss Petrie took the problem out of my hands.

"Oh, but Mrs. Majesty, I found a wonderful book I think you'll love."

"Great! Thanks!" I was so glad to get off the lowering subjects of murder and inequality, I didn't even care what book she'd found. Fortunately for me, it turned out to be *The Girl on the Boat*, by Mr. P.G. Wodehouse. He wrote very funny books, so I was pleased to take it from Miss Petrie's hands.

"It's quite entertaining," said she as she handed it over.

"I've enjoyed everything I've ever read of his."

"You're in for a treat. The catalogue department is preparing another Mary Roberts Rinehart book that should be available next week, and another book by Edgar Wallace. I know you like those."

"As long as Mrs. Rinehart didn't write about the war again," I said, leery of reading any of her books after Miss Petrie had given me *The Amazing Interlude* a couple of years prior.

"No. Neither of those books is about the war." Miss Petrie patted my hand.

"Thank you very much for this one," said I, lifting *The Girl on the Boat* to show her.

"You're more than welcome."

I tried to think of anything else of a pertinent nature I might ask her about the case Sam was investigating, but couldn't. So I checked out my book and headed back to Mrs. Pinkerton's house. I still had to warn Vi that Sam aimed to come to dinner that night, after all.

Because I didn't want Mrs. Pinkerton to know I was there—she might waylay me and make me read the cards or something—I pulled up to the back entrance and entered the kitchen that way. Vi had her hands in a bowl of bread dough, punching it savagely. She glanced up when I walked in.

"Daisy! What are you doing here? I thought you'd come and gone hours ago."

"I had. I looked for you before I left, but you weren't in the kitchen."

"Even I have to visit the ladies' room from time to time," she said drily.

After having practically raced through the library to visit their ladies' room, I could fully appreciate Vi's need. "Indeed. After I had lunch with Sam, I used the library's facilities."

Instantly, I knew I shouldn't have mentioned having lunch with Sam, because Vi beamed at me. "Oh! How nice that you had luncheon with your young man."

"Sam's not my young man," I said, knowing my words would do no good. "I was talking to him about the case."

"What case?"

"The *Jackson* case, Vi! For heaven's sake, somebody shot the man after almost killing his brother's children and wrecking the Pinkertons' gatehouse and bombing their mailbox." I decided not to tell her about the murdered Officer Petrie. He didn't deserve her consideration. Not that I'm the least little bit judgmental or anything.

"Nonsense, Daisy. Those are police matters, and they don't require you dining with Detective Rotondo."

"Well, I hadn't planned to dine with him. I actually went to the police department to tell him the name of man who, I believe, is mixed up in a phony financial deal."

"What does that have to do with the Jackson case?" asked Vi. And reasonably, too, I must admit.

"I'm not altogether sure, but a fellow who was involved in both the Klan and the financial scheme was murdered last night." Oh, piddle. I hadn't meant to bring Petrie into the conversation.

Vi's eyes went round as billiard balls. Not that I've ever seen a billiard ball in person, but I've seen pictures. "For heaven's sake! You'd better just stay away from this case until Sam solves it, Daisy. You're liable to find yourself in hot water if you don't watch out. You do tend to get involved in things better left alone, you know."

Darn it! Here was my wonderful aunt virtually parroting the words Sam had flung at me over Chinese noodles. It wasn't fair!

"Sam himself has asked me to go with him to question people involved in the Jackson case, Vi," I pointed out rather hotly.

"Yes, yes, I know." She dumped her punched-down dough onto a floured board and divided the dough into little balls. Guess she was preparing dinner rolls.

"Anyhow," I said, getting to the purpose of my second visit to the Pinkerton place that day. "I invited Sam to dinner tonight. I hope that's all right with you. We're going to compare notes after dinner and see where they lead us. If they lead us anywhere. Sam is going to visit Jackson in the hospital."

"He doesn't think Jackson had anything to do with that man's death, does he?"

I lied. "Oh, no. He just needs to talk to Jackson again. One of Jackson's friends was going to take photographs of where Jackson was shot. You never know. The photos might provide a clue."

"If you say so," said my aunt, making neat little knots of the dough balls she'd created and putting them on a baking sheet. Then she covered the knots with a damp towel. I hoped we'd get some of those little knots for our own dinner, but I didn't say so, not wanting to prolong my visit in case Vi had anything else of an equivocal nature to ask of or impart unto me.

TWENTY

By the time I got home, the only other being in the house was Spike, who greeted me with his usual exuberant ecstasy. I greeted him the same way, and then took us both to my bedroom, where I plopped *The Girl on the Boat* on the bedside table, slipped out of my dress and lay down to take a nap. It had been an eventful day, and I was beat.

What woke me up was the heavenly aroma of baking bread. Have I mentioned that the room Billy and I used to share, and that I kept after his death, is right off the kitchen? Well, it is. I got up, rubbed my eyes, threw on a faded blue day dress and stumbled into the kitchen.

"It smells *so good* in here!" I told my adorable aunt just as she withdrew the dinner rolls from the oven.

"They are good."

"What do you call them?" I asked, peering at the perfectly browned knots. Vi must have brushed them with egg before baking them, because they glistened gorgeously. I wouldn't have known to do that, but once, when Vi had tried teaching me to cook (the lessons didn't take), she suggested brushing bread or dinner rolls with beaten eggs or egg whites in order to create that glisten. I hadn't been able to successfully separate an egg white from an egg yolk, so Vi hasn't bothered with me since.

With a shrug, she said, "I just call them dinner rolls. I thought they'd be pretty tied into knots—you know, for a change from plain old dinner rolls."

"There's nothing plain about your dinner rolls, Vi." In fact, I wanted one. Badly. However, I knew my aunt. Also, when I glanced at the kitchen clock, I saw it was five o'clock, and Aunt Vi would probably smack my hand if I grabbed for one. We Gumms and Majestys dined at six p.m. every day.

"Thank you, Daisy. You still can't have one." She laughed.

"I know. I wasn't going to snatch one. I want one, though."

"Well, we'll eat at six, and you can have one or two then."

"What are you fixing for dinner?"

"Plain old beef stew. Easy as pie. Easier than pie, actually."

I vividly recalled my mother and me puzzling over a recipe for raisin pie one day a couple of years earlier. Neither of us could figure out what a capital T meant. We finally decided upon tablespoon, and the pie came out all right, so I think we'd guessed correctly. "Pretty much anything is easier than pie," I told her, meaning it.

"For you. I love to cook. You have your own gifts, sweetheart."

That was nice of her. "Thanks, Vi."

Spike had reluctantly left the warmth of my bed and strolled into the kitchen, too. Vi actually tossed him a piece of extraneous something-or-other, and I felt she was treating my dog better than she treated me, but I didn't say so. "I'll set the table."

"Thank you, Daisy."

So I set the table, making sure I put both bowls and bread plates at each setting. Then I fetched *The Girl on the Boat* and retired to the living room, where I plopped myself on the sofa, Spike at my side, and read until about five forty-five, giving greetings to Pa and Ma when they both came home. Then I thought perhaps I'd better spiff myself up some, so I retired to my bedroom and selected a plain but pretty brown-checked dress from my closet. The dress had a slightly scooped neck and I'd decorated the neckline, loose sleeves, pocket and skirt with rows of rickrack. The belt was wide and tied just below my waist.

Eyeing myself critically in the cheval glass mirror, I decided I'd do. The dress wasn't so fancy that it would make anyone think I'd dressed up especially for Sam, but I looked quite respectable. Glancing down at Spike and worrying I'd spiffed up a trifle *too* much, I said, "What do you think, Spike?"

His tail swept back and forth across the floor, and I took that as a sign of approval, so I left off tidying myself and went back to the kitchen. There I donned an apron and helped Vi dish up the various courses. There weren't many of them, beef stew being a relatively self-contained meal unto itself.

"Boy, this smells spectacular, Vi. It's not the usual beef stew you make, is it?"

"If you won't tell Sam, I'll let you in on my secret ingredient," she said with a sly grin.

"I won't tell. Promise."

"I fixed the same thing for the Pinkertons today, only *they* call it beef *bourguignon*."

I eyed the stew, looking for anything new and exciting. Pearl onions, potatoes, carrots, chunks of beef. Nope. Couldn't find a single unusual ingredient. Oh, wait. There were some mushrooms. I wasn't necessarily a fan of mushrooms, but I figured they'd soak up the flavor of the delicious sauce and wouldn't taste like dirt, as they usually did. To me. Other people liked them.

"What does *bourguignon* mean?"

"It means I put some Burgundy wine into the regular sauce."

My mouth dropped open. "Vi! Where in the world did you get Burgundy wine? We're supposed to be in the throes of Prohibition!"

"Indeed, we are, but Mr. Pinkerton has himself quite a wine cellar." She slid me another sly glance. "I'm sure he bought it all before the law was passed."

"I'm sure," said I, as sly as she.

Here, once again, is proof that rich people are different from the rest of us. If anyone in my family had a wine cellar, we'd all be locked in the clink. Oh, well. I made a good living off the Mrs. Pinkertons of the world. Besides, the stew smelled *really* good, so I wasn't about to complain.

As I was setting dishes on the table, Spike set up an uproariously gleeful barking frenzy at the front door. Sam. I said, "I'll get the door."

So I did, and Sam walked in, looking like a big, tired policeman in his overcoat, hat and big policemanly shoes. Without my prompting, he hung his hat and coat on the hall rack and headed for the food and Pa, who had just entered the dining room with Ma on his arm. Ma, too, had put on a nice day dress, I suppose for Sam's benefit. Generally speaking, we Gumms and Majestys didn't "dress" for dinner. We just wore whatever clothes we had on when Vi called us to the table.

Sort of like my own beloved hound dog, only much larger and less beloved, Sam lifted his face and sniffed the fragrant air. "Oh, my, is that beef *bourguignon* I smell? I haven't had that since I last ate at Delmonico's, and that was years ago. It smells wonderful."

"But it's made with wine," I said. Then I could have slapped my own face for giving away Vi's secret. Not that it seemed to be much of a secret if Sam knew instantly what it was.

He shrugged. "So what? Your aunt made it, so I know it's good. And I'm not on duty."

"How'd it go at the hospital?"

I knew I shouldn't have asked when I saw the expression on his face. "Let's talk about it later. Is that all right with you?"

"Sure, Sam." Guess I couldn't fault him for wanting to eat a good meal before he started talking murder and mayhem again.

So we gathered around the table, Sam and I on opposite sides. A lovely bouquet of orchid sprays sat in the middle of the table, so Sam and I couldn't see each other very well. That was all right by me.

Vi passed the bowl of stew to her right, so Sam got first crack at it. I noticed, through the branches, that he filled his bowl to the brim before he passed the bowl to Ma. She did nearly the same thing before she passed it to Pa, who then passed it to me. I didn't take much, since there wasn't a whole lot left, and I wanted Vi to get some.

When I passed the bowl back to her, she eyed it and then frowned at me. "There's a gallon more of this stuff in the kitchen, Daisy. Take more if you want it." She shoved the bowl back at me, so I filled my bowl almost to the brim. Then Vi took the bowl back to the kitchen, refilled it, and began passing the rolls and butter.

"This is delicious, Vi," said Ma after tentatively taking a bite of carrot she'd carefully picked from her bowl. It's fun watching my mother eat new stuff, because she's so unadventurous when it comes to foodstuffs.

"It's marvelous," said Sam, sounding almost worshipful. "I haven't eaten anything like this since I moved away from New York City. You can't get the variety of food here that you can get back East."

"That's true," said Pa. "When I visited New York City with Ernie"—Ernie, Aunt Vi's late husband, was Pa's older brother—"we ate all kinds of food. Chinese, East Indian, German—You all right, Daisy?"

At the word German, I'd almost raised a protest, but I'd cut it off. I'd learned not to loathe all Germans, but I still struggled with the concept of eating anything a German might eat. Except a good sausage every now and then. "I'm fine, Pa. Carry on."

"Well, they had all kinds of food there, was all I was trying to say." He looked up the table at Sam. "Guess you can miss food, too, can't you?"

"You bet," said Sam.

"We're lucky," I said, trying to redeem myself. "Our relations in Massachusetts send us real maple syrup every year, and Vi makes Boston baked beans and brown bread from time to time."

"And you've broadened all our horizons with that Turkish cooking book," said Vi with a smile for me.

"Guess so," I said, pleased. The food in Turkey had been *very* good. Even though I'd been too sick to eat it most of the time I was there.

Good food, and chatter about more food, carried us through the meal. Vi brought in tapioca pudding for dessert, and we all liked that, too. Then the men went to the living room to talk and/or play gin rummy—although Sam had looked worn to a frazzle when he came in —so Ma and I washed the dishes, and I put them all away.

When I entered the living room, Vi, Pa and Sam were chatting about, of all things, the Longneckers. I eyed them with interest and, perhaps, a soupcon of skepticism mixed in.

Pa glanced up at me with his innocent blue eyes—eyes I'd inherited—and said, "I was just telling Vi and Sam about talking to Mrs. Longnecker today, Daisy?"

"Oh?"

"Yep. I asked if she could recommend a good cleaning lady to come every couple of weeks or so to help out here."

"*What?* We don't need a cleaning lady! I keep house very well when I'm home, and I don't work so often that the house suffers!" I was, as you can probably tell, indignant.

"Calm down, sweetie," said Vi. "Your father was being sly."

I plunked myself on the piano bench. "Sly?"

"You wanted to know about the woman Mrs. Longnecker has come in to clean on Thursdays, don't you?"

"Oh." Now I felt silly. "Yes, I did want to know about her. Actually, I already knew about her, but thanks for your ruse, Pa. What did Mrs. Longnecker say? I'm sure she's going to tell all the neighbors that Daisy Majesty refuses to help her mother and aunt with the housework, so poor Mr. Gumm has to hire a cleaning lady. The woman is a poisonous gossip."

"Daisy," said Ma in the voice she uses when I'm being bad.

I huffed. "It's true, Ma. You know it as well as I do."

"Sorry I smirched your reputation, but I did get the name of the woman. You're right. It's Georgia Akers. Mrs. Longnecker said she does fairly well, for one of *those* people."

I felt heat rise up my neck and invade my cheeks, not from embarrassment, but from rage. "And precisely whom does she consider *those* people?"

"Negroes, of course," said Sam, as if this were a matter-of-fact observation and I shouldn't take it amiss.

"I hate that woman."

"Daisy," said Ma again.

"Nuts. She's mean as a snake—actually, Pudge Wilson told me snakes aren't mean. They just have a bad reputation because people think they're slimy, but they aren't—but that's not the point. She's awful!"

"Daisy," said Ma yet again, but without much conviction.

"No, Peggy. Daisy's right. I don't like her much myself, but at least I spared you the trouble of being nice to her," said Pa with a grin.

Sam grinned, too. He would.

But they were both right. Deflating, I said, "Thanks, Pa. I appreciate it. I'll try to look out for Mrs. Akers on Thursday and say hello to her. I don't want her to think the entire neighborhood is full of people like Mrs. Longnecker."

"Actually," said Sam, "it probably is. It's a sad fact of life that people don't look at people who are different from themselves as being as good as they are."

"I know it," I said, defeated.

"But I need to talk to you about the Jacksons," said Sam. Then he glanced at the rest of my family. "Do you mind if Daisy and I consult on the porch? Not that it's anything secret, but..."

"Of course," said Ma, entirely too quickly. She thought we were going to canoodle. I knew it. "In fact, I'm going to our room. Why don't you chat here?"

"I'm going to bed. You can chat to your hearts' content," said Vi.

"Me, too," said Pa. "I'm going to read for a while."

I watched my family depart the room with something akin to amusement, although not a whole lot of it.

Sam said, after they'd all departed, "Guess we don't have to chat on the porch."

"No. Might as well just tell me how it went right here."

"Not well," said he.

"You mean your interview with the Jacksons didn't go well?"

"Exactly. They resented me questioning them about Petrie."

I shrugged. "Well, you expected that, didn't you?"

"Yeah, but I didn't expect quite so much hostility from the door guards."

"Oh, dear. They didn't threaten you or anything, did they?"

"No, but they hated my guts by the time I finally got out of there."

"I'm sorry." I heaved a sigh. "But you did expect that reaction," I reminded him.

"Yes, I did." He heaved a sigh, too. "However, I also got some photographs. Mr. Armistead showed up to see Jackson, and he'd brought the photos with him and gave them to me. Saved him a trip to the police station. He seems like a nice boy, and he wasn't as hostile as the rest of the bunch."

"I'm sure he is a nice boy. He was doing you a favor, and I'm sure he hopes his photographs can help you solve at least part of the crime."

"He's an excellent photographer." Sam walked to the coat tree and withdrew an envelope from his overcoat pocket. He opened it as he walked back to the sofa, where I joined him. I didn't sit close to him, but left a big gap so we could look at the photographs together. I didn't want to hear snickers from my family if any of them should peek in while Sam and I were alone.

After he'd shaken a pile of photographs from the envelope, Sam laid them on the sofa cushion facing me. I peered down at them, fascinated. I didn't know Marshall Armistead, but he was definitely a good photographer. He'd taken photos from every angle imaginable, and even some I wasn't sure why he'd taken at all. I pointed to a blotch on what looked like a sidewalk. "Is that blood?" I think my nose wrinkled.

"Yes. Here's another picture from another angle. After I looked at all the photos, I think I can picture what happened and why the shooter ran off."

"He probably didn't want to be murdered by a crowd of bystanders," I said, stating what I considered the obvious.

"Maybe, but he had a gun, don't forget. But look here. The shooter evidently came up to Jackson from between these two buildings." He pointed.

I squinted. "How do you figure that?" Not that I doubted him; I just wondered, was all.

It took him a while, but after putting the photographs in a certain order, Sam showed them to me one at a time, explaining the sequence of events as he perceived them—and, apparently, as Jackson confirmed them—so that I, too, got the picture. I think.

"May I pick them up?" I asked Sam, not wanting to get a tongue-lashing for not asking first.

He shrugged. "Don't know why not." He handed me the bundle of pictures.

I set them on my lap and lifted each one individually. The place where Mr. Jackson had been shot was quite close to John Muir Technical High School, whose mascot was a terrier for some reason. Not that the location of the high school matters; I just mention it in passing. A sign on a building caught my eye, and I squinted harder.

"What?" said Sam. "Do you see something I missed?"

He didn't sound grumpy, only interested. I lifted the photograph nearer to the table lamp and leaned over to peer at it even more closely. "I don't know. Do you see the sign on this building? I think it says C.S. Smith, Dry Process Cleaning." I pointed at the signage painted on the side of the building, not quite sure if I was reading it correctly.

Sam rose from his end of the sofa, snatched the photo from my hand and held it close to the same light I'd used. To my astonishment, he withdrew a pair of eyeglasses from his coat pocket and perched them on his nose. I'd never seen Sam in specs before.

"I didn't know you wore spectacles," I said, sounding a little accusatory, although I'm not sure why.

"Just got 'em," he said absently, intent on the photograph. "I need them for close work."

"Oh," said I, feeling a little left out, although there was no good reason I could think of why Sam should apprise me of every appointment he kept. Or every pair of eyeglasses he bought.

"By God," he said after a considerable silence, "I think you're right." He lowered the photo and looked at me.

I looked up at him. "C.S. Smith," I said.

"Yeah," he said. "C.S. Smith." He folded his specs and put them back into his pocket.

He left the house shortly thereafter, taking his photographs with him, but not before telling me he'd be visiting Charlie Smith again on the morrow.

If this case got any more complicated, I didn't think I could stand it.

TWENTY-ONE

On Tuesday morning, I woke up befuddled. I didn't know what to make of anything at all, much less who'd done damage to the Pinkerton home, Jackson, Mr. Merton, and Officer Petrie. And where did Mr. Enoch Billingsgate fit into the picture? Had Petrie been part of the consortium? What about Charlie Smith? And if that building belonged to a member of his family, was it of significance?

Who the heck knew?

I considered pulling the quilt over my head and hiding out in bed for a day or three, but I couldn't do that to my family, which needed the income I generated by being a fraudulent medium. For another thing, I had a feeling I'd be hearing from Mrs. Pinkerton any minute now. When I looked at the clock on the bedside table, I saw it was seven a.m. She didn't generally call before eight.

Then I bethought me of Flossie and Johnny Buckingham. Johnny was a captain in the Salvation Army, and Flossie was his wife. For quite a while now, Flossie's credited me with not merely introducing her to Johnny, but for saving her life. She'd been a gangster's moll, but she claims I rescued her from her abysmal circumstances. In a way she was correct, but it wasn't on purpose. I'd been trying to get her out of my hair at the time. However, that's not very nice, and I preferred Flossie's opinion on the matter to my own, even though mine was closer to reality.

And why, you might ask, did I think of Johnny and Flossie? I'll tell you: because Stacy Kincaid was making her mother's life even more of a misery than it already was, and she was one of Johnny's flock of Salvation Army maidens. Maybe Johnny could talk her into going easier on her poor mother. Besides, the Salvation Army, sitting as it did on the corner of Walnut and Fair Oaks, was right on the way to the Castleton Hospital, and I wanted to visit Jackson again.

Pa sat at the kitchen table reading the *Star News* when I walked out to join him. I'd put on my old pink housedress, but still wore my slippers. Spike, naturally, sat at my father's feet, peering up at him with pleading eyes, as though to say he hadn't had a decent meal in weeks, if not decades. If anyone bothered to look at the rest of him, they could tell those soulful brown eyes fibbed. Spike was a trifle plump. Mrs. Pansy Hanratty, who'd taught Spike and me at her dog obedience class at Brookside Park, would be horrified.

"Don't give him any treats," I advised my father. "He's getting fat, and that's bad for his back."

Pa eyed me over his newspaper. "I'm not the one who's always giving him treats, Daisy Majesty."

I let out a sigh at least as soulful as Spike's eyes and said, "I know. I'm sorry, Pa."

"That's all right. How's my girl this morning?"

I'd made it all the way to the stove, where I poured myself a cup of coffee. "All right, I guess." I thought of the photos Sam and I had studied the night before. "Say, Pa, do you know if Charlie Smith or one of his relations has a dry-cleaning establishment on Lincoln? Near Washington?"

I peered into the oven to see if Vi had left any enticing goodies for breakfast. No luck. Nuts. That meant I was on my own when it came to breakfast. I could at least fix toast without burning it too badly. Most of the time.

"Let me think," said Pa, and proceeded to do same. Before he was through thinking, he said, "Vi left one of her wonderful casseroles on top of the stove, Daisy. On the warming rack."

"Oh." There had been food, delicious food, right smack in front of me when I'd stooped to open the oven door. Guess I wasn't quite awake yet. I'd tossed and turned for a long time after I'd gone to bed, worrying over the case and all of its many angles and intricacies, and still hadn't been able to put everything together. Actually, I hadn't been able to put much of anything together. "Thanks."

"Don't thank me. It's your aunt who's the miracle worker."

"She certainly is." I scooped out potatoes, eggs, sausage and cheese from a casserole dish and thanked my lucky stars we had Vi in the family. I could burn water, and Ma was almost as much of a disaster in the kitchen as I was. But I think I've mentioned that several times already.

I took my plate and coffee cup to the table and sat down opposite my father, who seemed to be still thinking. I'd forked in a mouthful of delicious breakfast casserole when he finally emerged from his thoughts.

"Yes. I do believe his family has a business on Lincoln near Washington. And now that you mention it, I think it's a dry process cleaning place. Why?"

Pooh. I should have anticipated this question, but hadn't. Another reason to assume I hadn't fully awakened yet. "Um...." Good Lord. Should I tell my father I suspected Charlie Smith of trying to murder Joseph Jackson? Oh, why not? "That's where Jackson was shot. Sam and I looked at photographs of the site yesterday evening, and it appears Jackson was shot right in front of C.S. Smith's Dry Process Cleaning Establishment."

I heard the paper crinkle and looked up to see that my father had crumpled it on the table and was staring at me. "Are you serious?"

"Dead serious."

"Good God. Do you actually think..." His voice trailed off.

"I don't know what to think, Pa. I do think it's curious that Mr.

205

Smith is a member of the Klan, and that Joseph Jackson was shot directly in front of his family's cleaning firm. Sam said he thinks that's where the shooter escaped to after he shot Jackson. He was walking up to Jackson, presumably to finish him off, when people began screaming and gathering around Jackson, who had fallen to the sidewalk. A couple of the folks who saw the attempted murder said the man ran off, but nobody saw him afterwards. It would make sense that he entered the dry-cleaning place. Lincoln's a long street, and it doesn't bend up that way, so if anyone ran up or down the street, someone would have seen him." Would Pa know if Charlie Smith aimed to invest money in a Florida land deal? I asked him.

Pa blinked at me several times. "Florida? Land? Is that connected to the Smith cleaning place? I'm still trying to come to terms with Charlie Smith shooting someone. Maybe."

After considering and rejecting the notion of arguing with my father about his use of the word "maybe", I said, "I don't know what's connected to what, Pa. But several people in Pasadena, including some folks who seem to be involved in the Klan, have joined together to form a financial consortium headed by a person nobody trusts, but who says they can all make a fortune if they give him money to buy and develop property in Florida?"

After a moment of silence, Pa said, "Why Florida?"

As my mouth was full, I only shrugged.

"What's this about Florida?" said Vi, coming into the kitchen, buttoning a sweater over her sensible brown day dress. "Isn't that where the crocodiles live?"

I swallowed and said, "Alligators. Crocodiles live in Africa. I think. Mr. Pinkerton, along with Mr. Hastings and several other men, including the head of the deal, a fellow named Enoch Billingsgate, are investing money in a land deal in Florida. But all the wives of the men involved think Billingsgate is a fraud and aims to steal their money and run away with it. The money, I mean. Billingsgate might also belong to the Klan, but I'm not sure."

"Why would anyone want to buy land in Florida?" asked Ma,

also stepping into the kitchen. She already had on her hat and gloves and sensible shoes, and was ready to walk up the street to the Hotel Marengo, where she worked every day except Sunday. Half days on Saturdays. "Isn't Florida full of swamps and crocodiles?"

"Alligators," I told her. "Not crocodiles, which live in Africa. Mrs. Hastings said Mr. Hastings believes Florida is the next California," I told the assembled listeners.

"What does that mean?" asked Ma. No imagination, my mother.

"It means that people are going to build lots of houses and buildings and hotels and so forth and make it into a place where people will want to live. Or at least visit."

"Isn't it hot and muggy there?" asked Ma. Sensible question, I have to admit.

"Probably. It's on the Atlantic seacoast, it's flat as a stretched-out pancake, and I don't think they ever get snow or anything. And they get those terrible storms during the summertime that wash out everything. They're called hurricanes, I think. I've seen pictures in *The National Geographic*." I ate another bite of casserole. "This is delicious, Vi."

"Glad you like it, sweetie. Well, I'm off to the salt mines." And she headed to the front door.

Ma said, "Salt mines?" shook her head in puzzlement, and she, too, went to the front door. Pa got up and walked her to the door, where he kissed her fondly. My parents' marriage might not be perfect in every way, but it sure looked good to me.

Clearly troubled, Pa returned to the kitchen table and sat across from me again. I continued to eat, tense, waiting for the telephone to ring. I snagged a corner of the back section of the newspaper and skewed it around so that I could read it as I ate, wishing the *Star News* would include a crossword puzzle every day instead of just on Mondays.

"Do you really think Charlie Smith is involved in these nefarious deeds, Daisy? Really? I've known the man for a few years now, and I never thought he'd ever do something so awful as shoot someone."

I shrugged and continued to eat my breakfast. The second part of the paper didn't really contain any good stuff, but I perused it anyway because I didn't want to get into an argument with my father.

"What's Sam doing about it?"

I lifted my gaze from the boring newspaper. "Doing about what?"

"Charlie Smith."

"He's going to question him again today. Face it, Pa. Mr. Smith belongs to the Klan, the Klan has been harassing the Jacksons since before they moved from Oklahoma to California, and Joseph Jackson was shot directly in front of one of the Smiths' businesses. And then whoever did the shooting disappeared. Sam *has* to look at Charlie Smith. No matter how long you've known him."

"I guess so."

The phone rang. Even though I was waiting for it, I jumped in my seat. I said, "That's Mrs. Pinkerton. I hope nothing else has happened at her house."

Pa said nothing, so I rose and approached the telephone. Sure enough, it was our ring. Not that it being our ring would thwart our party-liners. When I picked the receiver from the cradle, I heard several other clicks and knew our party-line neighbors were on full alert. Nevertheless, I sucked in a deep breath and said, "Gumm-Majesty residence. Mrs. Majesty speaking."

"*Daisy!*" squealed Mrs. Pinkerton.

"One moment, please, Mrs. Pinkerton. Will our party-line neighbors please hang up? This telephone call is for me."

"Well, really!" said Mrs. Barrow. I knew it was her, because she had a hideous New York accent. Sam's accent wasn't nearly so ugly. "You do hog the line, Mrs. Majesty!"

"I'll be away from home all day, Mrs. Barrow. I'm sure you'll find plenty of free time to use the wire."

I guess Mrs. Barrow slammed her receiver into the cradle, because the noise it made was rather loud. Two other softer clicks followed hers.

Mrs. Pinkerton sniffled. She was loud, too. "Oh, Daisy, can you come to my house today?"

"I'll be happy to, Mrs. Pinkerton." It wasn't much of a lie. I wanted to know what had been going on since I'd seen her last... yesterday? It seemed longer ago than that. Yesterday had been a busy day. "Has anything else of an unsettling nature happened?" I caught my father's eye and he winked at me. I'd have winked back, but I've never acquired the knack of shutting only one eye at a time.

She sniffled again. "Not...not really. But I'm worried about Algie."

"Mr. Pinkerton?" Good grief, now what? "What's the matter with Mr. Pinkerton?"

"He's becoming more and more disgruntled with that horrid man who's running the Florida scheme. He told me last night that he thinks Mr. Stephen Hastings is an idiot. Algie's going to withdraw his funds from the consortium."

"Good for him!" Mr. P had more sense than I'd given him credit for.

"Well, perhaps, but now I'm worried that Algie might be in danger."

That woke me up in a hurry. I straightened and said, "What? What kind of danger?"

"I'm not sure, but he thinks someone followed him home from a meeting of the Florida Club last night, where he voiced his dissatisfaction with the way the consortium is being run. I don't trust that Billingsgate creature."

"My goodness. Perhaps you should telephone Detective Rotondo —" I stopped speaking abruptly, having learned from ample experience that Mrs. Pinkerton did *not* telephone policemen. "Um...I'll telephone Detective Rotondo and tell him about this. You say Mr. Pinkerton believes someone followed him home from the meeting of the Florida consortium?"

"Yes."

"Do you know where the meeting was held?"

"At Mr. Stephen Hastings' offices. Algie says Mr. Hastings is not happy with the way things are going, either. I'm afraid that Billingsgate fellow will take off with everyone's money in a day or two. That won't matter much to Algie or Mr. Hastings, but there are other people in the consortium who can't afford to lose money."

Like Officer Petrie. Only Petrie was dead, so Billingsgate taking off with money wasn't any concern of his. Unless, of course, he'd already gypped his parents out of some moola and given it to Billingsgate. Instantly I wished I hadn't thought about that. "It's nice of you to think of the smaller investors, Mrs. Pinkerton."

"You've taught me to think of other people, Daisy. You should thank yourself."

I had? You could have fooled me. "Nonsense," I said, although I could feel my cheeks heat from her compliment.

"It's not nonsense. You've taught me not to knuckle under to Stacy, and that people like Jackson are worthwhile citizens, and that there's a lot of suffering in the world from which I'm shielded by my wealth. I think you're a true godsend."

Very well, now I was blushing in earnest. This was ridiculous. I made my voice low, spiritualistic and humble—the humble part wasn't difficult. Well, neither were the other two, since I'd practiced. "Thank you very much for saying so, Mrs. Pinkerton, but you have a good heart. Otherwise you wouldn't be of so much help to others." A little thick, perhaps, but she'd stood up to her idiot daughter and was paying Jackson's hospital bills. That was a whole lot of help to the Jacksons.

"So when can you come over, dear?"

"Let me call Detective Rotondo." And walk my dog. I didn't add that part. "Would..." I glanced at the kitchen clock. Golly! It was only seven-thirty! "I'll be over at ten," I told her firmly. Shoot, the woman might be good for a few things, but I wasn't going to allow her to dictate when I got up in the morning.

"Ten o'clock?" she asked, as if there could be another meaning for ten in this context.

"Yes," I said firmly. "I'll only be able to stay an hour or so, but I'll be sure to bring the cards and the Ouija board. I want to visit Jackson again."

"And you'll call the police department?"

"Yes. I'll telephone the police department."

"Thank you *so* much, Daisy. I'll see you at ten."

We both hung up our receivers. Well, I presume she hung hers up. For all I knew, she made Featherstone hang up her telephone receiver for her. As I waited a few seconds, I considered one of the words I'd been thinking: gypped. I'm sure it originated with Gypsies and was, therefore, another obnoxious word people had coined to represent a perceived flaw in an entire group of people. Oh, dear. The world could be quite depressing if one really studied these things. I decided not to do so any more that day.

I clicked our cradle a couple of times to make sure Mrs. P and I had disconnected properly, and then I telephoned the Pasadena Police Department. It wasn't even eight o'clock yet, so Sam might not be there, but Sam was a tenacious so-and-so, so I took the chance.

An officer on the other end of the wire picked up the police department's receiver and said in a grim voice, "Pasadena Police Department."

"Detective Sam Rotondo, please. This is Mrs. Majesty and it's kind of an emergency." Bother. I'd just lied to a policeman. But I didn't want the guy on the other end to think I'd called just to chat with Sam.

"I'll see if he's in, madam."

Madam? Very well, so I was a madam. It was better than a snicker, I supposed.

I heard a few clicking noises that I recognized as my telephone call being transferred through some intricate process known only to operators at various telephone exchanges, and a moment or two later, I heard Sam's gravelly, "Yeah? What now?"

TWENTY-TWO

"For pity's sake, Sam Rotondo! What if it had been someone other than me on the other end of the wire?" Or should that have been I? Well, never mind. Irritated, I fingered my juju, wishing it did contain magical properties. I'd wish for Sam to sweeten up.

"Doan said it was you when he buzzed me."

"Oh. I didn't recognize Officer Doan's voice." Wait a minute. Sam had been *buzzed*? What in the world did that mean?

"Well, what do you want?" Sam repeated, and I decided to ask about buzzing later.

"Mrs. Pinkerton just called—"

"Huh," said Sam, interrupting my narrative.

"*Mrs. Pinkerton* just called," I said once more. "She told me Mr. Pinkerton smells a rat in the Florida deal. He thinks Mr. Hastings is getting nervous about it, too. Have you made any headway with Enoch Billingsgate."

"No. Except to learn he doesn't exist."

"What do you mean?"

"Just what I said."

"Doggone it, Sam Rotondo! How'd you find that out? That he doesn't exist, I mean."

"Ever heard of a cable gram? Or a telegraph?"

"Oh. So, who'd you cable to find that out?"

"The Dade County Sheriff's office."

"Oh. And they'd never heard of Enoch Billingsgate."

"I just told you that."

Darn him! "Thank you, Sam." I didn't want to rouse the bear, but since he seemed to be already roused, I decided to ask him anyway. "Have you found out who all else is included in the consortium?"

"According to your pal, Farrington—"

"He's not my pal!" Very well, I liked Del, but it was Harold who was my pal.

"Huh. Anyhow, this fellow who doesn't exist has duped Pinkerton, Hastings, your friend Mr. Smith—"

"And *he's* not my friend! Darn you, Sam!"

"Do you want to know this stuff, or not?"

I sucked in a gallon or two of breakfast-scented air and said, "Go on."

"Did I mention Hastings?"

"Yes, although you needn't have, since I'm the one who told you Hastings was involved."

"Yeah, whatever. Anyhow, Hastings, Pinkerton, Smith, Petrie— well, if he weren't dead—and two fellows named Johnstone and Delaney. Johnstone is part-owner of the Hertel Department Store, and Delaney is the vice-president of the Pasadena Public Bank. Oh, and Dr. Wagner, the guy whose daughter you stole a couple of years ago."

"I didn't *steal* her! She ran away from home because Dr. Wagner is a monster!"

"Huh."

Because I already knew it didn't do any good to argue with Sam, I held in further indignation on the Wagner front and concentrated on the Florida consortium. "So except for Smith and Petrie, all the investors are rich."

"Wagner's not so rich now. He lost a lot of patients because of you."

"Good."

Sam didn't even bother to grunt at that comment. "Anyhow, all the other ones we've found out about so far are quite wealthy. There may be more. But we're going to pick up Billingsgate today, if we can find him. Or whatever his name is. Once we get fingerprints, we might be able to find a match in Dade County."

"Oh, boy, I never realized what has to go into a nation-wide investigation. It really isn't much trouble for people to disappear in one place and re-invent themselves in another one, is it?"

"Used to be worse. Before we had proper fingerprinting equipment."

"I guess so. Still...."

"Yeah. I know. Anything else?"

I remembered the other reason for my call. "Mr. Pinkerton thinks someone followed him home from Mr. Hastings' law firm last night after he voiced disapproval of the way the Florida deal is being handled."

"I don't suppose he bothered to look at who was following him or take down the number plate on the follower's car, did he?"

"We're talking about a Pinkerton here, Sam," I said a bit stiffly.

"Yeah. Right. Anything else?"

"No. Thanks, Sam."

He hung up the receiver on his end without another word. The man was *such* a grump. I went back to my breakfast, fuming.

A bowl of oranges sat in the middle of our kitchen table. We had both a Valencia and a navel orange tree on our property, so we had oranges pretty much year-round. Yet another bonus we received for living in Southern California. I grabbed an orange and began peeling it viciously.

"Peeved with Sam?" asked Pa mildly.

I ripped off a big piece of skin from my orange which, fortunately for me, was a navel and easy to peel. "Yes. He's so grouchy."

"Well, it's only seven thirty. He's probably bone-tired."

"I suppose. But that's no excuse for being rude to me. All I was doing was relaying information."

Pa chuckled. "The problem is that you only give him bad news, sweetheart. If you ever called him up with a bit of good news, he probably wouldn't be so grumpy."

"Pooh. I'm doing my duty as a citizen. Coppers should be polite to the citizens of their city."

"Whatever you say, sweetie."

Pa went back to reading his newspaper, and I broke off sections of my orange and ate them. Delicious! My mood improved slightly.

After I washed the dishes and put them away, I changed from slippers to walking shoes, and Pa and I took Spike for a walk. The weather continued warm, so I didn't bother with a sweater, although I did wear a hat, since no woman would appear outside without one. This one was a straw number, and I'd tied a pink ribbon around it to go with my dress. When I looked in the mirror, I was pleased to see I didn't look as shabby as I'd felt when I woke up.

Because Spike was a trifle plump, I decided to walk extra far that morning. Pa, whose heart wasn't in great shape, decided to walk back home without us. Spike and I had a good time together.

We'd almost made it back home when a big black automobile drove slowly past Spike and me. Often people would stop me on the street and tell me what a good-looking dog Spike was—and they were right. I expected a comment of that nature to come from the people in the machine.

You could have knocked me over with a peacock feather when a gun appeared through the partly rolled-down window, and whoever rode in the passenger side of the machine took a shot at me! Spike jumped and started barking hysterically, and neighbors rushed out of their houses. As for me, as soon as I saw the gun, and even before it fired, I plastered myself on the sidewalk on top of all the dried leaves, dust, and hard little pepper-tree peppercorns and yelled. Don't ask me what I yelled, because I don't remember. Talk about being scared out of your wits. I was. And then some.

Spike had begun licking my face when the first neighbor rushed up to me.

"Daisy! Are you all right? What happened?"

Afraid to open my eyes, I managed to chatter out, "S-s-somebody shot at me."

"Good Lord!"

I recognized the voice as belonging to Mrs. Wilson, our neighbor to the north, and mother to Pudge Wilson. Pudge was at school, I expect.

"I called the police! I called the police!" came another voice. I recognized this one as belonging to the supremely nosy Mrs. Long-necker. Oh, well. I really couldn't blame neighbors for gossiping about me if people were going to take potshots at me.

Very slowly, Mrs. Wilson helped me to my feet. For some reason, I hadn't let go of Spike's leash, but gripped it as if it were a lifeline. In a way, I guess it was, since Spike was my main source of comfort and happiness back then. Other neighbors had gathered around. Mrs. Killebrew brushed the dust and peppercorns from my dress, another neighbor patted me on the back, and Mrs. Wilson and Mrs. Longnecker helped me home. I didn't really need their help, but I was glad for it, although I'm sure Mrs. Longnecker would have a field day gossiping about how Daisy Majesty must have done something *really* awful this time if people were shooting at her.

Lord, I was frightened. When I reached the house, Pa stood on the porch, looking worried. "Are you all right, Daisy?" said he.

"I think so. The bullet didn't hit me, anyway."

"Good God. Somebody *shot* at you?"

"You didn't hear it?" I asked, puzzled. Heck, all the rest of the people in our neighborhood had heard it, to judge by the crowd that had gathered.

"I thought I heard a car backfiring. I came outside to see whose it was." Ever the automobile mechanic, my father.

"No. It was a gunshot, and I'm only lucky the guy missed me. And Spike." The thought of my darling dog being shot hit me in the stomach, and I burst into tears. Pa and Mrs. Wilson led me into the house, Spike cavorting at our feet—he didn't know what all the fuss was about—and I was still crying when Sam Rotondo banged on the door and barged in without being invited. For once, I didn't mind his lack of manners.

"All right, what's going on here?" he demanded, standing before the sofa upon which Spike and I sat, his fists on his hips, glaring up a storm. Spike jumped up and wagged at him. Sam petted Spike, but kept looking at me.

"Someone took a shot at Daisy when she was out walking the dog," said Pa, succinctly summarizing events.

"This business is getting totally out of hand," said Sam. Need I say he was angry? I didn't think so.

"It-it's not my fault," I said, blubbering and embarrassed. My pink day dress, which wasn't new to begin with, was now stained and blotchy, as was, I'm sure, my face. I scowled at Sam Rotondo, who scowled back.

"You didn't see who shot at you, did you?"

"No! And I didn't look at the license plate, either! Darn it, I was scared to death."

"Figures," said Sam, disgruntled.

Well, I was disgruntled, too. "You try being shot and see how interested *you* are in looking at license plates and people!"

"You'd better stay in your house for a few days until we pick up whoever's responsible for the mess you've got yourself in to."

"*I* didn't get myself into any mess, Sam Rotondo!" I cried, my tears drying up like magic. "It's those horrible Klan and Florida people who are behind all the awful things that have been happening lately! If you coppers would do your jobs, decent folks could walk their dogs on their own streets without being shot at!"

"Daisy," said Pa. He didn't say it forcefully, but I'm sure he didn't like me hollering at Sam. Too bad. I didn't like Sam blaming everything on me.

"Anyhow, I can't stay home. I have an appointment with Ms. Pinkerton at ten o'clock this morning, and then I'm going to visit Flossie and Johnny, and then I'm going to visit Jackson in the hospital. At least the crazed gunman *missed* me, which is more than poor Jackson can say!"

"For God's sake, do you *want* to be killed?" bellowed Sam.

"*No!*" I bellowed back.

"And we *are* doing our jobs! Dammit, we're working our hardest to catch the perpetrators of all the crimes being committed in the city!"

"You could have fooled me." I added a sniff at the end of my sentence, mainly because my nose was running. Oh, but I was angry with Sam.

"You don't *have* to leave your house," Sam snarled. "If you *choose* to do so, thereby putting yourself and anyone near you in danger, you can't blame it on the police."

"I wouldn't dream of it," I told him, as acidly as possible.

To my surprise, Sam plumped down on the sofa next to me and took my hand. I jerked back, not expecting this.

"Please, Daisy. Can't you just make life easier on all of us for a couple of days and stay indoors where those idiots can't get at you?"

"Sam's right, Daisy," said Pa, concern evident in his voice.

Fuming, feeling mulish, yet knowing Sam and Pa were right, I considered the matter. If I left the house even though someone clearly knew where I lived and had already taken a shot at me, I'd be an idiot.

After some thought on the matter, I decided I aimed to be an idiot. "I'm sorry, Pa and Sam, but I'm not going to desert my friends. You know who's doing these things, Sam. I know you claim you don't have evidence, but you still know. I don't expect you to put a guard on me or anything, but I promise I won't do anything more foolish than drive to the Pinkertons' place, the Salvation Army, and the Castleton Hospital."

"Dammit," Sam grumbled. "Wait here a minute." He dropped my hand, got up from the sofa, and stomped to the front door, which he opened and left open.

I blinked at Pa a few times and got shakily to my feet. Being shot at is truly a shocking experience, and one I advise everyone else in the world to avoid, if possible. Nevertheless, I made my way to the door and stared outside. People still milled about. As for Sam, he seemed to be searching his Hudson for something. I guess he found it, because he turned abruptly, gave the assembled neighbors a comprehensive frown, and stormed back to our house. I barely got out of his way before he could barrel into me.

"If," he said as nastily as he could, "you insist on making a target of yourself, at least put this on your dashboard when you're at the hospital. Then you can park right up front and won't have to walk a mile from the parking lot to the building."

And, by golly, he handed me a cardboard sign that read: PASADENA POLICE DEPARTMENT. OFFICIAL BUSINESS.

"You won't need it at the Pinkertons' or the Salvation Army, I don't suppose," said he, doubling his negative and thereby telling me I *would* need it at those places. But I understood. In fact, I appreciated his thoughtfulness.

"Thanks, Sam."

"You're welcome."

"I appreciate this." I waved the sign at him.

"Yeah. Well, use the damned thing, will you?"

"I will. You needn't swear at me."

"Like hell."

With that, Sam exited the house once more and stormed to his Hudson. He took off with a roar that seemed to scatter the last remaining neighbors back into their houses.

I stared at the sign and then at Pa. I didn't know what to say.

"That was nice of him," said Pa.

"Yes, it was."

"I wish you wouldn't leave the house today, Daisy."

"I know you do, Pa, but I...I don't know. I just think I have to. If I don't...well, all I know is that after Billy died, I nearly became a hermit, and I don't want that to happen again."

"These circumstances are entirely different, sweetie."

"I know they are. But they're making me feel sort of the same." I pressed a hand to my still-palpitating heart and felt my juju. Hmm. Maybe it *was* bringing me luck. I mean, getting shot at wasn't lucky, but the fact that the bullet hadn't hit me was. It then occurred to me that it was fortunate the person behind the gun had held a pistol. Or maybe it was a revolver. I don't know the difference. Anyway, if he'd held one of those Thompson submachine guns, I'd be splattered all over the sidewalk on South Marengo Avenue instead of standing, safe and secure, in my own home.

With that not-quite-comforting thought in mind, I decided to take a long, soaking bath, in hopes it would relax me. I wished Spike could bathe with me, but he didn't enjoy bubble baths as much as I did, so I didn't force the issue.

When I got out of the bath, I felt a little better, albeit not much. Face it, getting shot at is an upsetting experience. It would probably take me some time—and the arrest of the participating villains—for me to feel absolutely secure again.

Nevertheless, I chose a nice cool dress made of a light brown, wool crepe fabric I'd bought when it was on sale at Nash's fabric department. The pattern was one I'd made myself after seeing and liking a Worth dress modeled by a tall, skinny woman gracing the pages of a fairly recent *Vogue Magazine*. The fact that I was neither tall nor skinny didn't matter much in this case. The bodice bloused slightly, was hip-length, and was secured on each side with a white disk. I'd had to search some to find the right kinds of disks and had ended up improvising, but they worked. The dress had a U-shaped neckline edged with a band of white silk. The sleeves were wide and had a broad cuff also edged with white silk, and I'd done some fancy beadwork at the neckline and cuffs, which gave the dress an elegance far greater than its price had been. It came to my mid-calf, and I wore flesh-colored stockings and my brown low-heeled shoes. I also wore my brown cloche hat.

When I gazed at my reflection in the mirror, I didn't look like a woman who'd had a near-death experience not an hour earlier. In fact, I was rather proud that I appeared so serene.

The front door slammed, and I jumped a foot in the air and slapped my hand over my heart. Whirling around, I saw Pa and Spike smiling at me. And don't tell me dogs can't smile. Spike could and did.

"Sorry," said Pa. "I had my hands full. Hope the slamming door didn't startle you."

I flipped my formerly flattened-to-my-chest hand in the air with as much nonchalance as I could muster. "Not at all, Pa."

"Brought these for you," said he, handing me a bouquet of chrysanthemums he'd clipped from our very own flower beds.

Oh, my, but I loved my father! "Thanks, Pa."

I slipped my juju over my head, made sure it was concealed under my fancy bodice, put the flowers in a vase—by the way, in case you wondered, chrysanthemums and orchids go splendidly together —slipped on my gloves, grabbed my tarot cards and Ouija board and the sign Sam had given me. Then I kissed Pa on the cheek, patted Spike three or four times for the sake of my soul, and left the house for the day.

TWENTY-THREE

I not only kept my eyes on the road as I proceeded to Mrs. Pinkerton's house, but I also craned my neck in every way it could crane as I watched out for slow-moving black automobiles. There were lots of black automobiles on the roads, but I didn't see the one out of which someone had shot at me.

The gate to the Pinkerton place stood open again today, but a uniformed man sat in a chair in the middle of the opening. He wasn't a policeman; at least not an official one. He jumped up as soon as he saw me pull into the drive, held up his hand, and I stopped the Chevrolet.

He whipped a notebook and pencil from his jacket pocket. "Name?" he barked, sounding older than he looked.

"Mrs. Majesty."

The guard peered down at his notebook, which apparently held a list of people authorized to drive up the deodar-lined way to the Pinkerton abode. Or palace. Choose either word; they both apply.

"Very well. Please drive on up."

He stood smartly to one side of the Chevrolet, whipped the chair out of my way, and I continued to the house. Harold's bright red

Stutz Bearcat wasn't parked in the circular drive in front of the porch, and I was disappointed, but his absence didn't deter me. I had an appointment.

Featherstone opened the door to my knock, said, "Please come this way," as he always did, and I followed him down the hallway to the drawing room. He announced me as I waltzed through the door.

Springing up from her chair—quite a feat, considering her bulk—Mrs. Pinkerton cried, "Daisy! I'm so glad you came!"

"Thank you, Mrs. Pinkerton." I smiled one of my mysterious spiritualist smiles at her. "I'm happy to be here." Not much of a lie.

So Mrs. Pinkerton talked to Rolly through the Ouija board, I consulted the tarot cards for her—they said the same thing today as they had the other sixty million times I'd consulted them for her—and Mrs. P was happy. I didn't upset her by telling her someone had taken a shot at me. No need to distress the woman any more than she was already distressed.

I did, however, ask her about Mr. Pinkerton's experience of the night before. "You said Mr. Pinkerton was followed from Mr. Hastings' law offices last night?"

"Yes, he was," she said, sounding indignant. I didn't blame her for that.

"But he doesn't know who followed him?"

"No, but he thinks that Billingsgate creature had one of his minions follow him."

The man had minions, did he? I envied him a little. "I see. Um... how many people does Mr. Billingsgate have in his employ? Do you know?"

After taking a moment or two to think over my question, Mrs. P said, "Well...I'm not sure they're actually *employed* by him. I do believe they're Pasadena men who are investing in the Florida plan. Only they're...not wealthy. In fact, they might be as unsuspecting as some of the other men in the group, although how anyone with half a brain can look at Mr. Billingsgate and not know him as a villain amazes me."

"I see. I think I understand." Billingsgate had himself a couple of henchmen who were too stupid to realize he was a crook and who did his bidding, probably believing they were performing good deeds. I wondered if one of his minions had shot at me that morning. But no. I think this morning's to-do had to do with the Klan. And the Klan might or might not have anything to do with Enoch Billingsgate. The fact that he said he was from a southern state made me lean toward the Klan side of the equation as far as he went, but that was complete supposition on my part. It wasn't evidence, as Sam so delighted in pointing out to me.

"Do you think Algie is in any danger? What with all the horrid things going on around here lately, I'm not sure what to think, myself."

"I...don't know. It's difficult to believe anyone would wish Mr. Pinkerton harm. He's so..." I searched my occasionally agile brain for a good word to describe Mr. P. Innocuous? Jolly? Bland? Innocent? Stupid? I didn't think Mrs. P would appreciate any of those. Anyhow, Mr. P clearly wasn't stupid, or he couldn't have helped save the bank when his help was needed. "He's so nice. I can't imagine anyone wanting to harm him." Very well, so nice wasn't a great word. He *was* nice.

"Yes," said Mrs. Pinkerton. "But Jackson is nice, too, and he's in the hospital nursing a gunshot wound."

"True. But Mr. Pinkerton isn't a Negro. It was probably a member of the KKK who shot Jackson." Then again, I wasn't a Negro, either, and someone had shot at me. I just hated what was going on in my beautiful home town!

"I wouldn't put it past Mr. Billingsgate to belong to that awful Klan," said Mrs. P in as stern a voice as I'd ever heard issue from her mouth.

"I was thinking the same thing," I told her because it was the truth. "If he's truly from Florida, he might just belong to the Klan." Being from a southern state didn't account for the Pasadenans who were stupid enough to join the Klan, but why bother with reason? Mrs. P and I agreed on the Klan issue, and I appreciated her for it.

"I'm going to visit Jackson after I leave your house," I said, figuring it wouldn't hurt to mention my benevolence. Which reminded me I probably ought to take something to Jackson and not show up in his room empty-handed. Well, I'd think about that later.

"That's kind of you, Daisy. I haven't been to see him, but Quincy Applewood has."

Quincy Applewood, who worked for Mr. P in his stables, was married to my good friend Edie, who worked as Mrs. P's lady's maid.

"That's nice of Quincy."

"Yes. He's a good boy. I don't know what we'd do without Quincy and Edie."

That was good to hear.

I took my leave of Mrs. Pinkerton then, and walked down the hall, through the servants' door, and into the kitchen, where my aunt reigned supreme. "Hey, Aunt Vi!" I said to her back. She was stirring something on the range when I entered her kingdom.

"Daisy!" she cried, turning and beaming at me. I did love my aunt. "Are you going to be visiting Jackson any time soon?"

Slightly taken aback, I said, "Why, yes. I aimed to visit him right after I stop by the Salvation Army to see Flossie and Johnny."

"Oh, good. I made some cookies for you to take to him in the hospital. Scotch shortbread. I already know he loves my Scotch shortbread."

"Who doesn't?" I asked, my mouth beginning to water. But really. If you've never tasted my aunt's Scotch shortbread, your life isn't yet complete.

"Yes, yes, I made some for the family, too," said Vi, laughing at me. "Here. You can have one of the family's batch now. But don't eat any of Jackson's."

"Thanks, Vi! I promise I won't eat any of Jackson's cookies."

And I didn't. I was extremely cautious as I drove south on Fair

Oaks to the Salvation Army, searching for and not finding the automobile that had crept past me that morning. I parked the Chevrolet on the street directly in front of the Salvation Army's front door and raced thereto, looking in all directions as I did so. No sinister car, thank God.

Unfortunately for me, all that running and looking didn't help me a single bit. Flossie and Johnny and, I presume, their baby, William, weren't there. They were undoubtedly on a Pasadena street corner, playing "Onward, Christian Soldiers," and trying to recruit sinners into their benevolent fold.

Nuts. I raced back to the car, still searching for evildoers and finding none. Then I drove to the Castleton Hospital. I positioned the sign Sam had given me on the dashboard of the Chevrolet, and parked as close to the hospital's front door as I could get. Then, holding the plate of shortbread to my chest, I ran like a bunny to the hospital's doors. The lady at the reception desk peered at me oddly, but I tried not to let her expression bother me.

Since I already knew the number of Jackson's room, I walked up the stairs and went directly there. Carl Simmons sat in a chair outside Jackson's room. When he saw me, he rose from his chair and smiled at me. "Mornin', Mrs. Majesty. Joseph'll be might pleased to see you."

"Good morning, Mr. Simmons. I brought him some of my aunt's shortbread cookies. Aunt Vi baked them especially for Mr. Jackson."

"That's mighty kind of the both of you."

"Jackson's been my friend for a long time, Mr. Simmons. It's awful, what those wicked people did to him."

"Yes, ma'am. I agree with you on that one."

When I walked into Jackson's room, I was surprised not to see Mrs. Jackson ruling it. Rather, a thin black man with huge glasses sat on a chair next to Jackson's bed. He rose when I entered the room and stared at me through the thick lenses of his spectacles. It looked to me as though Jackson was asleep.

"Good morning," I whispered to the stranger. "I'm Mrs. Majesty, and I came to see how Mr. Jackson's doing."

"Good morning, ma'am," the young man said. "I'm Marshall Armistead, a friend of the Jackson family."

"Oh! You're the one who took the pictures!"

He appeared pleased that I knew even that much about him. "Yes, ma'am. Photography is my hobby. I aim to turn it into my life's work."

"Oh, my. How do you do plan on doing that?" Perhaps that wasn't altogether polite, but I wanted to know.

"Have a seat, Mrs. Majesty," said Mr. Armistead.

So I did, carefully setting the plate of cookies, covered with waxed paper, on the table next to Jackson's bed. "I'm really curious, Mr. Armistead. How do you go about making a career out of photography?"

"I'm putting together a portfolio of my photographs. Then I'll send photographs to various venues. Lots of magazines and newspapers are using photographs these days. I'm hoping my color won't be a topic of concern, since they won't even know what I look like."

His calm statement regarding the color of his skin and people's prejudices hit me in the heart. How awful it was for people to judge a person's character by the color of his skin. But Mr. Armistead was correct. If anyone knew he was a black man, his chances for employment at a good magazine were probably zero.

"Oh, my, I'm sorry you have to go through that. It's not fair."

He shrugged. "It's the way the world works. I'm just going to try to circumvent some of the problems by showing my work to folks without showing them my face, too. If they like my work, maybe they won't care that I'm a Negro."

"Best of luck," I told him sincerely. "The photographs you took of the scene where Mr. Jackson was shot have been of tremendous help to the Pasadena Police Department. I know, because I went through them myself with Detective Rotondo, and he put together a sensible pattern of how the events occurred by studying them."

I got a smile from the serious Mr. Armistead for that. "Thanks for telling me."

"I think I even know who the shooter was, but Sam—that's Detective Rotondo—requires proof. He doesn't think my guess, even though I believe it's a valid one, is enough evidence."

With a chuckle, Mr. Armistead said, "Yeah, the police are like that."

Conversation sort of stalled at that point. Mr. Armistead and I smiled at each other, but neither of us knew what to say. Well, I didn't, anyway. Not sure about him, but if he thought of anything to say, he didn't say it.

Eventually, I said, "I'm surprised Mrs. Jackson isn't here. I expected to find her with her son."

"Everyone expected her to be here," said Mr. Armistead, his countenance taking on a worried mien. "My mother went up to the Jacksons' place to see if she's all right."

Alarmed, I said, "Does your mother think Mrs. Jackson may be ill?" Oh, dear. I suppose having one's son nearly murdered might cause any number of heart palpitations or whatever in a fond mother's bosom.

"I think she's more worried about the Klan, to tell you the truth." No more smiles from Mr. Armistead. He was dead serious.

That word, dead, gave me the shivers.

"Oh, dear. I can't believe that awful organization has actually gained a foothold in Pasadena, California, of all places."

He shrugged. "The Klan drove some of the Jackson family out of Tulsa, Oklahoma."

"I know." I sighed, hating the knowledge.

"Some folks are strange, I reckon."

"I reckon."

Mr. Armistead and I ceased speaking at that point, and I sat there, contemplating the Klan and the Jacksons. It was most unlike the Mrs. Jackson I'd sort of come to know not to be at her wounded son's bedside.

"How long ago did your mother go to the Jacksons' place?" I asked after a space of silence.

Shaking up his long sleeve and looking at his wristwatch, Mr. Armistead frowned. "An hour and a half. She should be back by now." He stood. "Maybe I'd better go and check."

I stood, too. "No, I'll go. I need to get a recipe from Mrs. Jackson anyway, and I think it would be better if you're here when Mr. Jackson's wakes up." Don't ask me why I said that, because I didn't know, but a creepy feeling that something was wrong had begun slithering up my spine, and I didn't want this nice young man anywhere near the Jackson home if all wasn't right there.

"Are you sure, Mrs. Majesty?" he asked, looking uncertain.

"I'm sure. I need to visit her again anyway."

"You'll be kind of conspicuous in that neighborhood," he said candidly.

"Maybe, but I know Mrs. Jackson. In fact, we're in the same profession."

His eyes widened behind his spectacle's lenses. "You're a voodoo mambo?"

I grinned. "Your mother and Mrs. Jackson call me a white mambo."

And then Mr. Armistead gave me an eye-roll that reminded me so much of Sam Rotondo, I nearly laughed. However, the circumstances didn't seem to call for humor, so I only pulled out the juju Mrs. Jackson had given me, and said, "Don't worry. I have my luck always with me."

"I expect Joseph was wearing one of those things when he got shot, too. Better not depend on it too much." Mr. Armistead's voice was as dry as alum.

"You're right. I won't. It was good to meet you. Best of luck in your chosen career."

"Thank you."

We shook hands across the sleeping Jackson, and I departed his room. I bade Mr. Simmons farewell, too, and decided it wouldn't hurt if he knew where I was going. You know; in case I never came back.

"Be careful," he advised me.

"I will be," I assured him.

I left the hospital's double fronted glass doors at a dead run and got to my Chevrolet so fast, I'd probably have won a race had anyone been running with me.

Then I made my way across California Boulevard, where the hospital was located, turned north on Lincoln Avenue, and tootled my way up to Mentone. I was still gazing around for big, black, slow-moving automobiles, but it wasn't until I found the Jacksons' house that I noticed, parked right smack in front of it, the very same machine from which someone had taken a shot at me only a few hours earlier.

TWENTY-FOUR

If anyone had been walking on Mentone, I'm sure he or she would have heard my cry of alarm. Fortunately for me, the street was deserted. Made sense. Most everyone in this neighborhood worked away from home during the day. Later, after my heart stopped trying to leap out of my chest, I realized how different life was for the black people in Pasadena from the lives of most of the rest of us. Except for us Gumms and Majestys. Most white women stayed home during the day to do their housework and cooking. The black population of my fair city didn't have that option. Life was *totally* unfair. But I'd known that for years.

However, at that moment in time, I thought not of fairness. I thought of gunmen. And I thought I knew where they were. If there was more than one, and I thought there must be since the fellow who shot at me hadn't been the same fellow driving the automobile from which he (the shooter) fired.

Good God. What to do now?

Well, for one thing, I got myself out of there. I drove past the Jacksons' house without pause, and turned right at the corner of the street where Mentone ended, which was called Zanja. I pulled over and stopped the Chevrolet, and allowed myself to panic for several minutes.

What to do?

Drive to the police department?

Would Sam listen to me?

But that was the car from which I'd been shot at!

Same question: would Sam listen to me? I, who hadn't bothered to look at the number plate on the automobile as it cruised past Spike and me?

If I went to the police department, would I be deserting Mrs. Jackson and/or Mrs. Armistead?

Well...yeah. I would be.

Very well. I, a white woman, was an outsider in this neighborhood and might perhaps be a trifle conspicuous walking on Mentone Avenue if I went to the Jacksons' home to see what was going on in there.

On the other hand, as mentioned above, most of the residents of Mentone were at work elsewhere that late September morning.

And I could sneak. At least I thought I could.

Taking my courage in both hands—which didn't leave a whole lot of fingers left over with which to touch my juju, although I managed —I exited the Chevrolet and very quietly shut the door. Then I assessed my options. I was, darn it, on the wrong side of the street to sneak up to the back of the Jackson home. I'd have to cross Mentone to do that, and what if those awful men saw me? I'd be one dead Daisy.

I should have turned left on Zanja, but my brain had been sending off alarm bells when I got to the end of Mentone, and my thought patterns had scrambled. Should I turn the Chevrolet around and park on the other side of Zanja where it crossed Mentone?

That would make a lot of noise.

On the other hand, it would get me to the correct side of the street from which to spy.

I commanded my brain to stop whirling and think. My brain

didn't pay any more attention to my commands than Sam generally did, curse it. I reminded myself that I'd thwarted a vicious criminal a month or so ago by sticking him up with a pair of chopsticks. That had been ingenious, hadn't it?

Well, yes, but only until the crook whacked my arm and I dropped the chopsticks.

But then I ran like a streak and managed to foil not merely that villain but two others, cracking a drug-smuggling ring and solving a murder in the process.

That particular villain hadn't been armed with anything more lethal than his fists. The guys who might or might not be in the Jacksons' house had already shot Jackson and Mr. Merton, tried to shoot me, and had probably smothered Officer Petrie. Mind you, Officer Petrie might have deserved his grisly fate, but neither Jackson nor I did. And neither did either Mrs. Jackson or Mrs. Armistead, whom I expected were in the Jackson house.

Bother.

I don't know how long I stood there, debating my choices of various evils, but I finally decided to attempt to sneak up to the Jacksons' house from the rear—which entailed crossing Mentone in full view of God and anyone else who might be watching—and see if I could figure out what was going on in there. If I saw a crime happening, I could...what? Run to the Chevrolet and drive hell for leather to the police department? Bang on a neighbor's door and ask to use the telephone? A glance upward told me that nobody on that section of Mentone had telephone service. Shoot. I mean shucks. The notion of shooting didn't appeal at that moment.

Very well. I was going to be a brave Daisy Gumm Majesty and see if I could affect a rescue, should one be required. If I peeked through a window and saw Mrs. Jackson and Mrs. Armistead dead in a welter of their own blood, I'd faint.

No, I wouldn't! Darn it, I'd help them! Unarmed. Against men with guns. Or at least one man with a gun.

I decided it would be best if I'd just stop thinking entirely and walk across Mentone and see if I could access an alleyway that would lead me past the rear of the Jacksons' house. So I did. Walk across Mentone, I mean. However, once I got (in one piece) to the other side of the street and scooted as fast as I could past the first house on the corner of Mentone and Zanja, I found no handy alleyway.

Blast! That meant I'd have to tromp through people's back yards. I hoped none of the Jacksons' neighbors had any vicious dogs chained up outside. Or any vicious residents, for that matter.

But never mind all that. I shoved my way through hedges and bushes—fortunately, nobody'd bothered to build fences around their properties—and made my sticky way to the back of the Jacksons' house. I knew it was their house, because I'd actually managed to count houses, in spite of my state of terror.

So. There I was, at the very back of the Jacksons' property. Now what?

Bearing in mind that someone with a firearm might be looking out the windows, checking for snoopy people, I decided I'd just have to sacrifice my beautiful imitation Worth creation, and crawled from the very back of the Jacksons' yard to the back porch. I could feel beads snagging on bushes as I crawled, and I cursed the man or men in that house holding Mrs. Jackson and/or Mrs. Armistead hostage. If they were there. By that time, I prayed they were so I wouldn't have sacrificed my gorgeous gown in vain.

The window curtains weren't drawn and the window was open, so I could, if I got close enough, peer into the house. Figuring my chance of silence would be better if I were unshod, I took off my shoes and set them neatly on the first porch stair. Then I crawled up the stairs. In order to do so, I had to lift my skirt above my knees and hold it at waist height, so my stockings got ripped, too. Darn those stupid Klansmen! They were no good for anything.

As carefully as possible, I rose slightly until only the upper part of my face was above the windowsill. An empty kitchen lay before me. Tidy and as neat as anything, all appliances shining fit to blind one, it was as empty as empty could be. I slumped back to the porch floor.

Very well. So nobody was in the kitchen. In my head, I plotted the outline of the Jacksons' house. Wasn't difficult to do. The house was pretty much a square. The living room was on the south side of the home, with the bedrooms on the north and the kitchen to the west and south. Hmm. What now?

I crawled to the southernmost part of the porch and peeked around the corner to see if there were any handy windows into which I could peer, unseen, at any lurking villains. There was a window, all right. It was not merely open to catch the September breezes, but it was also about as high off the ground as I was, which meant I wouldn't be able to see through it with any ease unless I found a handy brick or something to stand on.

Rescuing damsels in distress was a darned annoying business.

Nevertheless, I found a flat rock in the yard, carefully made my way to it, making sure no one was observing me from the house, and picked it up. Dang, it was heavy! But never mind. I was on a mission here.

I lugged the rock to the side window, crouching all the while so that no one looking out of the window could see me, and set the rock beneath the window. Then I carefully climbed up on the rock and inch by inch lifted my head and peered inside.

They were there! I almost fell off my rock. In truth, I kind of did, but I caught myself before I could land on the ground and make a noise. I did scrape my hand pretty badly, but that was nothing to the point.

Two men sat in two chairs in the Jacksons' front room, pointing guns at Mrs. Jackson and Mrs. Armistead, who occupied two other chairs in front of the fireplace. It was fortunate for me that the two men had their backs toward me. It occurred to me that leaving their backs exposed to anyone peeking in the window was a stupid thing to do. Then I remembered they were members of the Ku Klux Klan and decided such behavior was only to be expected.

After I caught my breath and managed to still my rampaging

heart a bit, I again climbed on the rock and squinted through the window. Lord, Lord, what was I supposed to do now?

Well, for one thing, I could listen, thanks to the window being open. As luck (or something) would have it, one of the men took that opportunity to threaten the two women.

"You'd better tell me where he is, lady, or you're not long for this world."

Charlie Smith! I'd recognize that voice anywhere! So he *was* a dirty crook! Ha. I'd thought so from the beginning. Almost. But who was the other guy?

"You can go right along and chase yourself, Mr. Smith and Mr. Petrie. I ain't tellin' where my Henry be. You done tried to run down his children, and I ain't goin' to give you another chance at 'em."

Mr. Petrie? Wasn't Petrie dead? How could that be Petrie? Unless he was yet another bad-apple Petrie from the Oklahoma branch of the family. I squinted harder. The man seated next to Charlie Smith was a fat, redheaded fellow. A fat, redheaded fellow was in charge of the phony Florida deal in which both Mr. Hastings and Mr. Pinkerton were losing faith. But I'd been told his name was Billingsgate.

Then I recalled that Mr. Billingsgate didn't exist. Was that fat, redheaded man a Petrie in disguise? For pity's sake. I was the only Majesty left alive, at least that I knew about, but the evil Petrie clan seemed to go on forever.

As stealthy as a cat creeping up on a bird, I again lifted myself and peeped through the window. Mrs. Armistead looked quite anxious, which made sense. Mrs. Jackson was fiddling with a pile of little person-shaped jujus. I wondered if I could catch her eye and, if I did, if she'd let on I was at the window.

Naw. She was smarter than that.

But what about Mrs. Armistead? Well, her son was smart as a whip, and it was she who'd brought him into the world and helped rear him. She was probably smart, too.

It then occurred to me that I should probably fetch myself a weapon. Not that any weapon I discovered in the Jacksons' back yard would provide much defense against a firearm, but it still wouldn't hurt to have something at hand. I recalled the collection of stuff on the back porch and remembered seeing a couple of porch chairs, a zinc bucket, a pot containing some kind of flowers, a baseball bat, and...my memory stretched no farther. Pooh.

Nevertheless, I silently crept back to the porch and picked up the baseball bat. Then, figuring what the heck, I took the bucket, too. If one of the men stuck his head out of the window, maybe I could shove the bucket over it.

I began to believe my senses were unraveling due to stress.

However, I once more made my way to the open living room window, stepped on my rock, and lifted myself so that I could see into the room. The men still weren't paying attention to anything that might be lurking at their backs, which might or might not be a good thing. I mean, if something gave my presence away, one of them could probably turn and fire a gun before I could duck. Maybe. Maybe not.

Since the men were both busy harassing the two women, I decided to let Mrs. Jackson know I was there. Maybe she could think of something for me to do that might prove useful. I sure wasn't coming up with anything on my own. For someone under the threat of imminent death, she was being mighty stoical. I thought she was swell.

Which didn't change anything. Therefore, I ducked under the window ledge and stuck my arm up, waving it slightly. Then I waited for what seemed like about eight hours but which was probably only a couple of seconds and again peeked through the mirror. Mrs. Jackson didn't look at me, but she did pick up one of the jujus on her lap. With great deliberation, she wrung its neck.

"You ain't gettin' Henry's address from me, Mr. Smith and Mr. Petrie. And if you kill me, you still won't know where he be. And if you shoot off a gun, it's goin' to make a mighty big noise."

"Yeah," said Mrs. Armistead, sounding truculent, for very good reason. "You'll still be as blind and stupid as you are now. And everybody will know it, 'cause they'll have heard the shootin'.'"

Because I figured it was safe for me to do so, I stood up on my rock and showed Mrs. Jackson the baseball bat in my hands. She carefully picked up another juju and pressed her finger against its head until its skull was crushed. I got the message, but didn't know quite how to put it into action. So, to give me time to think, I also lifted the bucket.

Darned if Mrs. Jackson didn't smile and bring her hand down over another juju, covering its head.

"What are you doing with them damned stick toys?" demanded the man whom I believed to be calling himself Billingsgate. "Put those damned things down."

"Them's jujus," said Mrs. Armistead, doing a credible imitation of appearing shocked. "They be magic."

"And they're gonna bring vengeance down upon the both of you, too." Mrs. Jackson picked up a book on the table beside her and dropped it on the floor, making a heck of a noise.

"Stop that!" cried Charlie Smith, who seemed much more rattled than his companion in villainy.

"Just tryin' to catch your attention, gentlemen," said Mrs. Jackson. And darned if she didn't wink at me!

Well, I guess I knew what she expected me to do. Ducking below the windowsill, I stepped down off my rock, held the baseball bat in both hands, ready to swing it, and set up a scream that would have done a banshee proud. I shrieked so loudly, I frightened several dogs on Mentone into barking frenzies.

"What the hell was that?" demanded Petrie/Billingsgate?

"Damned if I know?"

"You fellers curse too much," said Mrs. Jackson serenely. "Go look to the window if you want to see who's screamin'. It sure ain't one of us."

"It's probably somebody callin' the police," said Mrs. Armistead, pronouncing the word *police*.

"Shut your damned black mouth," said the fellow who wasn't Charlie Smith. "Go see what's going on out there, Smith. Whatever it is, shoot it."

"Yes, sir," said Charlie Smith, making me believe I had just seen the broad, fat back of Pasadena's exalted cyclops.

My heart hammered like a thunderstorm as I waited, bat poised, for Charlie Smith to stick his head out of the window. When he did, I brought the bat down on his skull as hard as I could. It was lucky for me that he'd stuck his hand holding the gun out before he did his head, because the gun fell from his grip and landed at my feet. It took me about a tenth of a second to scoop it up. Not that I knew what to do with a gun, but better I have it than Charlie Smith.

"What the...? Smith, what the hell's going on?"

But Charlie was unconscious and couldn't answer him.

Whoever the other man was, he said, "Dammit, if one of you black bastards did anything to Charlie, I'll kill all of you!"

"We didn't do nothin' at all," Mrs. Jackson pointed out. "We's just been sittin' here. But your friend don't look so good."

"Stay there and don't move," the man warned the two women.

And darned if he, too, didn't come over and stick his head out of the window, also leading with his gun-toting hand. So I whacked his arm with the baseball bat and, before he could figure out what was going on and as he hollered in pain, I slammed the bucked over his head. Since he was leaning out, he went into the bucket head-first. I hope his nose broke when I shoved the bucket, hard, to make sure it was stuck tight.

"Mrs. Jackson! Mrs. Armistead! Can you tie these men up?"

"Come on in, Mrs. Majesty. You done good!" said Mrs. Jackson. I could tell she was laughing. Whoo boy, if I'd been held hostage at gunpoint, I don't think I'd have been amused at the denouement of the action, but evidently she was of a more tranquil disposition than I.

So I went to the back porch, put on my shoes, walked through the back door into the kitchen and hurried to the living room.

Ew. I'd whacked Charlie Smith pretty hard. His head was streaming blood onto the Jacksons' pretty hardwood floor. Fortunately, Mrs. Jackson hauled a braided area rug away from his head so the rug wouldn't soak up any blood.

"They's rope in the kitchen. Can you get it, Vera?"

"Why don't you get it? I'll just sit on that there one that's still movin'. With me on him, he won't go nowhere."

That was the truth. Both Mrs. Jackson and Mrs. Armistead were very large women.

"Good idea. Mrs. Majesty, you done real good. You done exactly what I hoped you'd do."

Although I felt extremely shaky, I said, "Happy to help."

The man who wasn't Charlie Smith was moving around, so it was a good thing Mrs. Jackson did sit on him. I thought, although my presumption wasn't confirmed until later that day, that I'd broken his arm with the baseball bat. He was sure making noises through that bucket, though. They weren't happy noises. I hoped I *had* broken his nose. And his arm. He was a bad man, and he deserved all the pain he got.

After both men had been trussed securely by Mrs. Jackson, Mrs. Armistead, and me, I pulled the bucket off the bad man's head. He cursed so loudly and proficiently, that I put it back on. The two ladies didn't need to listen to *that* while they waited for me to fetch a policeman.

But I didn't have to drive to the Pasadena Police Department. As soon as I stepped out of the Jacksons' house and onto their front porch, darned if a whole squadron (or whatever you call it) of police cars, sirens screaming, didn't race up Mentone, being led by a black Hudson with no siren. Sam.

For once I was glad to see him.

TWENTY-FIVE

"**P**etrie's a died-in-the-wool criminal," said Sam at the dinner table that night. "We couldn't break him, although we're going to keep trying. Fortunately for us, Charlie Smith is a much weaker vessel. He told us everything." He gave me a sour look. "After he had his head bandaged and woke up from his concussion. The citizens of Pasadena are going to be paying for a hospital stay, thanks to you."

My family sat, goggle-eyed, at the table, alternately lifting bites of roast beef and vegetables to their mouths, watching Sam, and looking at me with something akin to awe. Unless it was horror.

I have a feeling it was horror. Oh, well.

"I'm glad I gave him a concussion. I wish I'd killed him." I slammed a bite of beef into my mouth and chewed savagely.

"Daisy," said Ma, although her voice was merely a faint approximation of the tone it usually achieved when she was telling me to be good.

"So was the guy who called himself Billingsgate actually another Petrie?" Pa asked.

To tell the truth I was a bit uncomfortable with my family's reaction to the events of the day. Not that I'd enjoyed said events. I'd been scared out of my wits and had ruined my best dress, not to mention an almost-new pair of stockings. But at least I hadn't been killed.

"Yes. He's one of the Tulsa Petries. I guess your librarian friend didn't know there was a whole nest of them up there who were bad eggs."

"I guess she didn't."

"I'm not sure I understand, Sam," said Ma. This was typical of her, but it was also reasonable.

Sam tried to explain. "Enoch Petrie, who was calling himself Enoch Billingsgate, was from Tulsa, Oklahoma. Evidently, Henry Jackson saw him kill another man in Tulsa, and Henry and his family fled Tulsa as a result. Well, as a result of Petrie trying to kill them all."

"Henry Jackson is Joseph Jackson's brother," I said. "Joseph is Mrs. Pinkerton's gatekeeper. I guess the Klan harassed him in order to get to Henry, whom I'm sure they aimed to murder when they found him."

"That's terrible!" said Ma. She might not have much imagination, but she was on the side of Good in the universe.

Pa shook his head. "I can't believe Charlie Smith was involved in such heinous activities."

"I think he was a weak man who got in over his head. His battered head," said Sam, eyeing me askance, but being more charitable than I was about Mr. Smith, who had finally admitted to murdering his neighbor, the fiend. Not the neighbor. Mr. Smith was the fiend.

I sniffed. Then I asked him, "Which one of them smothered Roland Petrie in the hospital?"

"Somebody was *smothered*?" Ma's voice was sort of squeaky.

"Yes. Roland Petrie, who was a police officer. Unfortunately, he also belonged to the Klan. He fell of a roof and broke his leg. According to Charlie Smith, Petrie was the one who smothered... Petrie." Sam frowned.

"It gets confusing," I said, attempting to mollify him slightly.

"I can't believe you faced two armed men with a baseball bat and a bucket," said Pa, gazing at me as if he'd never seen me before.

"Huh," said Sam. "I can believe anything she does."

I frowned at him. "It worked out just fine, Pa. I caught Mrs. Jackson's attention, and she showed me precisely what to do."

"She showed you how to bash in a man's head and stick another man's head in a bucket?" Sam, of course.

"Yes, she did, Sam Rotondo! She demonstrated what I should do with those little juju dolls she makes. Then she threw a book on the floor in order to signify that I should make a racket outside the window so both men would rush to the window to discover the source of the noise."

"What's a juju doll?" asked Ma, completely ignoring the marvelous unspoken communication that had taken place between Mrs. Jackson and me. Oh, well. That was Ma all over.

Using my bandaged right hand, which had been thoroughly washed, iodined (at great pain to me) and bandaged by a fellow at the police station, I fished my own personal juju from the front of my old pink day dress. I'd laid my Worth copy on the bed, hoping I'd be able to fix it, but I had grave doubts. "This is a juju. Mrs. Jackson gave it to me the first time I met her." I squinted down at my little juju. "They're supposed to be good luck."

"Unless the juju mambo breaks its arm or cracks its head, in which case the person represented by the juju is supposed to have the same thing happen to him," said Sam, giving a more or less coherent explanation of how jujus work.

"Right," said I. "Only, while Mrs. Jackson broke Officer Petrie's juju's leg and he fell off a roof and broke his leg for real, I don't think she ever smothered him. I mean his juju."

"It was probably Petrie who smothered Petrie," said Sam. By that time I doubt anyone was confused as to which Petrie did what to the other Petrie.

"But I followed Mrs. Jackson's instructions, bashed Charlie Smith on the head with the baseball bat, then broke Mr. Petrie's arm with it, and then I shoved the bucket over his head." I thought I'd acted in a darned near heroic fashion.

Aunt Vi, Pa and Ma all stared at me, aghast, which irked me.

"It's not my fault. Voodoo's just a different type of spiritualism. Jackson's told me lots of stories about voodoo mambos and jujus and stuff like that."

"Good Lord," said Ma, faintly.

"Do you actually believe in voodoo magic?" asked Vi, sounding incredulous.

"Of course not! But I took Mrs. Jackson's advice when she demonstrated on the jujus in her lap, and it worked. It's not magic. It's common sense. Heck, all I had were a baseball bat and a bucket. Petrie and Smith had loaded guns. I couldn't very well barge in there, could I?"

"You could have driven to the police station instead of putting yourself in danger," said Sam, snapping a biscuit in half with his strong teeth.

"Piffle. Mrs. Jackson and Mrs. Armistead were in danger. I didn't want to just leave them." Which reminded me of something. "How'd you know to come up to the Jacksons' house, by the way? You could have bowled me over with a fall leaf when I raced out on their front porch and saw that stream of police cars with their sirens wailing."

"I went to see Jackson at the hospital, and Carl Simmons told me what you were up to," said Sam, sounding as if everything that had ever gone wrong in the City of Pasadena during his tenure at the police department was all my fault. He would.

"And this Enoch Petrie, who was calling himself Enoch Billingsgate, also tried to bilk a bunch of Pasadena residents out of their hard-earned money by selling them swampland in Florida and calling it development property," I said, hoping to distract everyone from my own actions of the day. In all fairness, perhaps I'd been a wee bit rash. But I couldn't have just walked away from those two women as they were being threatened with guns, could I? No, darn it. I couldn't.

"My goodness gracious," said Ma faintly.

"Mercy sakes," said Vi, also a trifle faint.

"You did a good job, Daisy," Pa said, and finally a member of my family smiled at me.

"Thanks, Pa."

"We were on our way," grumbled Sam.

"Well, how was I supposed to know that?" I snapped back.

The telephone rang. It was our ring. Everyone at the table looked at me. I slumped in my chair for a couple of seconds, but I knew where my duty—not to mention my livelihood—lay, so I excused myself and went to the kitchen, where the telephone hung on the far wall, making a racket.

After heaving a huge sigh, I plucked the receiver from the cradle. "Gumm-Majesty residence. Mrs. Majesty speaking."

"*Daisy!*"

I pulled the ear piece away from my head in order to save my hearing. I heard a couple of clicks on the wire, signifying that a couple of our party-line neighbors had hung up.

"One moment, please, Mrs. Pinkerton," said I. "Mrs. Barrow, please hang up your receiver."

"Well, really!" said an irate New York accent. But the stupid woman hung up her receiver.

"I'm sorry, Mrs. Pinkerton. Did you wish to speak to me?" Silly question, but oh, well.

"Oh, yes, Daisy! I'm so thankful that you managed to thwart those evil men! And I understand that Billingsgate person is in jail because of you! You're so brave!"

Gee, maybe I should get my family into the kitchen so they could listen to the woman gush my praises. "Thank you, Mrs. Pinkerton. But I really didn't do much." Huh.

"Oh, yes, you did. Harold told me all about it!"

"Harold told you?" How the heck did Harold learn about the incident at the Jacksons' home?

"Yes, he did! He went to the hospital to see Jackson, and all sorts of people where there singing your praises. You're a true heroine!"

"Um...thank you."

"And Mr. Pinkerton was right about that dreadful Billingsgate fellow. He's a low crook, and his name isn't even Billingsgate."

"No. It's Petrie."

"You simply *must* come to the party I'm holding next Tuesday! I want all my friends to learn about your bravery. Why, this is...what? The fourth or fifth time you've solved a vicious crime?"

"Well, I wouldn't put it precisely like that—"

"*I* would! You're simply too wonderful, Daisy! Do say you'll come on Tuesday. And bring that detective fellow with you. He can tell everyone about how you foiled the villains!"

"I'm not sure that's such a good idea, Mrs. Pinkerton. Detective Rotondo is a very busy man, and he doesn't always approve of my involvement in thwarting criminals."

"Nonsense! Tell him to come on Tuesday. Eight o'clock. We'll have dinner, and then you and that Rotund fellow can tell us all about the iniquitous behavior of that wretched Klan."

Feeling beleaguered—not an unaccustomed feeling when dealing with Mrs. Pinkerton—I said, "I'll be happy to come on Tuesday. And I'll try to get Detective Rotondo to go, too."

"*Thank* you, dear! Darling Del had just discovered that Florida consortium to be shady, and then you went and caught the culprits! This is so exciting!"

Exciting, was it? And darling Del? If Mrs. Pinkerton ever figured out the true relationship between Delray Farrington and her son, Harold Kincaid, I wondered how darling she'd consider Del. But never mind. This was the second time that Del had helped save Mrs. Pinkerton from financial disaster.

"Do you think you can visit me tomorrow, Daisy? Just to use the Ouija board?"

Darn her! I considered for a moment. Tomorrow was Wednesday, and I had other things I wanted to do with my Wednesday, not the least of which was to let Miss Petrie know that the Klan in Pasadena had been squashed. I hoped. But really, if the exalted cyclops was in prison for murder, surely it couldn't continue. Could it?

I'd learned long ago that the stupidity of people could be vast, so I guessed I'd better ask Sam about the Klan as it related to Pasadena.

"I won't be able to visit you tomorrow, Mrs. Pinkerton, but I'll come at ten on Thursday, and I'll be happy to attend your party next Tuesday."

"Oh, very well." She sounded disappointed. Too bad. "Thank you, dear. You're a true heroine."

"Thank you." And I replaced the receiver on its hook and went back to the dinner table.

Naturally, everyone gazed at me speculatively when I entered the room. I focused on Sam.

"Hey, Sam, want to go to a party at the Pinkertons' next Tuesday? They want to grill the two of us like little fishies about the Klan affair."

I didn't deserve the glare I got from Sam.

However, when he said, "Yeah. Why not?" I darned near fell over in a dead faint.

The End

SPIRITS ONSTAGE

A DAISY GUMM MAJESTY MYSTERY, BOOK 9

"Aha! Here are some other folks you know. Mr. and Mrs. Hastings."

Oh, dear. I did indeed know Mrs. Hastings. I'd never actually met Mr. Hastings, although he'd banned me from his law offices a year or so prior, when I was in pursuit of a murderer. Not that I pursue murderers on a regular basis, you understand. It just worked out that way.

"Mrs. Majesty! How lovely to see you this evening." Laura Hastings, whose only son had died several months before this—which was why I'd been in Mr. Hastings' law offices—was delighted to see me. I could tell.

"It's wonderful to see you, too," I said, trying to ignore her husband's glare.

"And here's Detective Sam Rotondo," said Harold, not mincing words this time.

I saw Mr. Hastings' lips writhe a little before he unbent. As well he should have. If not for Sam and me, he'd have been fleeced of a good deal of money and his son's murderer would never have been apprehended.

"How do you do, Mrs. Majesty. Detective Rotondo." His voice

softened when he spoke Sam's name. "I appreciate the good work you people did in breaking up that land swindle."

"You're welcome," said Sam. Stolidly, I'm sure I needn't add. He shook hands with both of the Hastings.

"Oh, and there's Connie and Max Van der Linden!" Harold cried with glee.

He hauled me over to a younger couple. I resisted slightly, but only because the couple's last name sounded German to me, and I'd held a grudge against Germans ever since they all but murdered my Billy. Irrational, I know. But I'm just a lowly human, and humans are irrational creatures.

Harold, who knew me well, leaned close and whispered in my ear, "They're Dutch, so you're free to like them if you want to."

I poked him in the ribs, but didn't respond. Sam, the rat, smiled slightly. I saw him. Well, I guess it was better than his usual scowl.

Harold said effusively, "Connie and Max, please allow me to introduce you to Mrs. Majesty and Detective Sam Rotondo. Daisy's the one I told you about, Connie."

The Van der Lindens were an attractive couple. He was tall and lean, and she was a little taller than I am—I'm five feet, four inches—and also lean. They both look fresh-faced and as if they didn't strive to achieve boredom. I instantly liked them for it—and the fact they weren't German—and smiled.

"How do you do?" I asked them both together.

"I'm so very happy to meet you, Mrs. Majesty. Harold has told us all about you. I understand you sing!" Mrs. Van der Linden grabbed my hand and pumped it as if she expected water to gush from my mouth.

Her words startled me. "Sing? Me?" I glanced at Harold, puzzled, but he only grinned more broadly.

"She has a good voice," said Sam. That startled me, too. Sam wasn't given to complimenting people, especially me.

"Sing? Well . . . I sing in the choir at the First Methodist-Episcopal Church, but I'm only an alto."

"Can you sing contralto?" asked Mr. Van der Linden. He, too, appeared rather avid.

What was going on here? And what in the world was a contralto? I vaguely remembered reading about a contralto in a Sherlock Holmes story, but darned if I could remember which one.

"I...I don't know. What's a contralto?" Then I felt stupid.

But the Van der Lindens only laughed. The mister said, "I'm sorry. You must think we've gone 'round the bend. But you see, we're interested in putting together a little musical operetta company. We're thinking of staging light operas like *The Merry Widow* and perhaps some of Gilbert and Sullivan's works."

"What fun," I said, still confused. Did they want the lowly me to sing in their operettas? Actually...that *did* sound like fun. "I loved *The Merry Widow*, when I saw it at the Shakespeare Club."

"Daisy is a wonderful seamstress, too," said Harold, sounding coy.

Was he volunteering me for something? I slipped him a glance. He looked innocent. I considered this a very bad sign.

"Oh, how marvelous!" cried Ms. Van der Linden, clasping her hands to her more or less nonexistent bosom.

"But—"

Didn't work. Harold interrupted me. "I'm a marvelous baritone," said he with his customary modesty (I'm joking).

"Yes, you are," said Mrs. Van der Linden, giggling. On her a giggle sounded just about right.

"Do you sing, Inspector?" Mr. V asked Sam.

"Detective," said Sam. "Not really."

"I beg your pardon. Detective. You have a deep voice. I'd bet, if I were a betting man, that you'd sing bass."

"Maybe," said Sam, as voluble as ever.

"Let's discuss this more after dinner," Harold suggested. "I want to introduce Daisy and Sam to a couple of other people."

He tugged on my arm, and I lurched after him, bringing Sam along with me. "Harold Kincaid, is this why your mother has been in such a lather this past week? Did she want to get me to sing in some stupid operetta?"

"That would be telling," said Harold with a laugh.

I wasn't sure I approved of this nonsense, and I was certain Sam didn't. His scowl could have wilted roses.

~

Available in Paperback and eBook From Your Favorite Online Retailer or Bookstore

~

ALSO BY ALICE DUNCAN

The Daisy Gumm Majesty Mystery Series

Strong Spirits

Fine Spirits

High Spirits

Hungry Spirits

Genteel Spirits

Ancient Spirits

Spirits Revived

Dark Spirits

Spirits Onstage

Unsettled Spirits

Bruised Spirits

Spirits United

Spirits Unearthed

Shaken Spirits

Scarlet Spirits

The Dream Maker Series

Cowboy for Hire

Beauty and the Brain

The Miner's Daughter

Her Leading Man

ABOUT THE AUTHOR

Award-winning author Alice Duncan lives with a herd of wild dachshunds (enriched from time to time with fosterees from New Mexico Dachshund Rescue) in Roswell, New Mexico. She's not a UFO enthusiast; she's in Roswell because her mother's family settled there fifty years before the aliens crashed (and living in Roswell, NM, is cheaper than living in Pasadena, CA, unfortunately). Alice would love to hear from you at alice@aliceduncan.net

www.aliceduncan.net

 facebook.com/alice.duncan.925

CPSIA information can be obtained
at www.ICGtesting.com
Printed in the USA
LVHW041125251120
672639LV00002B/176